To Nick and Theny

from Dean

VOWS OF THREE SISTERS

VOWS OF THREE SISTERS

Novel
By C. Dean A. Papas

iUniverse, Inc.
New York Lincoln Shanghai

Vows of Three Sisters

iUniverse, Inc.

For information address:
iUniverse, Inc.
2021 Pine Lake Road, Suite 100
Lincoln, NE 68512
www.iuniverse.com

ISBN: 0-595-30657-8 (pbk)
ISBN: 0-595-66188-2 (cloth)

Printed in the United States of America

To my daughter Leah

Contents

CHAPTER 1

The Beginning of Friendship

Lucia Antonelli, Margo Martinez, and Barbara Hendricks first met at 17 when their parents brought them to Marie Curie Academy, a preparatory school for women offering only junior and senior classes as a completion of high school curriculum.

The Academy was a *finishing* school of the mind.

It was named after Marie Skoldowska Curie, the famous Polish chemist. In 1903, Curie, working in Paris with her husband Pierre and A. H. Becquerel, won the Nobel Prize in physics for the discovery of radium, a rare radioactive element in the Uranium decay series. In 1913, Mme Curie herself won a second Nobel Prize, this time in chemistry, for isolating and measuring Uranium.

A boarding school for exceptionally intelligent and mature girls, the Academy accepted a maximum of 20 students each year. It was expensive, highly selective, and competitive.

In addition to other qualifications, to be considered for admission, a student had to pass a specially designed psychometric test to assess the depth of cognitive skills. There were twenty to thirty candidates for each opening.

The mission of the Academy was not only to provide knowledge and information, but also to prepare young women to become scholars and excel as leaders in their chosen fields. All faculty members held doctorates and could have been easily appointed tenured professors at any prestigious university.

Traveling was part of the curriculum to expose, stimulate, and make the students think about their own participation and contributions to constantly changing societies influenced by the dynamics of instant information and globalization.

Students came from well to do families and were typical upper class all-American girls raised by ambitious and educated parents with strong family values.

There was something unusual about this year's junior class.

For the first time in the 96-year history of the Academy, there were three hyphenated Americans: Lucia Antonelli, an Italian-American; Margo Martinez, a Mexican-American; and Barbara Hendricks, an African-American.

Lucia Antonelli had an interesting paternal family history. Her grandfather, Augustino, was killed on Omaha Beach during World War II when her father, Rick, was just three years old. Augustino's wife (Lucia's grandmother), Theresa, was widowed at 28 and never remarried. She kept the small grocery store her husband had left that became the main source of income for the family, in addition to a small government pension.

Rick helped his mother at the store and did his homework in between serving customers, as far as he could remember. He was a straight A student, but never thought of going to college. It wasn't only a matter of economics. Even though his mother was 42 and in excellent health, he wouldn't think leaving her. She had made so many sacrifices for him. He was her whole life.

Rick kept his perfect grade point average through the first semester of his senior year.

It was late Christmas Eve. After dinner and with all relatives gone, Theresa asked Rick to sit next to her on the small sofa by the Christmas tree. She took his hand and smiled.

"Rick, your father, God bless his soul, had a dream. He wanted to educate his children so that they could have a better life. It's time for you to start thinking about college."

Rick was caught by surprise.

"Mother, there's no way I'm going to college. The state college is over one hundred miles away, and tuition for the private university in town is beyond our means."

"Who said anything about going away to state college? I want you to stay in town as much as you do. Whenever you are free, perhaps on weekends, you can help at the store.

"As far as tuition is concerned, there's nothing to worry about. Your father didn't have formal education beyond junior high school, but he was a wise man. As soon as you were born he took out a life insurance policy. The money was never touched. There's enough to cover undergraduate and even graduate school tuition."

Rick was surprised and happy, but sad, too. He remembered how his mother had scrimped and saved over the years, depriving herself of anything she considered unnecessary, like a pair of shoes or a new dress for Easter.

He recalled how many times she took him shopping for shoes and clothes, but after looking around and checking price tags, bought nothing for herself. All the while there had been plenty of money in the bank—money that had been set aside for his education. He kissed his mother hand and hugged her, barely holding back his tears.

"Mom, there's nothing to say now. I could say *thank you*, but would be a redundant euphemism and expected nicety. I hope to thank you with my deeds and make you proud of me. I barely remember my father. His foresight and dreams, and your love and sacrifices you made for me would be the inspiring and compelling force, and the guiding light in my life to help me succeed, honor, and thank you both."

Rick and his mother were close.

She wanted especially to be sure that Rick did not feel that he was the reason she had not remarried after his father's death. She had made that decision for herself, not for her son.

In fact, she had received several proposals over the years, but her husband's memory stayed with her all her life. He was a generous, kind, loving man who put her above every one else, including his own family. The five years of happiness she had shared with him were enough for a lifetime.

After his death, she was much admired by friends and family for her aggressiveness and tenacity in keeping the family business strong and profitable.

She would have been happy for Rick to go away to college, but she knew that he would worry more about her than she would about him. She wanted him to be happy and independent.

❧   ❧   ❧

Rick attended the prestigious School of Management at Trinity University; a loosely church affiliated, non-Sectarian institution of high academic standards, and graduated third in his class.

Several companies, in and out of town including a number of banking firms, tried to entice him with many good offers, some of which included tuition for his MBA, but Rick returned to the grocery store his mother had so successfully run. If she made it on her own and became successful, why couldn't he? This was America, after all.

Rick, after expanding the business, pleaded with and convinced his mother to sell the family business and take some time off. She was still young, in her mid-fifties, but the wrinkles on her face and withered skin on her hands bore witness to a hard life and exposure to the punishing elements of nature.

Yet she never complained. Rather, she emanated a divine grace and faith and hoped that her son would have an easier life. For his part, Rick was always grateful for what he had and never envious over the things he didn't.

Within a year after graduation, Rick took over a large store of a supermarket chain that was filing for bankruptcy.

Three years later, he opened a brand new and much larger supermarket in a more affluent neighborhood, and through a program that required only week-end classes, he went back to school to earn an MBA in marketing.

Rick's business continued to grow, and fifteen years later the Ricki Super-market chain had expanded to seventy-five stores across five states.

Rick and his mother were named Business Man and Business Woman of the Year by the local Chamber of Commerce.

Under his mother's supervision, items not selling but still in good condition were donated to the needy through various churches and missions around the community.

Rick married his college sweetheart, Roxanne, a music major and an excel-lent violinist.

Later, with his finances secured, he built his dream house—a 3 ½ story mansion, on top of a hill overlooking the city.

Devoutly religious, Rick had the architect redesign the seventh bedroom, facing east, into a chapel.

The morning sun through the stained-glass windows reflected a playful rainbow of colors that made the air cheerful, and the Antonellis morning thanksgiving prayers more celebratory for the gifts with which they had been blessed.

The chapel was dedicated to Saint Augustine, in memory of Rick's father, Augustino; his mother lived happily with them until her death at 75.

Roxanne was an accomplished violin teacher. She was on the faculty at the Institute of Music, and also gave private lessons. She taught both her children to play the violin. Lucia was the more talented and progressed faster than her brother, John.

❧   ❧   ❧

Margo Martinez came from a family with a strong background in music and the arts.

Her father, Julio, a Judge in the U.S. Court of Appeals, was an accomplished guitarist during his college years.

A graduate of Yale Law School, he was among the first Hispanic to be appointed to a federal appellate judgeship, and it was felt that, given the right political climate and a vacancy, he could be a candidate for the Supreme Court.

He came to United States from Mexico with his parents at the age of five. He was extremely bright and went to Yale on a full scholarship. Following graduation, he spent two years in South America with the Peace Corps.

Upon his return, he clerked for one of the Supreme Court Justices. After the clerkship, he worked as legal counselor for various government agencies, including the Justice Department, the Office of Solicitor General, and the FBI.

He made his mark as constitutional scholar ensuring that people's rights guaranteed by the Constitution were protected in the process of introducing and upholding federal laws.

The A.C.L.U. would rarely challenge his decisions.

His book *Federal Laws and the Constitution: Partners in Justice and Social Order* was a classic and had become a standard textbook for students of constitutional law.

Her mother Clara was a graduate of the Institute of Arts with a double major in music and art, and minor in business; her instrument was the cello, and she was a pretty good illustrator.

Of Irish, Scot, and English ancestry, she was the typical all-American girl—blond, blue-eyed, athletic, and entrepreneurial. Clara, when Margo started junior high, went back to graduate school and got her MBA in arts management.

She owned and operated a large art gallery and represented young and older well-known artists. She kept a cello at home and another in the gallery and practiced whenever possible. She was a member of a chamber music group that performed at various charitable and fundraising events.

Margo had a brother, Pedro, who was in college, a freshman pre-law student. She was good in math, and like her brother, had her own computer since she was five years old. She was a serious child and seldom used her PC to play games or other forms of entertainment. Margo was musical, started cello lessons at the age of six, and played well for a seventeen year old.

She was happy that the Academy encouraged students to bring their instruments and to continue practicing and studying. Teachers from the Institute of Music and members of the Symphony Orchestra, through special arrangements, would be available for those students wishing to continue taking lessons.

❁   ❁   ❁

Barbara Hendricks was adopted and an only child. Both her parents were physicians in academic medicine and professors at the medical school.

Cedric, her father, an ob/gyn sub-specialist in high-risk pregnancies, was the director of the Perineonatology Unit. Janice, her mother, an ob/gyn sub-specialist in reproductive medicine and genetics, was the director of the Reproductive and Human Genetics Center.

Her parents met and got married during their residency training, and after finishing stayed with the medical school. They had no interest in private practice, but loved research and enjoyed teaching medical students and young resident physicians.

Barbara had never forgotten her first birthday, she could ever remember; the rendition of *Happy Birthday to You* sang by her mother, accompanied by her father at the piano.

Janice, Barbara's mother, had a booming contralto voice, with secure low notes that shook the heart and the guts of your body.

She took voice lessons and was told she had the range, timbre, and musical temperament to become an opera singer.

Being the daughter of a nurse and exposed to medicine from early age, she considered nothing else but medicine, despite the fact that she was offered scholarships by several conservatories, including Julliard, to study voice.

During college, she was the soloist, and getting paid for, of the Bethany Baptist Church Choir. She sang *The Star Spangled Banner* for all her college football games, including the game for the national championship.

Cedric, Barbara's father, took piano lessons as a kid but played mostly by ear, endowed with a perfect pitch. He was a natural, with uncanny musical instinct for the blues and improvisational jazz.

One of the highlights of the faculty's Christmas parties was her mother singing spirituals and the blues accompanied by her father at the piano.

Barbara liked music in general, but her real love and passion was for classical piano. With a Steinway grand piano in the house, she started fooling around with the keyboard as soon as she was able to stand. By the time she was three, seating on her father lap, she was able to play certain tunes.

Cedric often thought;

For some mysterious reason or coincidence Barbara has a perfect pitch and gifted ear for music like me. There is no question that biological connection and continuity could transfer certain traits from parents to children, but not in this family.

Could be possible that destiny and fate, by circumventing biological imperatives and predilection, can accomplish the same? Who knows?

Unexplainable reality will always tease and humble our human wisdom, knowledge, and reasoning until the end of time; human wisdom, being human by nature and irrespective of its accomplishments, would never be perfect and have all the answers, for its origin is not divine.

Barbara started taking piano lessons at the Institute of Music several months after her seventh birthday, and within two years, she was advanced to the intermediate level.

One evening, Barbara's mother, supposed to be attending an emergency, came home unexpectedly. And what did she find? Father and daughter, at the piano, improvising jazz for four hands!

She almost exploded but the scene was so loving and endearing.

Priorities were set and practice time was allocated accordingly.

With Barbara, picking—up tunes so quick and easy, her mother was afraid, that her daughter's musical pedagogy and discipline could be compromised; so she was told by Barbara's teacher. Her technical skills steadily progressed, and was elated that she would be able to continuing taking lessons and practicing.

The Academy, way ahead of time, had sent a packet to all juniors with instructions and other details concerning registration. The junior class was to report and meet with representatives of the faculty at 11 o'clock in the morning, the Sunday following Labor Day weekend. The packet also included information for various events that were scheduled for that weekend.

On Saturday evening, the long anticipated debut of the famous Russian Minsky Chamber Music Ensemble of St. Petersburg Conservatory was to take place, performing Tchaikovsky's Trio in A minor for violin, cello, and piano.

Students and parents, if interested, were advised to get tickets as soon as possible.

Lucia Antonelli, the violinist, Margo Martinez, the cellist, and Barbara Hendricks, the pianist all amateur performers, but serious music students and lovers were thrilled to hear the *Trio* live.

They had all their records and enjoyed listening to chamber music while doing their homework; they liked pop music, too, if doing something that wouldn't demand concentration. Chamber music, being so intellectual and contemplative can induce and restore inner peace of mind that would keep its creative and thinking process in sharp focus.

On Sunday, around 10:30 am, students and parents started arriving. Differences in shape, appearance, and beauty notwithstanding, the girls had two things in common—intelligence and intellectual curiosity. Eyes, body movement, and voice inflexion denoted determination, confidence, maturity, imagination, and self-control.

Bright people with brilliant minds and similar intellectual pursuits meeting for the first time maybe reserved.

In spite of some initial hesitancy, sooner or later they gravitate to each other; their minds having analyzed external signals and images, respond to intuitive magnetism that pulls them together.

Lucia and Margo met over their respective musical instrument cases.

'Hi; I'm Lucia; what's your name? I see you brought your cello. I play the violin. Maybe we can play something together."

"I love to; my name is Margo. I wished we had a pianist! We could play, or at least try to, Tchaikovsky's Trio. What a beautiful music, but so demanding! I went to the concert last night and heard the Minsky Trio; it was purely Heaven."

"So did I; what a coincidence."

Barbara was standing by. When she heard the word *Minsky* approached the two girls.

"Hi guys; I'm Barbara. I went to the concert last night, too. What a magnificent piece of music; and how well was played. Of course, dexterity was there, but the outpouring pathos of soul was overwhelming. I noticed, among suitcases and luggage, a violin and cello case. Do you know these students? Have you met them? I'd like to meet them right away."

"It's us," Lucia and Margo answered hastily in unison, and introduced themselves.

"Barbara, my name's Lucia, and I play the violin."

"Hi Barbara; I'm Margo; I play the cello. We plan to continue practicing and taking lessons. The Academy is accommodating and encourages students to continue with their music education. All student quarters are soundproof, and there're pianos available on campus."

"I know; I play the piano; when I was accepted at the Academy the first thing I inquired was about the opportunity and facilities available to continue my piano studies. I don't plan a career in music, but for the time being piano for me is as important as the rest of my education. I've invested so much time and effort; besides, it gives me so much pleasure and joy. Making music can become a spiritual experience that only people like you can understand."

Lucia and Margo looked at each other with an expression of astonishment and happiness. Their enigmatic smile, laced with whimsicality and impetuousness, projected enthusiasm to create and accomplish, that only youth, with its unabated energy and the gift of time hardly used not only dreams of, but also does.

"Oh my! What a coincidence. Margo and I plan to continue taking lessons. After last night's experience, we just discussed how uplifting would be to find a classmate, who plays the piano, and try to learn and play the *Trio* together."

Barbara, as she was facing the two girls, took Lucia's left hand with her left and Margo's right hand with her right. Her beautiful big brown eyes sparkled with exuberance.

"That's fantastic; count me in. This is going to be our music project. I'm sure our individual music teachers would be more than happy to coach us; weekends we could practice."

The three girls, instantly, intuitively, and instinctively got connected with a blithe spirit, like falling in love on a blind date. They hugged and kissed as if they had known each other since kindergarten, but hadn't seen one another for years.

They felt a composite power that emanated from their minds, hearts and souls, and as it reached each other's became more powerful, resolute, committed, and loving. They had found in one another the sisters had wished for, but never had.

How long these feelings would last? Maybe, it was too early to tell.

Human feelings of any kind of love, with their fleeting nature and intertwined weaknesses like jalousie, possessiveness, mistrust, intellectual dishonesty, ego, and arrogance could disrupt and disconnect love, relationships, and friendships that were intended and committed to last a life time.

Time and circumstances eventually would test the depth and power of any love and friendship. Logic and sentiment alone wouldn't do it, unless supported by a mutually and deeply rooted faith and trust in one another, no matter how unusual, irrational, and even illogical circumstances might be.

Friendship untested is not friendship forever; would be like a boat on a dry dock. Its seaworthiness is a given, but not proven until sailing time comes.

Or like a vintage wine. Color, aroma, bouquet, body, and fruitiness would be anxiously anticipated but not fulfilled until the bottle is uncorked, the wine poured, the sun caresses the glass, and the senses slowly and cautiously surrender with an intoxicating but conscious abandon.

🍁   🍁   🍁

The instant rapport and camaraderie the three girls exhibited dumbfounded their parents. They walked to where the girls stood and met each other.

The Martinez living west and the Hendricks south, almost six hundred miles away from the Academy, were ecstatic that their daughters made friends so quickly.

Rick and Roxanne, being sort of the *locals*-living thirty-five miles way from the Academy, appointed themselves surrogate guardians for Barbara and Margo.

On Fridays, whenever Lucia would be picked up to spend weekends at home, Barbara and Margo would join her, and come along to relax, have fun, and make music together. The Antonelli house had a beautiful music room furnished with a Steinway grand piano.

The Academy strongly believed in, and promoted friendship among students, as much as it did in privacy and contemplation, as absolutely necessary elements in the process of self-growth, maturity, and completion of one's character.

If individuals couldn't stand or were afraid to be alone, dependency would impede creative power and hamper innovative and inspirational thinking.

The sleeping quarters were designed to address both the promotion of friendship and the protection of privacy.

The decision how far to go to either direction was left up to the judgment and will of each student.

The bedrooms were large self-contained private units, with a bathroom, two large walk-in closets, and storage space.

Outside the bedroom, and within each unit, there was a comfortable sitting area furnished with a desk, telephone, PC with high speed internet connection, printer, desk chair, two armchairs, and wall built-in bookshelves.

All rooms, in addition to the main entrance door leading to an outside long hallway, had two more access doors across from each other built in the well insulated, sound-proof partition walls. The doors, when left unlocked, allowed access to the adjoining bedrooms. For the doors to open had to be unlocked from both sides; the decision was left up to each student when to be alone or with others.

TVs weren't permitted in the rooms, but radios and CD players were. There were three large lounges with digital, high definition, wide plasma TV screens for the students to watch television. The lounges were empty during the week, with some activity picking up over the weekend.

House rules per se weren't existent, and there was no curfew.

A student could stay out all night or have gentlemen visitors in her room provided the parents had given permission, and the academic performance wasn't compromised.

The philosophy of the Academy was idiomatic concerning students' behavior.

The premise was that highly intelligent seventeen year old young ladies, performing at the ninety-nine percentile weren't recruited, but sought and competed to attend the Academy for its history of academic excellence, and for offering the best and most unique education and preparation for college.

On the other hand the parents were responsible for teaching and setting standards of behavior and social decorum for their daughters. The Academy simply functioned as the *executor* and *trustee* of the parents to ensure that the agreement and consent between them and their daughters were honored.

The final step for a student to be accepted was for the parents to answer, sign, and return a detailed questionnaire sent by the Academy. The questions were specific; for example:

What time do you expect your daughter to be on campus weekdays and weekends? 7:00 pm? 9:00 pm? 11:00 pm? No specific time. Please, check.

Is your daughter allowed to have male visitors in her room? Never or doesn't matter. Please, check.

The document had to be signed before a notary public and certified copies were given to the Academy, parents, and students. If the parents were divorced both had to sign, unless one parent had been granted sole custody by a court order.

There was zero tolerance. Once the student violated her parents' directives, she was dismissed.

The Academy had high expectations from the students. Their mental capacity, capabilities, and intelligence were tested and found to top the scale at the highest level possible; all were honor students, and academic performance was a given.

Any lapse in academic performance, unless specific reason existed, like illness, and the student was dismissed. Tuition, which was steep and paid in advance for the entire year, wasn't refundable. Per prior agreement, the balance would be donated to the parents' charity of choice.

Despite the zero tolerance policy, it was highly unlikely that any student would be asked to leave. The students were so motivated, mentally endowed, and intellectually curious, that the two years ahead of them weren't viewed as burden or constrain, but as a unique opportunity, given only once in one's lifetime, to developed critical and analytical thinking, in a highly charged environment of learning.

Lucia, Margo, and Barbara, who from now on would be known among themselves as "the trio," requested adjoining rooms from the house manager. Lucia got the room in the middle; Barbara, the room to Lucia's right, and Margo the room to her left.

Once inside, they unlocked the doors and began jumping up and down and running through the rooms like first graders on recess. A few minutes later, out of breath and faces red from excitement, they separated and Margo and Barbara went to their rooms to unpack.

They would meet back in Lucia's room later for the official declaration of the union of the three "territories" into a single state and to write the *Constitution of the Three Sisters.*

When Lucia was accepted by the Academy, she was happy and lucky to have the best of both worlds being only thirty-five miles away from home. She, like everyone else, during growing up times dreamt of going away to school; she was.

Nevertheless, no matter how sweet, glamorous, and romanticized independence in the rogue mind of youth might seem, there would be moments of loneliness and longing for family and home. Her home would be Barbara and Margo's home, too. After all, what are sisters for?

Lucia opened first a small overnight bag. On top of a purse there was a large envelope. She picked the envelope and took out a framed family photograph and a small Crucifix set on a polished granite base. She placed the Crucifix and the family picture side by side on the top shelf of the bookcase.

The photograph of the couple and both children, sitting by the fireplace, was taken in the Antonelli's living room last Christmas. Above the mantle, a beautiful portrait of Grandmother Theresa Antonelli hung. Her facial expression, both in characteristics and nuance, was serene. Like in real life, she kept her inner peace through hardship and success, for hardship was overcome with faith, and success was accepted with more humility than pride.

Lucia continued unpacking. After she finished sat down and gazed at the Crucifix. For the first in her life, she would be alone and away from family and friends. Would be moments she could be scared, apprehensive, isolated, and lonely? Not at all; for she had faith, a family who loved her, and now two sisters and soul-mates living one door away from her. And to top this all, she would be able to expand and feed her mind in a highly charged learning environment that at times seemed so surreal and perfect.

Margo put one of her suitcases on top of the bed, unzipped the outside storage pocket, and removed a box. She opened it and took out a family picture and a small painting of Virgin Mary. She placed the painting and the family photograph next to each other on the top shelf of the built-in bookcase. The picture was taken outside of a monastery in Mexico last summer.

For the first time, the Martinez's family decided to visit Mexico, and tour not only the big cities but the countryside as well.

Clara, Margo's mother, was particularly interested in a well known and successful artist that later in life became a nun. She left all her fortune and unsold paintings to the monastery where she spent the later years of her life until she died.

Proceeds from the sales of the paintings, which were expensive and professionally appraised, had become the sole source of income for the remaining four nuns. Larger paintings were shipped and sold abroad through various dealers and auctions.

The monastery was built on a cliff, had no full time priest, and was accessible only by mules and burrows. The nun, two years before she died, had limited her work to iconography. She had painted several murals on the walls of the small chapel, and small icons in oil that were for sale.

Margo was the first one to enter the chapel; it was dark.

There were two small windows and the main source of light came from candles. The afternoon balmy breeze crossing through the windows and the door made the candles flames flicker and brought the fresco images to life.

As the shadow of the flickering flames moved made the frescos not only more mystical, but also more alive and joyous. Angels appeared to be moving in a celebratory dance, and the faces of saints became less austere, and more human and forgiving.

Margo, on her way out, visited the small exhibit where several paintings of the deceased nun were on display. She fell in love with an oil painting depicting Mary. It was expensive, but she couldn't take her eyes off, especially after her mother's comments.

Clara, an artist herself, art gallery owner, and familiar with the artist, was taken by the intelligent and intended use of pastel colors throughout the painting except when it came to the eyes and lips. Both were well defined with vivid colors. The gaze and smile were enigmatic and emanated an undefined changing expression somewhere between happiness and sadness.

Margo insisted on having the painting as a going away present and would be more than happy to forgo up-coming Christmas and birthday presents! Typical teenage promises, never to be taken too seriously by parents. Margo got her wish and was thrilled to display the icon that had became her most precious and priceless possession.

Barbara's first unpacking move was to open her briefcase she had placed on top of the desk. She took out a beautiful black velvet case with a name on, embroidered in gold letters-Leroy Cedric Hendricks-her father great-great-great grand father's name. She opened the case and took out what appeared to be an old book.

The black withered cover had cracks and was partially defaced. The pages, some torn, were yellow, wrinkled and full of stains. As Barbara brought the book to her lips to kiss, the title became readable. It was The Holy Bible.

Leroy, a cotton-picker and preacher in the Deep South, took care of the spiritual needs of his co-workers and was known as *the preacher of the white fields*.

Every stained yellow and wrinkled page of the Bible had witnessed birth and death; hope and despair; laughter and tears; thirst and hunger; love and hate; faith and abandonment; humiliation and deliverance; patience and courage; hot burning sunsets and cool balmy promising sunrises. Whenever possible, Leroy would gather his flock and preach:

Brothers and sisters; Jesus wants and loves our souls like the souls of our masters and white folks. When we reach the Promised Land not even God, who created us, could tell no difference. In His wisdom gave no color to the soul.

Barbara's father took the Bible with him when he went away to school. It was his most valuable possession and a connection to his family past. He wanted her to value it as well and to feel that familial connection.

Next to the Bible, Barbara put a photograph of her parents taken two years earlier at a fund raising dinner to support expansion of the University Hospital Newborn Intensive Care Unit. Attired in formal dress, they stood holding hands after her mother sang *Amazing Grace* accompanied by her father at the concert grand piano. They looked stunning and victorious.

If there were African-American royalty and aristocracy in the history of this country, Barbara thought her parents were surely the finest example.

Beyond the love of music, the three sisters shared many things of which they were not initially aware. Not least among those things was a deep faith and spirituality. Was their faith contradictory to intelligence, and their spirituality laced with idolatry? Did they need props to confirm and express that faith? Did they confuse faith with religiosity, symbolism, and paganism? Was their intelligence tainted with primitivism?

Barbara had never forgotten what the pastor said to her last Sunday after the service when she went to say goodbye.

Barbara, I have known you since you were a little girl. Now you are an exemplary young lady. I'm proud that you will be attending an exceptional school.

Your father told me that the he gave you the family Bible, a unique symbol in his family history, to take to school. Hold on to and safeguard your family's faith and traditions while you are learning and expanding your mind. Be careful to keep all the values your parents gave you.

When the human mind, supposedly to be permeated with objectivity and critical thinking, comes to matters of faith, becomes somewhat feeble, confused, and forgetful.

In ancient times, after defeat or victory, how hostilities ended? With the offering of an olive tree branch; the symbol of peace.

Why do we salute the American Flag? Because is the symbol of national unity and what U.S. stand for.

Why do Christians venerate the Cross, and Jews, the Star of David? These are the symbols of their faith.

Yet some teenage girls would kill to possess, feel, or kiss the dirty, sweat-stained, and smelly T-shirt of their favorite rock star. That shirt is a symbol of adoration and exuberant frenzy.

Symbols, like your family bible, are an integral part of any society from the most civilized to the most primitive. Symbols become instruments of connection.

It's up to each of us to search for and discover the symbols to which we would like to be connected, and the value, importance, meaning, and redeeming power that connection may bring in the course of our life's journey.

The right symbols will enhance, rather than impede, our learning and our intelligence. Good luck, hold on the family symbol, and keep the faith.

Barbara, Lucia, and Margo were happy with the symbols of connection they would carry for the rest of their lives.

※   ※   ※

Their unpacking done, Margo and Barbara returned to Lucia's room. Noting the Crucifix on the shelf, Margo smiled.

"I feel better now. Some people might think I am a freak if they came to my room."

"What do you mean?" Barbara asked.

"Well, I brought an icon of the Virgin Mary, which I love, but which may be too much for others."

"We shouldn't be concerned about the opinions of others. I brought my family Bible. It is over one hundred years old, and I am proud to have it on the shelf in my room to remind me of love, perseverance, and liberating power.

"My father told me that if he had to choose between keeping his graduate diplomas or the family Bible, he would choose the Bible.

"We're all intelligent people and everybody knows that. If there is something else inside us that make us tick and shows with signs of faith, more power to us. If others don't understand and question it, becomes their problem."

Lucia, all excited, looked Barbara directly in the eyes.

"Barbara, listening to what you expressed so well, and what Margo said before you, I realized now, that we're in a totally different ballgame.

"When we met, a little over three hours ago, we seemed to find in each other the sisters we had hoped for all our lives. There is no question; our mutual love for music became the link of an unbreakable, life long lasting chain. Now, we have discovered other dimensions of power that will strengthen and reinforce that link in our chain of love with unprecedented resilience and fortitude; faith and spirituality."

The trio became pensive and remained silent for a few moments.

Margo raised her head for a second or two and stared at the Crucifix.

"Our intent, getting back together this afternoon, was to solidify our friendship by declaring the unification of the three territories in to a single state, and write the *Constitution of Three Sisters*.

"In view of the new dynamics that have raised our level of communion to new heights, definitions like *territories, state, constitution,* don't represent the spirit in writing a document inspired and directed by faith and spirituality. We need a document to reflect solemnity, promise, and reverence. Don't you think would be more appropriate if we name the document *Vows of Three Sisters*?" Margo asked.

"That's fantastic and so appropriate," Barbara remarked.

Lucia sat on her desk chair.

"I agree. Let me read you what I wrote after I finished unpacking, but first I'll make some changes to reflect Margo's suggestions."

Lucia typed a few words, and then read aloud.

We, Barbara, Lucia, and Margo, take the solemn Vows of Three Sisters, and promise that we shall love, respect, honor, and cherish one another like sisters, until the end of our natural lives.

Our hearts, minds, spirits, and souls shall always be in complete communion to understand one another's feelings and provide support, help, and encouragement.

Above and most of all, our communion under any circumstances, irrespective how demanding, challenging, and unexplainable might be, shall be guided with absolute and unconditional faith, truth, and trust in one another, so help us God.

"What do you think?" Lucia asked.

"I love it. It couldn't be better," Barbara answered.

"That's beautiful, Lucia," Margo said. "Make three copies. I'm ready to take the *Vows of Three Sisters*, if you are.

"Your wording is perfect. I think I have found the best and most unique sisters in the Universe. I'm already feeling positive power coming from both of you. Barbara reminded me to stand for what I believe in, and you articulated the depth and the sensitivity how to express it."

"Come on, Margo! You're so generous. Barbara and I are so thankful to you for your inspirational input. You raised the bar so high.

"Your concept of *Vows*, instead of the technical, humanly conceived term *Constitution*, ensures spirituality that could transform a casual, on and off, communication mode to a mode of communion of divine origin that would connect uninterruptedly our hearts, minds, spirits, and souls for as long as we live."

"I can sense we're already getting so many positive vibes from one another. That's great! We should be so grateful to God, who in his wisdom brought us together and made us sisters for ever. I think it's time to take our vows now. I can sense we're ready and willing. Let's do it," Barbara said.

The trio holding hands, bowed the heads, and recited the vows in unison. When finished, the girls signed all three copies, and each kept one.

The trio made the decision to keep the vows secret. There wasn't anything spooky in them, but the concern was that nobody would understand what the vows meant to them, and out of nowhere, how their lives irrevocably had changed. It was like an epiphany!

To dispel any perception of snobbery, aloofness, or superiority, the trio decided to mix at random with the other students in group situations, like in the dining room and classrooms.

Avoiding others could also be seen as a sign of insecurity. To the contrary, the trio never felt so secure. Their personal values, believes, and heritage in the voyage of shaping character had increased tenfold. On the other hand, by being open-minded, they could learn and benefit from experiences of others.

The three families had dinner together.

The first time Barbara and Margo addressed the Antonellis as *Mr.* and *Mrs.* were stopped. They wanted to be called *Uncle* and *Aunt* and meant it. Later, it was time to say goodbye.

It seemed that the parents, and especially the Martinez and Hendricks living so far away, were sadder than their daughters. They wouldn't see them again until Thanksgiving. They were happy though that Margo, Barbara, and Lucia had become such good friends so quickly never knowing how well and deeply they were connected.

The Antonellis were almost in the same boat.

Although thirty-five miles away from the Academy, it was highly unlikely that Lucia would have time to visit; maybe they could meet for dinner once in a while.

All parents were aware that the Academy's philosophy and only priority was to meet their daughters' educational needs and intellectual development; and that included allocation of weekend time.

With all the tears dried, and kisses, hugs, and sighs gone, the long day had finally come to an end.

In the infinite course of time, End wouldn't exist unless there was a Beginning. Beginning and End are not synchronous, but alternate, precede or follow, define, and compete against each other for value and quality they offer during one's life journey.

Today, the trio had a glorious beginning. The sadness at end of the day was part of the human psyche.

Happiness can end with sadness, and sadness can end with the beginning of happiness. That will never change.

What could determine the overall quality of life, in pursuing happiness, would be to relentlessly seek opportunities and the tenacity to make happy beginnings last longer and sad endings shorter, with long…long intervals in between.

The saga of the three sisters that would also entangle their families had just begun.

Three seventeen year old girls, unusually intelligent and spiritual, made a lifetime commitment with the *Vows of Three Sisters*. Were they way above their heads? They had intelligence; but did they have the maturity and depth at this age to comprehend the weight of the promise? Did they put the cart before the horse?

CHAPTER 2

Knowledge and Critical Thinking

Monday was the first day of school.

After all the hustling and buzzing of the weekend, the students were ready to start the new school year. Returning senior class students were expected to be in the classroom at 8 o'clock in the morning, and the new class of juniors, at 9:00.

The leadership of the Academy, on the first day of school, concentrated primarily on the orientation of the new class.

The original packet included general information, but no specifics, especially about the methodology of teaching. At first glance, and not knowing the educational philosophy of the institution, classes could be perceived as rather un-orthodox and deviating from accepted standards. Being a privately funded school required no state accreditation.

On the other hand the Academy was well known for excellence and considered to be probably the best preparatory school for girls in the nation. Directly communicating with students had worked well in the past and all questions could be answered in real time, avoiding any confusion.

The director of the Academy, for the past five years, was Martha Fuller.

She was in her early sixties, never married, spirited, engaging, and always on the go. She resigned as university Dean, two years prior to joining the Academy, to concentrate on writing.

She had a Ph.D. in Drama and English, authored several books, and during the summer, traveled extensively to attend seminars, and teach as a visiting professor in U.S. and abroad.

Last year she was elected member of U.S. Academy of Arts and Sciences.

What attracted her to the Academy were the freedom to be innovative and the intelligence and quality of the students. It was the director's responsibility to meet and welcome the junior class and present the core of the school's philosophy.

The students started arriving by 8:30. Within fifteen minutes all girls, after greeting each other, took their seats.

At exactly 9 o'clock Martha Fuller walked in.

She was thin, about five feet seven inches tall and her pleasant smile underlined the wrinkles of the lower eyelids and corners of the mouth.

Her gray hair, parted in the middle, was combed back and held with a clip, reached the lower part of her neck. Her long sleeve light brown dress, hemmed at the knee, showed that her legs were noticeable even for a woman in her sixties.

Beauty is in the eyes of the beholder, but nobody would argue that Martha wasn't graceful and maybe even attractive to a certain degree. Her towering forehead and light make up made her cheekbones less prominent and gave her eyes a glimpse of hollowness.

One would wonder; why a woman like Martha never got married? Maybe she wasn't interested or never found love; and if she did, was she frightened or disappointed?

Who knows? Does everybody have to follow the same expected path and mold in life and be like all others? And if he or she is different and not like others, why others are so curious and want to know why? Does the difference make them jealous, envious or insecure?

Martha pulled the desk chair out, sat on, put her hands on top of the desk, and addressed the class:

"Good morning young ladies.

"My name is Dr. Martha Fuller, I'm the Director of the Academy, and it's my pleasure to welcome you. It's important, and you must understand this from the first day of school. You're here because we're here. And we're here because of you. We complement and fill each other's needs and purpose.

"The Academy wouldn't exist if it weren't for young exceptional young women like you; and you wouldn't come here, unless the Academy had the structure and capability to meet your expectations and offer the highest level of excellence in education.

"Over the years, there has been an unprecedented synergy between the Academy and its students. The product has been phenomenal and unique.

"Leaders in Academia, Sciences, Politics, Government, Literature, Medicine, Law, and Industry have been graduates of this institution.

"After the last appointment to the U.S. Supreme Court, there is only one mountain left for a graduate of Marie Curie Academy to climb; the presidency of U. S. There is no question in my mind that the first woman U.S. president would be a graduate of this Academy. Maybe one of you; who knows. Your intellectual gifts and desire to excel are as good as your predecessors."

Martha looked at her watch.

"It's only 9:15.

"I expect this meeting to be rather long. Everything of importance about your stay at this school, and your education, will be discussed openly and frankly. After the meeting, you are free for the rest of the day, as you will need time to digest and discuss what you have heard here.

"If someone has to be excused, please let me know and I'll wait until you come back before I continue.

"There will be no time for questions at the end of the meeting, but you can meet me in my office at any time and I'll be happy to address any concerns. Just leave your name with my secretary.

"You will find that classes here at the Academy operate differently than what you have been used to.

"Classes, in other schools, meet for 45 to 50 minutes mornings and afternoons with a lunch break in between. There is a different teacher for each period.

"But before I describe our system and our philosophy, and the reasoning behind it, let me take you on an imaginary trip.

"The *Utopian Taste Bud* is the most famous restaurant in the world.

"Reservations have to be made at least four years in advance, and patrons fly in from every corner of the globe. There is a long waiting list, although reservations can be moved up in case of a cancellation. We're lucky. The Academy is only two hundred miles from the restaurant.

"We were on the waiting list for two and a half years.

"Around 9 o'clock in the morning, I received a frantic call from the restaurant; a private plane flying from Chile, with twenty-one prospective diners aboard, was hijacked! Our day miraculously had come. I made transportation arrangements and hotel reservations for one night stay and took you to the restaurant.

"The appetizers were divine; a perfect herald to the main course, which was carved into such small pieces to make it last forever. Unfortunately, it was interrupted half way through, and pleasure was taken away to allocate time for dessert. Alas, time is the enemy of pleasure. Yet if our senses rebel against untimely interruptions, can our minds be any less sensitive when the creative process is victimized by time, as often happens?"

The students were aghast.

They knew that the imaginary and allegoric trip was a metaphor. What did Martha have in mind? For the first time, they realized what was ahead of them.

A school uniquely structured to meet their demanding intellectual curiosity not only to possess and expand knowledge, but also apply knowledge to reason and develop critical thinking. And if rest of the faculty was half as good as Martha, attending this school would be a real feast.

Martha, being experienced and a wizard of how impressionable, inquisitive, impatient, and eager young intelligent minds could be, paused for a few minutes. They needed a break to contemplate.

The effect and impression of a metaphor would be diminished or even wasted if its real meaning was revealed without a pause. It would be like opening a present lacking festive wrapping and a colorful ribbon. No matter how fancy (or ugly) the box, opening it to get directly to the gift shortened the time of excitement and anticipation.

Martha stood, took a few steps, tried to make eye contact with every student, and continued.

"The Academy does not subscribe to the traditional several morning and afternoon periods. It has only two sessions; one in the morning and one in the afternoon, with one hour lunch break in between. And there is only one, I repeat only one, teacher assigned for each sessions. Why? To free you and your teacher from the prison of time, and make time your slave, not your master.

"From our trip we established the fact that our body becomes angry, protests, and rebels when pleasurable senses are untimely interrupted; like an exquisite, majestic, elaborate, long planned and anticipated meal of imperial quality and cost to accommodate time constrains.

"One of the fundamental instruments in the process of opening, reaching, and enriching our minds, from early on in our cognitive development, is dialogue; the process of intellectual exchange and communication among minds.

"How would you feel, if one of you had an intelligent, challenging, and provocative question and the teacher, after checking the time, said was sorry; time was up, and wouldn't like to be late for the next class and keep the students waiting.

"How would you react if a vivid, stimulating, and interesting discussion, debate, or presentation by you or your teacher was interrupted because of time constraints? Starved? Disappointed? Frustrated? Intellectually cheated?"

The meaning of the metaphor was obvious. The analogy of the importance of seamless stimulation of the senses to experience pleasure, and that of the curious mind to acquire knowledge and wisdom, was well taken.

Martha took her seat back at the desk.

"The advantage of having the same teacher for the entire session makes both, teacher and students, responsible for intelligently controlling time to their benefit.

"Short brakes within the morning and afternoon sessions can be moved up or down to accommodate you. If a topic generated interest and questions had to be answered, the teacher would delay the next class.

"You will take the same number of short breaks within a session, as you would have with periods, but vacuums in your minds, in the process of learning, would be avoided. You should become the master of time.

"The art of managing time determines not only productivity, but also quality of output and the value of the product, irrespective whether it comes from thinking minds or laboring hands.

"Every student is concerned about testing and grades.

"There would be no specific time scheduled testing, like *term* exams or *final* exams. We started with the premise that all of you are straight A-plus honor students, and you would continue performing at the same level.

"Your participation in the class and your written assignments and papers would be of such quality and depth that would convince your teachers your performance level hasn't changed.

"All top colleges are aware of our policy and have no problem with. To them, all our graduates are top students. Every student of the senior class, usually by Thanksgiving, if not earlier, has received unsolicited applications from the twenty top U.S. colleges that include all Ivy League schools.

"What about studying and homework?

"Everyone develops personal habits and allocates time accordingly.

"Experience has shown us, that in order to cover all material, do research, and write papers, you need about four to five hours every day after school; and about ten hours total over the weekend, which starts Friday after the morning session is over. There're no afternoon sessions on Fridays.

"On Friday evenings, if you want to go shopping, eat out, attend artistic performances, like theater, movies, or the Symphony Orchestra, the school van will drop you off wherever you want to go and bring you back later. That also goes for Saturdays and Sundays, too, if some of you like to attend services at various churches, synagogues, or other houses of worship.

"Remember: The Academy is responsible for all activities related to your education; however, all other activities both in and outside of this building fall under the directives of your parents, which you have agreed to honor and by which you have agreed to abide.

"I would like to close our meeting with some personal thoughts.

"Intelligence guarantees neither success nor sound judgment.

"During my carrier and having dealt with so many young women and followed them later in life, it seems that certain patterns prevail. They go to college, work for a while, get married, have kids, become unhappy, half get divorced, go back to school, etc. A great number, even in their late thirties, complain they haven't found themselves yet, and want to get away from it all.

"To find one's self is not possible unless spends time alone. Societal structure and peer pressure compel everybody to think and act alike. If one's time is not filled as expected insecurity may take over; for example:

"There are five college students; bright, good looking, and close friends.

"One Saturday all have dates except one. They tried to *fix* her up, but didn't work out. What a pity! She was going to be alone. So what? If one cannot stand, or not expect ever to be alone, will never become a mature individual.

"Being alone makes you think and focus on your own life, expectations, and goals. Being alone not only empowers your independence, but also elevates your maturity level.

"The Academy is proud to have you as students and will make every effort possible to help you become critical, analytical, and independent thinkers; individuals not only of knowledge, but also of charisma."

Martha got up, and after hugging and shaking hands with each student, left the classroom. The room became pleasantly noisy with laughter and enthusiasm. The girls greeted one another, and friendships of different qualities and depth were in the making, for sure.

Martha, after leaving the classroom was wondering what the future would hold for these young women of unusual intelligence?

There's no question, they were the "chosen" ones; but intelligence alone wouldn't have been enough to bring them where they are now, unless supported by life of privilege and wealth.

On the other hand, how many girls of the same or even greater mental gifts were left out, in the masses of humanity, and not been given the same opportunity to feed and expand their minds, and meet their potential for lack of means?

Is success of the "privileged" a given? Absolutely, not, as failure of the "unprivileged" isn't.

Choices made, timing of execution, and will, tenacity, and fortitude, or lack of, could fail the former and make successful the latter.

Means may help reach the end easier, but will never determine its worthiness, utility, and value.

Barbara, Lucia, and Margo were gifted. How will they use their intelligence? Will the deep commitment of friendship and the *Vows* enhance individual growth and help them become better persons?

CHAPTER 3

Families and Outreaching Love

The first two months went by quickly.

The trio met the academic challenge well, and their friendship continued to grow.

Like Barbara and Margo, the only contact Lucia had with her family was by phone. Although only thirty-five miles away, she never had the time to visit her family and stay for the weekend.

Weekends were taken with homework, music lessons, and practice. In whatever time remained, the trio practiced their musical project, Tchaikovsky's Trio, which was to become a sort of anthem for them, and an integral part of their vows.

Playing together deepened their connection with each other. It seemed to provide a new source of life, supplying them with energy and emotional sustenance, as though they were all sharing the same oxygen tank. Of course they missed their parents, relatives, and friends back home, but what they had found in one another soon made that separation a little distant.

At times, and not without some guilt, missing home was something they seemed to experience on a subconscious level. They loved their parents, and with Thanksgiving coming-the Academy was closed for the entire week-were looking forward to be with them.

Nevertheless, the trio wouldn't mind spending Thanksgiving week together. They had something special to celebrate this year and be thankful for; the out of nowhere, and never expected gift of sisters!

Could be possible for the trio to be together without disappointing or even offending their parents? Who knows? Love and the minds of these girls could work in mysterious ways. What kind of parents would say, no to a beautiful, intelligent, integrated, and pleading daughter without feeling guilty for the rest of their lives?

It was Sunday 9 o'clock in the evening; the time Lucia and her parents had set aside for the last routine weekend call. With all the homework done and the last paper typed, she called home.

"Hi, Mom and Dad. How are you? I'm fine…I'm doing well in school…It's no tougher than I expected it to be. Barbara and Margo are fine, too…We're having a ball! We're like sisters now. I missed you, too…I know. It's been a long time. Thanksgiving is only less than a month away. I have an idea. Why don't you come up to school next Sunday around 5:30 and take us out to dinner. We'll try to work harder Saturday and have all our homework done. We're going to have fun. The girls are going to be so excited. I love you, too…Good-night."

After the call the trio got together.

They were singing, acted giggly, and their faces exuded happiness. They planned and looked forward to have some fun time off campus, and enjoy a nice dinner out.

Before saying goodnight, they bowed their head and went into a huddle formation. They mumbled a few words, then jumped and screamed at the top of their lungs in unison:

"Let's go for!"

Next Sunday, around 5:15 pm, Lucia's parents arrived at the school and parked by the main entrance.

Rick and Roxanne walked into the building, and there were the three girls standing in the large hall, anxiously waiting.

Immediately, a human mass of hugs and kisses was formed. You couldn't tell who belongs to whom, but didn't matter.

Outpouring love and longing had taken over, throwing their unbreakable nets around everybody to ensure that their captivating power would take any shape and form to accommodate and capture the needs of the moment.

"Hi girls; we missed you; I'm sure, so did your parent," Lucia's mother said.

Hurriedly, everybody left the building and rushed into the car. Lucia's parents took the front seat with her father driving, and the girls sat in the back.

While driving to the restaurant, the bubbling and camaraderie coming from the backseat took over.

The bond and the comfort among the girls continued not only to surprise Lucia's parents, but also affected them. When love moves and expands directly can also make lateral moves. The bond of Lucia to Barbara and Margo deeply affected her parents, too, as if they had not one but three daughters.

As the dinner progressed the girls became quieter, and by the time dessert was served they were silent and maybe sad. It was natural for Barbara and Margo; they hadn't seen their parents for two months and missed them. What about Lucia? She had no reason to. What happened to their enthusiasm and laughter?

Roxanne, Lucia's mother became curious if not suspicious, broke the silence.

"Well, girls what is going on? Cheer up. What are you up to? I thought we were going to have a good time, and now, the only thing I see is long faces."

"Mom, there is something on my mind, and I don't know how to tell you. Pretty soon, with Thanksgiving coming and all, Barbara and Margo will go home. For some reason I wish we could be together for our first Thanksgiving. This is extremely important for the three of us."

"That's fine with your father and me. What about Barbara, Margo, and their parents and Pedro? I'm sure they've missed each other and looking forward to spend Thanksgiving together."

Lucia's father looked at her and said;

"I have an idea! Why don't we invite Barbara and Margo's parents and Pedro to come and spend Thanksgiving with us? For the first time since mother died we're going to use all our bedrooms.

"The third floor, my mother's two bedroom two bath suite, can comfortably accommodate the two couples. To help mother with her arthritis, three years before she died, we installed an elevator right off the breakfast room.

"We have three empty bedrooms on the second floor. That will take care of Barbara, Margo, and her brother Pedro. I think would nice for John and Pedro to meet and talk about their experiences as college freshmen.

"The first thing in the morning, I'm calling Barbara and Margo's parents to invite them. I think we're going to have a blast. There would be no formalities and we'd be like a big family. It's up to Barbara and Margo to convince them to come."

Lucia got up and started repeatedly kissing her father on both cheeks.

"Thank you, thank you Daddy. I love you. You can't imagine how much it means to the three of us to be together this Thanksgiving."

Lucia's parents got up, hugged, and kissed Barbara and Margo. Their reassured them that would be a pleasure and honor to have their parents as guests. After all, what are uncles and aunts for?

The girls were driven back to the Academy.

After kissing and saying goodbye to Lucia's parents from the backseat of the car, the trio opened the doors, waved hurriedly, and rushed to their rooms. It was about 8 o'clock. The trio changed into their nightgowns, and met in Lucia's room to congratulate her and celebrate the successful outcome of their plan.

Spending the first Thanksgiving together was so important to them. It would take them to a different level of understanding that they couldn't articulate either internally or externally.

Nevertheless, there were unanswered questions.

Discovering one another and the immediate bonding was an accident? How their connection, even if remained unbroken, would affect the future? Who knows? Only circumstances of the future might shed light to appreciate the depth of connection, and value its importance.

On Monday, after several tries, Roxanne and Rick Antonelli were able to reach Judge and Clara Martinez and Doctors Cedric and Janice Hendricks.

Roxanne spoke with the wives, after Rick had spoken with the husbands. They were, with some reservations, delighted to come and happily accepted the invitation. Their concern was that Roxanne would be overwhelmed and overworked with so many guests.

To begin with, they insisted to be addressed only by their first name and not as *Judge* or *Doctor*, be part of the family, and not be treated as formal guests. They flatly refused to be picked up at airport; it made more sense to them to get a cab. The house was only fifteen mile away from the airport.

The Antonellis reassured them that everything was going to be informal and family oriented. And with three young ladies at home ready and willing to help, Roxanne would be sort of acting, more likely, in a supervisory capacity.

The Martinez and Hendricks would be arriving later Wednesday evening, were not to be expected for dinner, and planned to leave early Sunday morning.

With all Thanksgiving plans finalized, the girls were beside themselves with joy.

To be together, and with families, too, was a dream come true. The intimate home settings filled with loved ones, and away from the formal, efficient, and sometimes cold, and emotionally sterile school environment, would forge their understanding and perception of being sisters to a higher level.

Being thankful on a holiday, like Thanksgiving, might be expressed, at times, hurriedly and take an undefined, blurred, and even abstract form in the twirl of a festive abandon.

The trio knew exactly the reason to be especially thankful for this year.

They were blessed with so many gifts and loving families. And to top this all, they have found the sisters that had enriched and changed their lives for ever.

Blood relationships are not by choice but a given, and do not always guarantee communion. On the other hand, non-blood relationships by choice could reach an unprecedented depth of communion that would put the former to shame!

Thanksgiving Day came with a great deal of anticipation by all.

The Antonelli household—they dislike the word estate, no matter how suitable-hadn't seen so much activity since last summer, when John, Lucia's brother, graduated from high school. But with three bubbly girls around, the atmosphere was different. Every corner of every room in the house was filled, in various sequences and at different times, with a perpetual motion of living, laughter, giggling, singing, teasing, and above all, loving.

The free, exuberant, and celebratory spirit of the girls quickly permeated everyone's heart and mind.

The parents felt comfortable with each other, and subconsciously dissociated themselves from the daily demanding activities and their complexities they were used to. The present surroundings were so peaceful, soothing, and relaxing, that made any pressing and preoccupying serious thoughts, at times so envious and jealous of leisure, fade away.

John Antonelli, a freshman at Georgetown, and Pedro, a freshman at Yale, became friends quickly.

Pedro was in pre-law, and like his father, had made up his mind to follow the legal profession in some capacity. John wasn't sure. He was considering, after graduation, staying at the same school, and getting his master's in government and diplomacy. He was thinking that he might like to join the U.S. Foreign Service. He liked languages, was taking German, and would continue into the second semester.

Next year, he would be tutored in Japanese, and planned to visit Japan the following summer.

The three couples were as diverse as similar.

The three husbands, a successful, astute, and educated businessman, a judge and legal scholar, and a physician and academic possessed totally different expertise. On the other hand, all came from a humble background, but were ambitious and used their intelligence to acquire knowledge that made them successful in their chosen fields.

Above all, they never forgot family and traditional values that they considered as important as knowledge in succeeding in life. They were committed and hoped to help their children follow the same path.

Every man or woman is entitled to make his or her own decision, but would be difficult to argue or ignore success. And what was the most extraordinary accomplishment that had in common, that brought them together? They were *fathers!*

The three wives, a violinist and teacher, a business woman, cellist, and artist, and a physician and researcher, were as diverse as their husbands; but like them, believed in the importance of family values in raising children. And what was the most extraordinary accomplishment that had in common, that brought them together? They were *mothers!*

The formal dining room, not often used, was large; a sliding double-panel oak door, when closed, separated it from the music-library room. The same arrangement was made to separate the other side of the music room from the living room.

When the house was designed, the Antonellis asked the architect to have the formal part of the house built to the left of the large entry hall, and the informal to the right, with the kitchen, pantry, and wine cellar behind the wall of the large entry hall facing the main entrance.

A set of double sliding oak doors to the right of the entry hall, when closed, separated the formal section of the house from a huge family room, bar, and a large breakfast room in the back, adjacent to the kitchen.

A wide stairway, from the family room, lead to an unusual high ceiling basement that was built and custom-made into a humongous entertainment center, with a billiard table and bar. The stairway also reached the second and the third floor of the house. The second floor, where the bedrooms were located, was also accessed by a formal staircase built to the left of the entrance hall.

Roxanne appointed the trio as junior hostesses, and their first assignment was to set the dining room table, while the parents sat in the family room enjoying assorted antipasto and sipping Chianti. John and Pedro were downstairs watching the traditional Thanksgiving football game.

The girls took their assignment seriously and followed Lucia's mother instructions to the last detail; when finished, everything was properly placed and looked perfect. Crystal, silverware, china, and napkins.

The deeply carved and ruby stained wooden napkin rings made in Mexico, a gift from the Martinez, contrasted the ecru tablecloth and napkins to a festive brilliance.

The centerpiece—a gift from the Hendricks, was made of a large oval wicker basket, exquisitely and intricately weaved, and lacquered to perfection; full of bright fall foliage-dry corn on the cob and pinecones-was decorated with three beautiful quails named Barbara, Margo, and Lucia, and two turkeys named John and Pedro! No offense intended.

When all came to the dining room and read the little name tags, attached to the birds, laughed and thought were cute.

After taking their seats held hands and recited the Lord's Prayer.

When finished, Barbara's father winked at her mother. He got up, excused himself, and hurriedly walked across to the music room, and sat on the piano bench. Everybody was caught by surprise. Janice got up on cue, and with her husband accompanying her at the piano, started singing:

We gather together to ask The Lord's blessings. He chastens and hastens His will to make known, the wicked, oppressing cease them from distressing. Sing praises to His Name, Amen.

Janice's soft velvety contralto voice filled the air, seizing and overtaking everyone on a spiritual level and causing a conscious outpouring of thanks for all the gifts received.

Everybody stood up and applauded.

Cedric returned to the dining room, and after kissing his wife, sat down next to her. The trio went to the side board, picked up platters with traditional food, and passed them around. With all served and sitting, and the wine poured, Lucia's father raised his glass to a toast:

"Thanksgiving is a unique day in our nation's history, families, and individuals. We all celebrate our blessings, but going back, would have never been any Thanksgiving at all, if it weren't for diverse inclusive friendships and extended families like we're here today.

"We came out of nowhere; we didn't even know the others existed, less than three months ago, and now we're breaking bread together as brothers and sisters.

"I raise this toast to thank God for all gifts received, and most of all this year, the gift of friendship; the friendship, the Antonelli family was blessed with this Thanksgiving, found in the Hendricks and Martinez families.

"Cheers to the Hendricks and Martinez families, who came from so far away, to enrich our lives with friendship, and help us celebrated the best Thanksgiving, ever!"

Cedric and Julio, after sipping wine, raised a toast to salute Rick and his family and thanked them for their hospitality; they were especially grateful to them for being such a good *uncle* and *aun*t to their daughters.

As soon as dinner was over, and the table was cleaned, the trio carried dessert from the kitchen, served on individual plates, and passed them around.

On every plate, besides the traditional pumpkin pie, there were a piece of black forest cake, and a slice of spumoni ice cream.

Later, with all eating done, the girls loaded the dishwasher. They were happy that were able to help, and Lucia's mother complemented them repeatedly for a job well done.

Now, the trio needed some time for themselves; they retired to Lucia's bedroom.

They were extremely pleased how well their parents and brothers got along, as if they had met before and had become close friends long time ago. Apparently the union and the love of the trio, for one another, had precipitately snowballed to include everybody else around.

Love can work on both sides of the spectrum.

It can be contagious and bring people together strengthening it, like the trio and their families, or competitive and jealous that could create distance, coldness, and even hatred.

Individuals opting for exclusive non-sharing love are basically insecure. If love loses its expansiveness would no longer be fresh, but mundane, old, wrinkled, unproductive, and probably dysfunctional.

Can Barbara, Lucia, and Margo continue to balance love of friendship and family? How the *Vows of Three Sisters* will hold in the future when romantic love and other personal commitments and pursuits come along?

CHAPTER 4

The Journey: A Window to the World

Almost a year and a half had gone by since the trio met. This year, each one took additional honor courses that gave a hint what their personal interests might be as they were approaching college.

Barbara took extra courses in physics, chemistry, and biology.

Lucia showed more interest in history, comparative literature, philosophy, and psychology.

Margo continued with her fascinations with advanced math and theorems. She took college courses in calculus and algebra, and studied variables and probabilities in predicting cyclic phenomena. She was overtaken how close math and music were in their logical sequence, and metric, rhythmic, and harmonic formulations.

The trio continued their individual studies in music, and practiced their instruments whenever possible.

Dexterity and interpretive skills had significantly advanced in the past six months, and their individual music teachers were impressed the last time they heard them playing together Tchaikovsky's Trio in A minor. The girls, whenever playing, reaffirmed again that this music score had become inseparable from their vows, communion, and sisterhood.

Part of the Academy's senior class curriculum was traveling abroad.

The intent, for the students, was not only to become and think as *accidental* tourists, but also observe, study, and assess circumstances under which other people lived and thought, and compare them to their own experiences. Each student, after the trip, was to make a presentation to the class concerning lessons learned, and what, if any, influence and affect had upon them.

The itinerary was flexible and could be different from one group to another.

Three students was the minimum number required to form a group. Each group was chaperoned, at least, by one faculty member or more, if the group was larger.

The trio formed their own group, and their choice surprised not only the faculty members, but their classmate as well. Not Europe but south of the border. Acapulco, Mexico and Rio de Janeiro, Brazil! They were so curious and had so many questions.

Those two cities were glamorized to death; constantly visited by the jet set, and their posters were conspicuously displayed in every travel establishment. What was the mystique? Beauty of nature, uninhibited exposure of flesh, free spirit, the sun, the sea, and the rain forest? It was up to them to find out.

It was in the middle of January and the peak season for both cities.

The trio flew from Miami to Acapulco, and six days later from Acapulco to Rio with a three hour stopover in Trinidad. They stayed eight days in Rio, and coming back, after a short stopover in Trinidad, flew back to Miami.

The trip, for a rather serious, intelligent, and conservative threesome of high school seniors, was an eye opener. The contrast of their own personal believes, experience and life, and to what they saw and observed was mind-boggling.

The girls were back for ten days and had worked hard to prepare their presentations, which was due the beginning of next week.

Although together and exposed to the same environment, they made an effort to choose and present different views, observations, and impressions in order to make each presentation more interesting for the rest of the class.

           ❧   ❧   ❧

It was Monday 8 o'clock in the morning, and the class was ready to begin.

Today, it was Barbara, Lucia, and Margo's turn to present and discuss their traveling experience.

The moderator was Alice Doyle, a Ph.D. in anthropology, with extensive knowledge of isolated islands of populations untouched by modern civilization. She was an only daughter of a missionary couple and had spent most of her childhood in small African and South American villages, some in the deep jungle.

Barbara was called first.

"Thank you Dr. Doyle.

"There is no doubt that traveling exposes you to a unique learning experience that would last for ever. There're no books, no matter how accurate and well written, that can substitute for the direct stimulation of the eyes and all other senses, and the real, live, and compelling images they generate.

"Many a time living and thriving in our secure and privileged environment forget the rest of the world.

"We forget that there're other people with faces, souls, hearts, and dreams like ours, but live in total hopelessness and desperation. They breathe, and the heart beats, but the spirit is dead.

"The street is home for food and shelter when alive, and the street would become the deathbed, when take their last breath, while aimlessly gazing the sun, the moon or the stars. And all this amid plenty, beauty, leisure, song and dance. What an absurd parallelism of existence!

"Our hotel in Acapulco, a beautiful building of pyramidal design with the top cut off, reminded me of an Aztec Temple. The lobby was wide open, and extended as an atrium all the way to the top floor. Plants and flowers hung from dimly lit balconies and wide corridors; and the surrounding gardens, interlocking with frolicking swimming pools and waterfalls, were a testimony to architectural sophistication imitating nature.

"The entire complex was away and isolated from Acapulco Bay, marketed as a resort, and was fenced around, with its own private beach.

"Although privacy was a given, was often interrupted by the through the fence passing hands of starving children—as small as toddlers, begging for food. The feeling was unsettling.

"Looking at the highly decorated enormous buffet luncheons, full of every delicacy possible, subconscious guilt might surface that could make even a lumberjack's hunger go away. The discrepancy between *have* and *have-nots* was incalculable.

"In Rio, the famous city of leisure, pleasure, and nature, the mind was overwhelmed with similar images.

"Along Copacabana Beach, in the evening, balconies of luxurious apartments and homes were full of vivacious chic women and deeply tanned men all dressed in the latest fashion, talking and enjoying themselves in the balmy breeze of the emerald sea, while being served cocktails and appetizers by properly attired house help.

"Through the windows crystal chandeliers were visible, competing with the full moon in illuminating large multicolor painting covering the walls.

"Farther inland and on the lower mountain slops another life, totally isolated and succumbed to despair existed, that would challenge the rational mind of any human being to the limit.

"There they were the cardboard and plywood sacks, the infamous favelas; homes to thousands upon thousands, without running water and electricity, densely wall to wall populated, with lethargically moving bodies of old and young, and with no hope for a better tomorrow.

"There's poverty all over the world, including U.S., but to directly witness such an overwhelming reality tests the balance of your own existence.

"How two, diametrically opposite levels of living, could exist side by side without challenging each other?

"Why such discrepancies are possible in a civilized world of plenty? Who would be responsible for helping the destitute and abandoned? Who has the means, the desire, and the task to restore dignity from a subhuman to a human level? The State, Government, individuals?

"Revolutions promised social justice and equity; but after unfulfilled promises, bloodshed, and oppression, brought more pain and suffering than joy and happiness.

"*Dialectical Materialism* of Karl Marx and *Communism* of Lenin failed miserably to restore human dignity and justice. Why?

"They took everything and gave back little. Their basic dictum of elevation of *matter* over *mind* bent the human spirit, controlled the mind, and compromised creativity, sophistication, and spirituality.

"They promised equality and common ownership, but when tumbled, it was discovered that their lives were deeply supported with consuming imperial opulence, while the rest of the people they fought for, lived in *equal* poverty.

"Any system of government, regardless how came to power, will perish if places matter over mind. Matter sustains, but only the mind creates. Matter's utility is time-limited. Mind's utility is timeless.

"I want to reassure you all, that I enjoyed my trip and had a good time. On the other hand, we shouldn't allow pleasure and happiness to blind our observational skills. After all, what is critical thinking for?"

After Barbara finished, Alice asked Lucia to proceed with her presentation.

"Our flight from Trinidad to Rio took about five and a half hours.

"Landing was an unforgettable experience. It was close to sunset, and the peaks of the mountains and hills, surrounding the city, reflected the fading sun.

"As the plane dropped with precision for landing, the statue of Herculean dimensions of Christ the Redeemer with his outstretched arms, on top of the highest point in Rio, came to view; as a protector and overseer of the city, he was welcoming the new visitors.

"To comprehend the massiveness of the statue certain numerical and quantitative references would be necessary. It weights one thousand metric tons of concrete that equals to a little over 2.2 million pounds! It's one third of a football field high and rests on a half a mile high hill.

"A human, standing next to the statue, affirms its miniscule, miniaturized, and insignificant physical presence.

"Human intelligence though, time and time again, has created, conceived, and produced outpouring accomplishment of excellence in thought, science, and art.

"I think, subconsciously us, as humans, we may have a complex about our physical nihilism. We build monuments to commemorate, but I wonder whether such massiveness is inspired by admiration and respect, or is instead a perfunctory response to compensate for the Lilliputian nature of our physical presence?

"From Athens, to Rome, to Washington D.C., to Rio larger than life monuments of all kinds attest in perpetuity the need of all humans for gigantic physical expressions. If not compensatory for human physical inadequacy, maybe they were built for catharsis and cleansing of the human soul; maybe, they unleash redeeming power mortals need to experience and relate.

"Brazil's slavery history is similar to that of U.S.

"Africans slaves were imported to Brazil by the Portuguese to work in plantations. The Africans brought, among other traditions, religious rituals, vestiges of which still practice, although generically have espoused Christianity.

"For the uninitiated, it was strange to see before sunrise burning candles flickering at the footsteps of closed church doors, with no services being conducted inside.

"Some Brazilians of African descendents still conduct old rituals at night, like exorcisms of evil spirits. Having been brought up as Christians, many feel guilty for participating in pagan practices that are incompatible with their faith. The candles brought and left in front of the churches signified remorse, supplication, repentance, and praying to God for forgiveness and absolution.

"Mardi gras, a three day feast, becomes a year long project for the Cariocas, the Rio natives. The various Samba Clubs, from the most endowed to the poorest and their members work hard the entire year, and pull all their resources, in order to participate and compete in the three day carnival. The preparation goes beyond dancing; it involves designing and making the multicolored, extravagant, and flashy costumes.

"A hotel nearby, with a huge auditorium and stage, presented nightly a two hour Carnival review show for the off Mardi gras season visitors; the experience was overwhelming!

"For the performers, it was a rhythmic, unstoppable, bacchanalian, celebratory, spiritual, abandoning, frenzied, uncontrollable, exhausting, and transposing trance; reminiscent of out of body experiences, religious revivals, and speaking incomprehensively in tongues.

"For the financially and socially challenged Cariocas, this outburst provided a release, with liberating power, and escape from the mentally fatiguing preoccupation of the daily needs and worries.

"Samba is not just a dance; it's a way of daily life.

"You need only drummer to start a slow beat, somewhere on the beach. The drumbeat quickly is transformed to a magnetic power that brings humans, men and women, poor and rich, old and young, close to the drummer. Before you know it, the drumbeat becomes faster and faster, and the crowd dances the samba to a frenzy!

"Soccer is the other passion of the Cariocas that frees the mind, and feeds the soul.

"The 200,000 plus-seat soccer stadium is another place to forget and scream at the top of one's lungs in celebrating victory and lamenting defeat. We can talk for ever, but those were the images that impressed the most."

Alice called Margo to make her presentation before the class went to recess.

"After we went through immigration and customs, we picked up our luggage and boarded the bus that took passengers to the hotel. Everyone on the bus was from the United States. When the hotel escort, a short stocky woman in her mid 50's, began to count us in German, she suddenly stopped and apologized—in perfect English.

"I'm sorry. I always forget, and I make the same mistake all the time. I was born in Brazil, but I'm German and my language is German, although I speak Portuguese like a native."

"Later we learned, that Europeans who migrated to Brazil the beginning of the twentieth century, and especially descendents of English and Germans, were brought up as they were born in their parents and grandparents lands; the English in particular.

They maintain their own day schools, and even have their own cemeteries.

The children speak perfect Portuguese, but when time comes for college, off they go to England, if they can afford it.

"How can you have a nation united with a national conscious, entity, and pride with this kind of mentality? It's difficult to comprehend.

"The difference between U.S. immigrants, with all their weaknesses and shortcomings, and others countries of immigrants in the Western Hemisphere is, that the former came to stay, work hard, and make this land their land, while the latter came to loot, steal, take the best, and return back home as conquerors but not victors.

Victors were those spirited men and women, who stayed, assimilated, overcame adversity, fought the elements, and created a new life.

"The hotel, where we stayed, overlooked the famous Ipanema beach, less crowded and away from the city; it was connected to the northern part of Copacabana beach where all the action was, and natives preferred.

"Exhibiting and showing body, beauty, flesh, and skin is part of all Cariocas' psyche.

"Women, all day long on the beach, wore the famous Tongas; the evolutionary bikini type of bathing suit for women, that is made of three triangles of material; two smaller and a larger, attached by strings, intending to cover strategic parts of the female anatomy.

Sudden turning, moving, or bending over defeats the intent and fulfills the imagination!

"Rio is the capital of plastic surgery of the world.

"With so much flesh and skin exposure, body imperfections cannot be tolerated and should be abated by all means. For those who cannot afford it, government programs would pay to avoid any psychological trauma and inferiority complex that may impact upon the wellbeing of people of no means.

"Anybody, who is anybody in Brazil, must live in Rio.

"San Paulo, the financial center of Brazil and South America, is only forty-five minutes away by plane from Rio. Important people live in Rio and commute to San Paulo for work. The airline providing services between the two cities is the biggest and busiest commuter airline in the world. Mornings take offs and evenings landings go through one after the other like taxi cabs.

"I think this trip was an eye opener.

"The *New World* of the Western Hemisphere started with the same dynamics for the Spaniards, English, French, Portuguese, Dutch, etc. It's amazing though, how U.S., as a nation, evolved and differentiated itself from all the others.

"We're still young by comparison, and the jury is not out yet; but it's up to each one of us to continue along the same path of excellence in building our nation, not out of ego, but out of respect and gratitude for our founding fathers."

After Margo finished with her presentation, Alice addressed the class:

"I would like to congratulate Barbara, Lucia, and Margo for their presentations.

"The places they visited are well known for their natural beauty and wonders, but they went beyond that. They used critical and analytical skills to study people. How they live. What make them tick? How social classes were formed, and how societies had responded in the past to correct inequities and restore social justice.

"Historically, we've seen it so often; the weakness of people when in power. Their ideas and ideals become murky, if not forgotten.

"How about the deep roots of faith? No matter where were originated can go on and on.

"You're all eighteen year olds, approaching graduation from high school.

"All your presentations, so far, have shown maturity and human understanding that goes beyond your chronological age. Not even one of you mentioned the word *shopping*, that no tourist, any place in the world, has ever escaped.

"Listening to your commentaries, observations, and thoughts made me proud to be on the staff of this Academy. With young women of your stature, mind, and intelligence to see and learn, I'm confident as a woman that the future of our nation will be in the hands of women of substance."

CHAPTER 5

Graduation and Separation

Two years had almost gone by since Barbara, Lucia and Margo met as juniors at the Marie Curie Academy. Their friendship became more solid and committed with the passage of every single day; it helped them to become not only better friends, but better persons as well.

Building one's character is a composite effort and process, that although is primarily influenced by family, peer pressure cannot be ignored. As matter of fact peers, under certain circumstances, could affect individuals much more than parents and siblings; that might lead to conflicts, mistrust, and even hostility.

The trio found themselves in a unique situation.

The value of their friendship reinforced personal values, and miraculous intertwined them with what their families stood for. They were all around winners!

Today was graduation day and Commencement Exercises for the trio. A milestone and a giant leap to the future.

What the future would bring and hold for them was unforeseeable, but what the future could become was dependent on every single moment of the present.

In their life's journey, choices and timing of execution would be as important as breathing air to sustaining life. Choices would reflect individual values, and timing of execution intelligence and judgment.

After the invocation, the trio played the first movement of Tchaikovsky's Trio in A minor, with Barbara, at the piano, Lucia the violin, and Margo the cello. The response was overwhelming. With audience clapping and standing, the trio walked back on stage and bowed several times; each received a bouquet of red roses, courtesy of the local florist, who made the flower arrangements for the auditorium and the dinning room.

With everyone sitting, Martha Fuller, the director of the Academy, got up, approached the lectern, and addressed the audience:

"Graduates, parents, and guests.

"On behalf of the faculty, administration, and the board of trustees, please accept our sincerest congratulations for what you have accomplished, as teams of students and parents, the past two years. It was hard for both of you.

"You endured separation, many a time loneliness, hard work, and concerns for the future. The Academy was by your side every step of the way. Do you know why? Because all of us—parents, students, and the Academy—have something in common: the pursuit of excellence.

"You, the parents, being accomplished yourselves, became an inspirational force for the students, who in return, challenged themselves in the process of learning. Of course native intelligence should take some credit for students who excel.

"Nevertheless, you will be amazed how much intelligence and brain power is wasted and lost every second, every minute, and every hour.

"Intelligence, that was destined to reach the skies, ended up in the gutter, instead.

"It's important to recognize, understand, and treasure what you've got; but what would more important, that will make the difference in the final analysis, is not what you've got, but what you did with what you've got.

"Gifts underused lose the original luster, become rusty, and never regain value.

"I'm sure you must have noticed certain differences between our Commencements Exercises and others you may have attended in the past.

"There was neither valedictorian nor salutatorian address today. It they were, you would be bored to death and fall asleep. Because every student, out of our twenty graduates, is a valedictorian and salutatorian!

This is the pride of the Academy; it attracts the best, and brings out best in the process of learning.

"Something else may have caught your eye, too.

"All faculty members are women, not by design, but by credentials.

"These are women like you in the audience, and they can be mothers, wives, sisters, and daughters; but all with extraordinary minds and unique backgrounds that enrich our faculty with depth, wisdom, and diversity, like Dr. Sue Chen, a wife and a mother of two, who offered the invocation.

She joined our faculty last year, after receiving her Ph.D. in Comparative Religions and Ethics from the Divinity School of Yale University.

"Our philosophy is that you as parents should be responsible for setting values and standards for your daughters.

"For the past two years, this Academy served as your trustee and executor to make sure that all your wishes for behavior and morality were carried out.

"On the other hand, when your daughters were exposed to these extraordinary women of the faculty, these women became role models, and your extenders in affirming your values, in addition to presenting inspiring paradigms of accomplishments of the highest level possible.

"Ladies and gentlemen, parents of the graduating class:

"I would like to reassure today that your daughters are leaving the Academy, thanks to you and our faculty, as mature, intellectually developed, and disciplined young ladies of substance; ready to achieve, create, lead, and determined to overcome all eventualities in their future.

"The synergy, between you the parents and teachers, remained the dynamic and the cornerstone responsible for forming the character and expanding the mind of these remarkable young women.

This synergy has been known since antiquity. To paraphrase Socrates, who said; *parents give life; teachers make life good.*

"In closing, I would like to say a few words to our graduates:

"When I look at you, I don't see twenty beautiful, smart, proper, highly intelligent, and disciplined women. I see an addition to our nation's aristocracy. I use the word *aristocracy* in its original concept that has nothing to do class, rank, privileges, hereditary nobility, and elitism.

"I am talking about the aristocracy of mind, character, heart, spirit, and soul of an individual, who through value principles, education, morality, justice, respect, discipline, sacrifices, and commitment, is equipped to be the best and offer the best to our communities, workforce, society, and nation.

"I see in you, the future CEOs of Fortune five-hundred companies, scientists, academicians, ambassadors, physicians, lawyers, jurists, university presidents, members of the House of Representatives, senators; and why not? A president of the United States!

"There is no question you are gifted; but what will make you the best is your fortitude not to rest on, or be overtaken by your gifts, but challenge them constantly. Good luck and don't forget; your intelligence is a blessing, never to be forsaken, neglected, or forgotten."

After Martha's address, the graduates received their diplomas, and the ceremony closed with a benediction offered by Dr. Chen.

An hour later, and around 5 o'clock, students, parents, and faculty reconvened in the dining room for supper. After supper, the trio excused themselves. They wanted to spend sometime together before leaving the Academy. The suitcases were all packed and loaded in their parents' cars.

❦   ❦   ❦

The trio gathered in Lucia's room, where they had held their first meeting, as juniors, two years ago.

The three young women shone with the beauty, demeanor, and grace of a lady. They eyes sparkled with fire. The bodies moved with the confidence and power of a finely trained warrior, ready to put the armor on, determined to fight with tenacity and perseverance in order win the war.

Victory wouldn't be taken for granted, easy or a given, but was a target that had to be fought for, hard.

The intelligence and the mental gifts were already there, and success was expected, but not guaranteed. The trio was convinced that by having become virtually sisters got the thrust of additional power that would give them more ammunition to make victory grater and more attainable.

Barbara was bound for Duke, and Margo for Stanford; both would be closer to their families.

Lucia decided to stay in the city and attend Trinity University.

Last year, her parents made a large donation to Trinity, worth several million dollars, in memory of her grandmother, and established the *Theresa Antonelli Chair in Business and Corporate Ethics.*

Grants would be also available for students pursuing Masters and Ph.D.s degrees in the business school, along the same venue.

Barbara, Lucia, and Margo agreed to meet once a year for a week, somewhere in a convenient location and after the academic year was over, for a retreat, to discuss their lives and renew the *Vows of Three Sisters.* In between retreats, they would correspond and talk to each other on the phone.

A letter from one would be addressed to the other two, and opted for a conference phone line, that would allow the three of them to communicate as a group, by having set a prearranged time call schedule convenient to all.

The trio was more pensive than sad.

Deep joy in their hearts affirmed the uniqueness of the bonding that had given them the best and the most integrated two years of their lives.

"Physical separation," Lucia said, "It's a fact that we have to accept with bravery and reasoning; our union is strong enough to sustain it.

"If physical presence was an absolute element necessary for our union to survive, would have indicated a defective foundation that sooner or later could compromise the future of its existence."

Barbara had packed everything except for her family's Bible. She took it out of her briefcase and placed it on the desk.

"I think before we go, there's nothing more appropriate than to renew our vows."

Barbara, Lucia, and Margo put one hand on top of the Bible and recited-they knew it by heart, the *Vows of Three Sisters*. The eyes became teary and the hearts beat faster. The arms extended to embrace with power, and the lips sealed the moment with the promise of unabated eternal friendship and sisterhood.

The saga of the three sisters, with the upcoming separation, had entered a new and more challenging phase. Will the *Vows* strengthen the friendship and help them overcome demands of the future?

CHAPTER 6

Aspirations and Commitments

Four years later, Barbara, Lucia, and Margo graduated from College, Summa Cum Laude-first in their class and bound for graduate school in the fall.

Barbara was going to medical school staying at Duke; Lucia for her Ph.D. in philosophy staying at Trinity; and Margo to Caltech for her Ph.D. in mathematics.

The trio kept their promise to meet every summer to renew the vows, play Tchaikovsky's Trio, and strengthen their friendship. It was like a retreat. They chose to meet and stay at Lucia's home, as being more convenient and centrally located.

This summer was different.

Demands of graduate school were forthcoming. They wanted to get away from it all, this time, and be more isolated, have more privacy, and spent more than a week together. They reserved three adjoining rooms in a mountainous resort, for the last two weeks of June.

The Hotel was built on a cliff with panoramic view of a leisurely and reluctantly moving waterfall, resonating more of a soothing and hypnotic than roaring sound presence. It was an hour and a half drive from the airport, but transportation was provided.

The trio's flights would be arriving within thirty minutes of each other.

Lucia arrived first, and after picking up her suitcases, took a seat in the lobby of the luggage claim area waiting for the other girls. Then Barbara came, and shortly after, Margo was seen on the escalator coming down.

The trio greeted each other with tears and laughter, hugs and kisses, words and sighs. Looking at these three beautiful young women, with sparkling eyes speaking with impatient, emotional, and hasty voices, no one could ever imagine the power and depth of a composite intelligence that existed among them.

Intelligence is not devoid of emotion.

In a well balance existence emotion shouldn't control intelligence, but definitely could inspire, stimulate, and initiate its creative power. Without emotion there would no music, poetry, art, politics nor even wars.

In life you have to take both; the good and the bad, hoping the balance tilts to the former and away from the latter, where emotion overtakes intelligence.

The winding road to the Hotel was breathtaking. Sharp turns kept the speed of the van down and allowed the eyes to see and admire, unhurriedly, the wonders of nature. Evergreens on steep slopes and pine trees bent to the winds still sheltered patches of stubborn snow.

The remnants of the winter bliss would soon succumb to the scorching rays of the mid-noon summer sun; and melting snow would bring back green pastures to life to sustain life, and feed crystal clear water springs to moist dry lips and abate thirst.

After checking in, the trio was escorted to the rooms by bellhops carrying the luggage.

Lucia took the middle room.

Once inside the original scene of six years ago, at the Academy, was repeated to its last detail. The partition doors were unlocked and left wide open.

The three women-recent college graduates-run from one room to the other until felt short of breath. They finally collapsed on Lucia's bed. Wisdom, knowledge, maturity, and age hadn't tampered girlishness, giggling, and silliness.

After drinking sodas from the mini bar, the trio unpacked, changed to denim shorts and T-shirts, and gathered again in Lucia's room. They sat on the bed in a circle, with their knees flexed.

"What six years have been since we first met," Lucia said. "I'm so happy to be together with you; I'm sure you feel the same. College was fine and fun, but my mind, on and off, drifted back to the Academy. Those two formative and intellectually challenging years wouldn't have been the same without you. What you gave me is so deep and expansive, that's difficult to put it in words.

"We all came from loving families that protected us and gave us values, security, spirituality, ambition, and positive role models.

"To share and energize all these with two sisters was an opportunity, a feast, and a dream come true. Nothing would ever matter in my life any more, as long as you're with me not only in flesh, but in spirit, too.

"Our friendship has not been tested as yet. I'm sure, no matter what the future would bring to each one of us, our love, devotion, and understanding for one another would give us the tenacity and the power to support and stand by one another.

"The effusion of our minds, hearts, souls, and spirits, always in communion, has become not only a powerful, but also a delicate instrument of quality and precision that transfers energy from one another to meet each other's needs.

"Our personal lives, in up or down moments, already have the infrastructure and support to overcome adversity, or celebrate blessings, and happiness. What are sisters for, after all?"

"To unconditionally love and understand," Barbara answered, "And you expressed it so well. You spoke my own mind."

"I'm sure the next two weeks," Margo said, "Will be awesome and a blast. It's a family away from family; the reunion of the family of three sisters! We can pick up from where we were left off last year; talking on the phone or corresponding by mail isn't the same.

"Physical presence, eye movements, facial expressions, and senses on guard transmit real time life images, uninterruptedly being lived.

"No matter how many photographs you have seen of *Mona Lisa*, looking at the real thing, you experience the complete, powerful, and unabated directness of communication; for the enormous and unimaginable space and distance in between have been conquered.

"Directness translates into warmth and comfort. Barbara, tell us the latest. What is new with you and Bob Brown? Any plans? How are your parents?"

"Well, as you know by now, Bob and I've been going steady through our senior year. His older sister, Arlene, got married last summer, and I was one of the bride's maids. My parents were invited to the wedding and there seemed to be positive vibes and chemistry between the two families.

"Bob is the first guy I've been serious with.

"There's no question; he is smart and nice. But right now, I can't tell for sure that this is the man I would like to spend the rest of my life with. He is going to graduate school up north to continue his studies in molecular biology. He loves research and teaching. He's already gone to work in the lab this summer, and we won't see each other until next year. We have to wait and see how we feel when we meet again.

"We haven't discussed this openly, but if either one of us would like to see other people wouldn't be any problem. In reality, I don't think this will ever happen. He is a bookworm and so obsessive with his work; and I, going to medical school with its pressure and demands, don't have any big plans for an active social life.

"Whatever time is left, if there is any, I'd like to practice my piano.

"My parents are doing fine and already gone.

"They took one year sabbatical and plan to visit and lecture in Africa and Australia. Right now, they are in Johannesburg. Former fellows, who worked and did research under my parents, already established back home, have been bugging them for years to come and visit them, and see other medical schools, outside the U.S.

"When they return will give up all administrative responsibilities and clinical work and concentrate on research and teaching. They plan to recruit four young physicians to work with them, for a year or two, upon the recommendation of their professors. Some funds, through grants from pharmaceutical companies and UNESCO, have already become available.

"What about you Margo? Have you found any particular guy you like? What's new with your family?"

"I dated a few, but nothing serious.

"Guys are still intimidated by women in math. They think we're *freaks*, but it doesn't bother me. Maybe I'll find another *freak* at Caltech! Even with all the progress we've made and all societal changes, men continue to have certain perceptions about women that it's strange.

"For some reason men in college, and at this time of their lives, gravitate more to the *bimbo* type of women and aren't serious about relationships. They're often driven by the immediacy of sexual impulses at the expense of dialogue and intellectual exchange. I've nothing against *bimbos*; maybe there are nicer and even more intelligent than I.

"On the other hand, I have no use for projecting kittenish vulnerability that melts the boys down!

"My family is doing well.

"My mother's gallery continues to thrive. She was approached and asked to establish sort of a franchise and chain with other galleries in various cities; the strategy would be to capture larger markets. She hasn't made up her mind yet. She's concerned that heavy traveling would be necessary.

"Pedro graduated from Yale Law School last year, finished his clerkship with a judge at the U.S. Court of Appeals in Washington, DC, passed the bar exam, and joined a large law firm in the city that represents several foreign banking and corporate concerns.

"As a result of NAFTA, his firm expanded to Mexico, and opened offices in other Central and South America countries.

He's the only lawyer in the firm with command of Spanish language, and with a last name like *Martinez* he will do well, indeed!"

"Lucia, what is going on with you?" Barbara asked. "You're so quiet. You spoke so eloquently at the beginning, preemptively expressing our feelings and the meaning of us being sisters, but nothing else. Are you still seeing Nick or somebody else? What's new? We're all ears!"

While Barbara and Margo were talking, Lucia remained attentive and was happy that her sisters and their families were doing so well. At times she became pensive and occasionally reacted with a happy but enigmatic smile.

"Well I've great news for you.

"John, courtesy of the State Department, graduated from the John F. Kennedy School of Government, at Harvard, with distinction last month. He entered the Foreign Service, two years ago, after getting his master's in diplomacy from Georgetown, and now is waiting for his first overseas assignment.

"Something else, totally unexpectedly, happened.

"Food Unlimited, the biggest supermarket chain in U.S., made an unbelievable offer to buy my father's seventy-five stores across the surrounding states. He hasn't decided yet. He might consider the offer, but there would be two stipulations: no management changes and no lay offs for the next two years.

"The buyer hasn't agreed yet, and my father is not in hurry to sell. If the deal goes through, they would keep the same name of my father's stores, and offered him the position of regional president, and membership to the board of directors of the parent company. He wants to make sure his employees are well protected by the new owner. This kind of a man he is. It'll take some time, if and when, before the deal is done"

"That's fine and dandy, kid. What about you and what about Nick," Barbara asked.

"Come on, spill the bean, sis! We're waiting," Margo said.

Lucia started laughing.

"You are funny.

"There's no more Nick or anybody else. Nick and I, as you recall, met during the spring semester of our junior year. We talked on the phone several times last summer, and corresponded twice.

"He's a nice fellow, smart, good looking, and mature; I think he was getting serious. The first week back in school he asked me out to dinner, but I declined. He was upset and concerned, if he had done something to offend me, or if there was somebody else. I tried to convince him that neither was true, and nothing personal. I told him simply, that for the time being, I decided not to date anymore, period."

"What is the matter with you?" Margo asked. "Are you a man-hater, or a lesbian? Is today your coming out day? Are you gay?"

The trio laughed to tears. Lucia started coughing an almost chocked. She went to the bathroom, closed the door, took a few sips of water, and later returned to the bedroom.

Barbara, still laughing, asked,

"Lucia, have you told your parents you're gay? Does John know?"

The uproar continued for several minutes until the trio became a little more sedated.

Lucia, trying to keep her cool, became more serious.

"I don't remember the last time we had such a good laugh; it was so therapeutic and we needed it badly, after four years of hard work. I hope we've more of the same the next two weeks. Now, let's be more serious.

"I've something important to share with you; I hope you'll understand and be supportive. Something personal that you, being my sisters, will be the first ones to know."

Barbara and Margo's faces changed in a flash. What could be?

They were honored by Lucia's trust, but also worried and concerned.

From Lucia's expression they knew it was something serious that was in the core of her life, and a top priority in her existence. They had been together for six years. Their intuitive power had become strong enough by now, and capable of sensing the feelings and thoughts in each other's hearts and minds.

For the first time, they realized the depth of their communion and understanding.

Lucia's stolid expression softened with the hint of a smile.

"What I'm about to tell you has been in and out of my mind, sort of subconsciously, from our first class at the Academy. I never paid too much attention thinking that was one of those vagaries of a dreaming, fantasizing, and romanticizing impetuous youth.

"This continued through out college in a rather undefined and murky mode. It became sharply focused during the last two months of the spring semester of our senior years. That's why I never brought that up until we had a chance to meet.

"I'm sure you remember our first day at the Academy when the director, Martha Fuller, welcomed the junior class. She mentioned her experience with many young intelligent women, who later in life felt unfulfilled and tried to find themselves; for some was too late.

"Martha emphasized the importance of spending time alone, if you want to find yourself, especially during your formative years; but some are afraid to be alone.

"Maybe, would have helped, if these women had some special and open friendship, counseling, and a *mentor* during college to prepare them for future challenges, as their lives were to change, with upcoming relationships, marriage, and motherhood.

"Margo, you were right when you asked me if today was my coming out day.

"It certainly is, and I'm sure we're all going to survive. You're the first ones to hear it from the horse's mouth; I have decided to become a nun! It's my *calling*, and I know that."

Barbara and Margo's faces froze.

At this moment, for them, Lucia was leaving and going to another world.

Was the sisterhood being dissolved before their own eyes? Feelings of bewilderment, confusion, anxiety, insecurity, and separation loomed over their minds.

The compelling need to express what they felt inside was halted to a standstill.

They had so many questions, but they didn't know where to start from. Relative and pertinent words to articulate their questions could not be recalled in order to make them logical, rational, sensible, and answerable.

Both remained speechless and their eyes rolled aimless at random.

Lucia could sense well how Barbara and Margo felt. It was so sudden and unexpected. They had no idea if, and how her decision would affect them. It was up to her to make some sense of her decision, and bring them aboard.

She moved closer and put her face between Barbara and Margo.

Tears started flowing from all directions.

In the six years they had known each other, this was the first time they wept.

Lucia kissed Barbara and Margo, went to the bathroom, brought a box of Kleenex, and passed it around. With all eyes dried and everyone composed, Lucia continued;

"I know exactly what're you thinking. I went through the same thing when I made my decision. What will happen to us? What will happen to our *Vows?* Absolutely nothing! Our union, communion, and love will continue uninterrupted.

"I don't expect any changes and neither should you. Would you expect any changes after one of us got married? I don't think so. What the three of us have is so unique and personal, that shouldn't affect or be affected by other pursuits or circumstances in our own lives."

Barbara and Margo took a deep breath in relief and smiled.

If a pursuit was good enough for one sister should be as good for the other two. Personal happiness and accomplishments of one sister would make the others cherish and applaud; and the trio should be prepared not only to share happiness, but also unforeseen changes, and even sadness.

Their union, from the start, wasn't founded on girlish and frivolous sentimentality, but on a concrete foundation reinforced by their own values and spirituality.

"What is the name of the order?" Margo asked.

"The House of Hope; it's an independent group of self-supported women not formally administered by the church. They're all working professionals, doctors, lawyers, teachers, etc.

"To be admitted, you have to be at least twenty-two years old, be in school or work full time. All students like me are or will be going to graduate school and have part time jobs. Of course there is no habit to wear or formal and structured ordination per se.

"The vows of chastity and to serve the community are between you and God, and taken by the altar in the presence of the other nuns; and you can quit any time. The nuns, known as *lay-nuns,* live in the same quarters, have at least one meal a day together, and meet in the chapel for mornings and evenings prayers.

"I became familiar with the order in the spring semester of our junior year.

"I saw several well and properly dressed single ladies, young and middle age, visiting the assistant dean's office for women, where I did my four-week internship in designing and writing curriculum in social studies.

"These women were given names of female students to meet, have lunch together, go to a show, and developed some kind of a rapport with them.

"The intent was for them to establish a communication line with students, and openly discuss whatever was in their mind.

Parents of out of town girls were particularly happy with the availability of these women outside the structured academic counseling services.

Some girls were so close with their *special* friend and *mentor* that invited her to visit sorority houses and meet with other students.

"For some bright young women, opting for a career in a specific profession, like law or medicine, was an eye opener to see what criteria successful professional women used in choosing a career that would keep them happy, productive, and fulfilled.

"If only I could help just one student, I'd be more than happy. We're lucky. During our formative years we got so much help and support from our parents, and from each other. Others weren't or wouldn't be as privileged and lucky as we were."

"Lucia, when are you going to tell your parents and John? And what is coming up next?" Barbara asked.

"When I get home.

"I've a hunch my mother may have suspected something. She met Nick once, and she thought he was a nice guy. When I told her I wouldn't be seeing him any more, she said I wound up being an old maid!

"Two weeks ago, I had a meeting with the membership committee, and the day before I left, Eunice, a member of the committee-she is an architect, called to inform me that I was welcomed to join. She designed and oversaw the conversion of an old hotel to residential units.

"Each nun has her own suite, and right now there are forty-five women living together. The facility can accommodate another fifty.

"Weekends we can leave and stay with family or friends. Considering the organization started seven years ago the growth has been consistent. I'll be moving in within a week after returning home. I got a part time job for the rest of the summer, at Trinity, teaching English literature to undergraduate students.

The residence is within walking distance from the main campus."

The trio had a fabulous time at the resort.

They enjoyed nature, went hiking, swam in the lake, greeted soaring hawks and eagles, and welcomed and saw off playful and impatient butterflies resting on a rainbow of flowers.

The silvery palette of the full moon brightened foliage and majestically transformed imposing amorphous monoliths to avant-garde sculptures of nature; and the balmy night breeze brought shadows of tree brunches to life in a oscillatory minimalist celebratory dance.

As the days past, Barbara and Margo were convinced that Lucia's choice wouldn't affect them after all. Unspoken concerns faded away.

The power and commitment that had amalgamated them for two years, at the Academy, remained as strong.

The trio, for the first time, realized that the future would challenge them with individual choices and personal circumstances.

Their friendship shouldn't be dictated by sameness, but diversity and freedom, for their love was inclusive and secure to not only to understand, but also thrive on differences.

The time to leave came too soon.

The night before departing, the trio was already making plans for next summer. This time though, they missed not playing music together, but didn't really matter.

When practicing alone, Tchaikovsky's Trio at home felt mentally connected.

Physical presence, by its nature, satisfies the eyes and tactile senses, but does not necessarily and automatically convey reciprocal connection and rapport of minds and hearts. Eyes were made only to see, but only minds and hearts were made to think and feel. The trio's connection was strong enough to sustain separation for another year without fear or regret.

The trio, right before checking out, gathered in Lucia's room to renew the *Vows of Three Sisters.*

Something extraordinary and unexpected happened this year; extreme and polarized differentiation of anticipated lifestyles.

Barbara and Margo's lives, from now on, would be diametrically opposite to Lucia's.

While Barbara and Margo would be looking forward to romance, marriage, and children, Lucia would be espousing in actuality monasticism and celibacy, despite the lack of habit and ordinary exterior appearance.

How these two antithetical existences would affect the *Vows of Three Sisters?* Are they resilient enough to accommodate both?

Would the *Vows* impede or enhance the future of these exceptional women in pursuing different but lofty goals in their own lives?

CHAPTER 7

Evolution and Accomplishments

Ten years had gone by since the trio met at the resort, surrounded by a serene and beautiful mountainous landscape.

Their lives had changed dramatically, as expected, but kept the promise to get together, at least for one week every year, preferably in the summer. The love for one another remained as strong, and was reinforced with more depth and maturity that came alone with age.

The trio shared and became part not only of each other's happiness, but also sorrows. They were lucky and blessed so far, that happiness, by far, had exceeded sorrows, which were rather insignificant and mundane, and nothing to speak off.

Barbara, after graduating from medical school, did a five year residency in obstetrics and gynecology. Although she followed her parent's path in choosing a specialty, after finishing, she joined a group of five women in private practice.

What attracted her to this particular group was that each member alternated and provided charity work-a few hours a week, by staffing the outpatient obstetrics clinic of the City Hospital.

She was appalled, during her training, to see pregnant women coming to the delivery room without having a single prenatal visit!

In the land of plenty-where the most technologically advanced healthcare was available, and more dollars were spent per capita than anywhere else in the world—no wonder U.S. fell behind in infant mortality per thousand life births in comparison to Japan and the Scandinavian countries.

Who was to blame? Everyone blamed everybody else-the government, people, the system, etc.-without offering any solutions. Barbara decided to be part of the solution leaving the debate to the *experts.*

She respected and admired her parents' academic life, contributions, and accomplishments, but she wanted to be in the *trenches* where the action was.

Barbara had never forgotten where she came from and what might have become of her. What she ended up to be wasn't by birth right, but by circumstance and fate, and above all by unconditional love and faith.

While examining unwed mothers-mostly teenagers-at the City Hospital clinic, her mind often galloped to some thirty years back contemplating the beginning of her own existence. She wasn't sad at all. She counted her blessings, and in her prayers thanked God for her parents, and the life she was provided with.

She never felt *chosen* but definitely grateful and humble.

She wanted to be part of *making the difference* aphorism, by helping in certain societal circumstances where the present was so bleak and the future so gloomy.

She wanted to ensure the babies coming to this world, no matter how compromising the environment was, weren't underweight, malnourished, or infested with drugs.

Barbara often thought,

Being born and coming to this world should be a celebration of love, life and hope, and not a calumniation of exploitation, despair, loneliness, abandonment, and destitution.

Barbara and Bob continued seeing each other during the summer and holidays, and as time went by, became more serious.

Bob got his Ph.D. in cellular biology by the time Barbara started the third year of her residency. He came back to town after he was offered a teaching position with a research project, as an assistant professor at the university.

They were engaged at the beginning of Barbara's chief residency year and got married two weeks after she finished. Besides being in love, it was a win-win situation for both.

Barbara was raised by parents in academic medicine, and she was aware of the demands and pressure of academic life; deadlines to meet, articles to write, waiting for tenure, books to publish, etc.

On the other hand, academic life provided more of a balanced structure for family. Barbara's specialty would require night calls that could be a problem when children came along. At least nights, when and if, she might be out delivering babies, Bob would be always home taking care of the children.

Barbara's wedding was a celebration of love, life, family, friendship, and tradition. She insisted, inconvenience and traveling notwithstanding, to be married in the Church of Bethany, where her mother sang in the choir as a college student.

The wedding would bring not only the trio together, but also their extended families.

The wedding ceremony was moving, original, idiomatic, and tailored to the celebrants' vision and taste.

Before the service began, Barbara's mother, standing in the back of the church, sang *Amazing Grace* with her father at the organ. As soon as the first unexpected word was sung and first note was played, heads turned and eyes were fixed in a gaze.

Janice, in her early sixties, tall, still beautiful with an imposing figure, hadn't lost the luster, timbre, and control of the booming and sweet sound of her contralto voice.

She was completely transposed, and while singing, slowly wept.

Her composite appearance was reminiscent of an African princess beseeching on behalf of her people, that the long famine had besieged them ends.

There wasn't a dry eye in the congregation that quickly became contemplative and introspective, sensing and comprehending not only the joyous, but also the sanctity and sacramental significance of the event.

The wedding party quickly assembled, entered the church, and started walking on the aisle, as the organist played the wedding march.

This was not your usual wedding with ushers, bridesmaids, ring bearers, and flower girls.

Classic simplicity combined with empowering commitment crowned the event and became the real essence.

The bride entered the church flanked by her parents. Behind, the maids of honor and bestwomen, Lucia and Margo, followed holding the train. For the service, Barbara's family Bible was used that had become her property now.

The trio was excited not only to celebrate Barbara's happiness, but also to see each other again.

The wedding convinced them that as their lives were changing, which was expected, had left their friendship unmarred and in full throttle. The vows they took as seventeen years old had remained meaningful and powerful as ever.

Three years after the wedding, Barbara's parents retired.

For reasons never planned or sought after, they had become a celebrity couple appearing on talk shows and the lecture circuit.

For their own catharsis and peace of mind, wrote a book titled *Living, Loving, and Healing*, chronicling their experience as physicians, teachers, researchers, spouses and parents, and how they had enriched and inspired each other in life. The book became an instant best seller and was an inspiration for professional couples striving and struggling to keep careers, marriages, and families together.

The emphasis was on deep spirituality, faith, and family values as the main commonalities that could provide everlasting and powerful connection.

They had seen so many couples in their own professional circle starting so ideally and promising to abysmally disintegrate later in life. Why? They had it all; beauty, success, wealth, but bored each other to death! Something was missing.

Slowly looking at each other saw a stranger; not a lover, soul mate, friend, or a committed and supporting partner in this life's journey. The sparkle in the eyes had changed to a glassy gaze; and unintentional and accidental touch had the warmth of a corpse. Was the condition terminal? Irreversible? Hopeless? Absolutely, not.

Each partner had to reactivate and reinvent his or her own spirituality and actualize the importance of faith in God beyond its abstract form, and faith in each other, in order to reconnect and rejuvenate love not as a fleeting sentiment, but as a spiritual experience.

Individual imperfections, lapses in judgment, selfishness, indifference, and the seduction of self-importance faded in the emergence of resurrected love reinforced by supplication.

While Barbara's parents were on a trip, the trio had an urgent and unexpected three-way phone call initiated by Barbara. She had big news! And Lucia and Margo would be the first ones to know.

After trying for two years she was pregnant!

They all laughed and cried, rejoiced and celebrated. Lucia and Margo weren't only expectant aunts but would go beyond that; they would be also godmothers for Barbara's baby.

Barbara had a baby girl and her christening was another opportunity for the trio to be together again. The baby was named Janice, after Barbara's mother, and her full name was Janice Lucia Margo Hendricks-Brown! The event not only solidified the trio, but also without a doubt, sealed and blessed it with irrevocable sanctity.

Lucia pursued her graduate studies and got her Ph.D. in philosophy from Trinity University.

The title of her doctoral dissertation was *Physical Laws and Metaphysics, and their Influence on Thought, Logic, and Reason.* The premise was that physical laws, even with their repetitive and predictable nature, weren't devoid of abstruseness.

The compelling intellectual force of the human mind to analyze and comprehend physical laws lead to the genesis of the concept of the theoretical principle of *inquiry,* which was championed by Aristotle, in the 4th Century B.C.

Thought, Logic, and Reason compel and dictate to deal with first principles, the relations of universals to particulars, and the *theological* doctrine of causation.

The Universe is so perfect. Was perfection self-made, accidental? How did the big *bang* get started and put everything in motion? Was any *mover* standing behind it? Who turned the switch on? Does the mind have to go beyond physical laws-maybe metaphysics-to understand perfection of the Universe and how all began?

The faculty was impressed. Lucia was offered a faculty position as an assistant professor, effective immediately, after her completion of one year of postdoctoral fellowship at Oxford University, in England.

As time passed, it was obvious that Lucia was becoming a woman of substance.

A combination of scholarship, leadership, intellectual curiosity, expanding knowledge, depth, personal growth, devotion, and faith had made her formidable in presence and stature.

Three years in a row, she was voted by the students the most influential member of the faculty, and at the age of thirty-two, she became a tenured professor.

Lucia was especially admired and idolized by young women, under-graduate and graduate students, not only for her intelligence and brain power, but also for her simplicity, humanity, and humility.

The lack of arrogance and sense of humor made her approachable.

Students, even with no pressing problems, sought her company for inspiration and comfort. All knew of her commitment to monastic life, with its sort of the twenty-first century concept and overtones in appearance, but admired and respected her.

She never had any second thoughts, was content with her decision, and was always at peace with herself.

Her family had originally accepted her decision to become a nun with a certain degree of skepticism, especially John, her brother. For a twenty-two year old woman to make a decision of that nature was rather premature. The hope was that she might change with the passage of time. Of course nothing happened.

Lucia continued to grow and meet the goals she had set for herself.

To her it was important, that Barbara and Margo not only understood the depth and significance of her decision, but they were also proud and supportive.

For Barbara and Margo to have a sister with such a commitment and mission gave them something special and unique. They felt somehow different; maybe more charismatic and enlightened by association and being so close, and be loved by another human being like Lucia.

She was exemplarily dedicated more to the spirit and mind, and less to the flesh and matter, considering her wealth.

The House of Hope, since Lucia moved in, grew dramatically.

All suites were occupied and expansion was planned. The architect designed an addition for seventy more suites and financing had been already obtained; with so many professional women, all in a high earning bracket, it was easy.

All of a sudden something unexpectedly happened.

Rick, Lucia's father, finally after a great deal of hesitation, and negotiations that took a long time, successfully completed the sale of his supermarket chain at an unbelievable profit. Taxes due would be steep, even after establishing substantial trust funds for his wife and two children.

The only option left that made sense was charitable contributions.

The main beneficiaries of millions of dollars became Trinity University and the House of Hope.

The Rick and Roxanne Antonelli Chair was endowed for graduate studies in *Philosophy of Natural Laws and Metaphysics,* reflecting Lucia's doctoral thesis, which was so highly thought of by the Philosophy Departments of top US universities. The endowment also provided full scholarships for four doctoral candidates, to be awarded each year.

The professorship was offered to Lucia, but she flatly refused to accept the appointment. In her written response indicated, that she was honored, but declined the position without giving any specific explanation as to why.

Deep inside, she believed that accepting the position would have been the worst kind of nepotism, as if her family fortune bought the Chair for her. Besides, she was only thirty-two, despite the fact that she had so successfully and impressively defended her thesis, had completed her doctorate four years ago, had lectured extensively, and was considered an authority on the subject.

The donation to the House of Hope covered the entire addition and construction of the seventy suites, and the bank loan was deferred. The chapel was enlarged and completely redone, an organ was added, and was officially dedicated to Saint Theresa as a memorial to Rick's mother.

Six months went by.

Lucia, busy with her work and ready to publish her second book, had all but forgotten about the offer.

Last Friday, late in the afternoon, she received a call from the secretary of the university president and was invited to attend the quarterly dinner-meeting of the University Board of Trustees, which was scheduled for Monday at 6:30 pm. She made nothing of this.

It was the policy of the board to alternate and periodically invite faculty members to acquaint them with certain administrative and financial issues of various departments and get feedback from senior and junior faculty members. Lucia knew there was something special about this meeting.

Paul Wallace was to be introduced as the new president of the board of trustees, along with four new members replacing those whose term had expired. She had heard of Paul Wallace from her father.

He was the president and CEO of the Midwestern Bank, the largest in the State that was also doing business in the neighboring states. By coincidence many of her father's supermarkets housed the same bank's branches, and offered discount cards to the bank's employees, like they did for their own.

Lucia arrived at the large and elegantly furnished dining room, located on the first floor of the administrative building, around 6:15.

As it was customary, Lesley Wilson, the university president, a Ph.D. in astrophysics, renowned authority in space thermodynamics, and an ordained priest, impeccable dressed in a suit and tie as usual, was at the main entrance greeting the dinner guests, as they were coming in.

At exactly 6:30 the door closed and Lesley asked Lucia to join and sit next to him. She was surprised that there weren't any other faculty members present.

There were at least four to six professors the other two times she was invited to attend.

After the university chaplain offered the invocation dinner was served.

Lesley formally introduced Lucia to Paul Wallace. He already knew of her, not from his association with her father's business, but from his predecessor and other board and faculty members he had met.

With dessert served Lesley greeted the guests and introduced Paul:

"Ladies and gentlemen, tonight, Trinity University enters a new chapter in its long history of academic excellence. Trinity, thanks to its faculty of renown and quality of students, stands in the vanguard of innovation and continues to challenge the young minds and molds the intellect of our scholars and leaders of tomorrow.

"Part of the American tradition is volunteerism.

"Institution like Trinity University could not exist if it weren't for individuals, who willingly and unselfishly sacrifice leisure and take time away from family and business to provide leadership and expertise to this institution. It is my honor and privilege to introduce Mr. Paul Wallace as our new president of the board of trustees.

"Paul is well known in our community for his many contributions and support of institutions that make all us proud.

"On behalf of the faculty, students, and the administration I would like to welcome and thank Paul for accepting to be a part of this institution and help its growth.

"One factor that continually helps the growth of this institution is the uninterrupted financial support and contributions we receive from our alumni.

"Rick Antonelli—a BS and MBA alumni of our business school, and his family have already endowed the Chair of *Business and Corporate Ethics* at the Graduate School of Management. Trinity University again has become the beneficiary of the Antonelli's family generosity.

"Eight month ago a second chair was endowed, the Chair *of Philosophy of Physical Law, and Metaphysics* at the Department of Philosophy in the Graduate School of Liberal Arts. So far the University has not found a suitable candidate to fill the position."

Lucia became a little uneasy, lowered her head, and shrugged her shoulders. She appeared somewhat bewildered, if not embarrassed.

Wilson continued;

"Several top schools were contacted and asked to submit suitable candidates from their own faculties or others and the answer, almost verbatim, was the same:

What you're looking for, you already have in your own back yard. What's your problem?

"The problem is that personal sensitivity and individual perception of integrity have been in our way. What we have been told, we knew it all along, but we weren't successful."

Lucia's head started spinning and all of a sudden hit her like a lightning rod!

Wilson was smart, if not shrewd, and knew exactly what he was doing.

What could she do? Get up and leave? Was she being blackmailed or publicly pressured to concede?

She quickly gained her composure and decided to leave it up to God and the school. She didn't ask for and made every effort to dissuade an offer she felt was inappropriate.

If she continued with her original decision, she might be perceived as stubborn, over-sensitive, and even immature. At least now, with overwhelming support and recognition of her peers gave her the credibility, moral authority, and power to stand on her own. If God had given her the talent and the brains she might as well use them for the benefit of the students.

She would pray, and be vigilant to accept God's will with humility, and use her talents wisely.

Wilson looked at Lucia with a happy smile.

"Trinity University has been blessed with constant influx of high caliber young scholars that join the ranks of our illustrious faculties.

"Four years ago, Dr. Lucia Antonelli joined the faculty of Liberal Arts College as an assistant professor. She is an authority on Physical Laws and Metaphysics; her second book will be out in a few weeks.

"Ladies and gentlemen, it is my distinct honor and privilege to introduce to you the professor of the newly endowed chair of Philosophy, Dr. Lucia Antonelli."

Wilson took Lucia by the left hand and asked her to stand. Everyone around the dining room table got up, and loudly applauded.

"Bravo, bravo, well deserved; bravo, bravo! Congratulations!"

✤   ✤   ✤

John, Lucia's brother, since joining the US Diplomatic Corps held various assignments in South America and Africa. He was stationed in Nairobi for the last two years. His dream was to serve in Japan. He was told it wouldn't happen for at least three years, until he was due for promotion and reassignment.

He finally got married last year at the age of thirty-six. With all his moving around and relocations was difficult to establish any serious and lasting contacts with American women. Luckily the first year in Nairobi, he met Patricia Colton from Boston when she joined the staff of the American Embassy.

She was a Georgetown graduate, like John, and this was her first post since joining the Foreign Service.

John became her mentor; both hit it on well, and soon became an item.

Patricia was from an old Bostonian family, and an only daughter among four brothers. She was pretty, reserve and serious, but not shy.

Six months later, they flew to Boston to get married and returned to Nairobi a week later. With the policy of the Sate Department to assign couples to the same post, John and Patricia envisioned a happy and uninterrupted family life.

Rick, Lucia's father, after he sold the supermarket chain, became member of the board of the holding company.

After pursuing him for several months, the board convinced him to accept the position of regional president that had especially designed for him. His knowledge of the market, business acumen, ability to communicate, and the respect he drew from the community were assets that couldn't be ignored.

He accepted the position only for two years to ensure that the transition wouldn't affect his employees that helped make his business so successful.

Roxanne, Lucia's mother, retired as a violin teacher from the Institute of Music, but continued to give private lessons for gifted students, and periodically performed as a guest soloist with the Civic Orchestra.

✤   ✤   ✤

Margo and her family weren't left behind. Like for Barbara, Lucia and their families, the Martinez's family last ten years were blessed; and with hard work and tenacity, brought their dreams to fruition.

Margo went to Graduate school at Caltech, where she got her Ph.D. in Mathematics with emphasis on the *Theory of Probabilities and Biostatistics*.

She was obsessed all her life with math and especially with probabilities and their applications to all disciplines, and especially in biosciences. She took all available courses in molecular biology, biochemistry, biotechnology, and genetics.

The professors, from early on, recognized Margo's talents, but when the time came to choose the subject for her Ph.D. thesis everyone was dumfounded! Was she a genius?

The common knowledge is that DNA could identify individuals like fingerprints or a photograph. Nevertheless, the scientific probability exists, that one in a billion or even billions, another individual could have identical DNA.

DNA is an extremely long macromolecule, and the main component of the chromosome, responsible for transferring genetic information. Two DNA strands coil around each other in a spiral ladder-like arrangement.

Margo was concept was to eliminate all odds, even one to a trillion, by slightly reshaping part of one coil or deleting one step from the ladder, or doing both.

The title of Margo's dissertation was *Single Macromolecule (DNA) Alteration in the Transfer of Genetic Information.*

Professors at Caltech had discussed Margo's graduate work with colleagues of other universities, and especially Stanford, where she went to undergraduate school.

Two years after Margo completed her graduate work at Caltech was honored with a special dinner, at Stanford, as the alumni of the year. After dinner, students mingled with her and asked about her work. One doctoral candidate was persistently annoying, and tried to question the significance of her doctoral thesis.

He questioned, that the subject being so abstract, if could ever have any practical and meaningful application.

Margo's face lit up; she looked first at his name tag, then in the eyes, and with a smile said,

"David, that's an intelligent question. I would like to remind you though, and I hope you agree that a scientist above all and before anything else, should be a profound thinker. One the other hand, you cannot be a thinker unless you're a dreamer.

A dreamer in the sense that your mind is capable of generating original and fundamental concepts away from the lab and devoid of intended utility.

"Democritos, a Greek philosopher, twenty-five centuries ago *dreamed* sort of, of the atomic theory, and his assertion was that the entire Universe was composed only of two invisible elements; *atoms* and *void*.

"An infinite number of eternal elements differing from each other only in shape, arrangement, and magnitude, moved through infinite space.

"And where had Democritos dream led us twenty-five centuries later? It had let us to Hiroshima, Nagasaki, Chernobyl, and Three Mile Island, and to the diagnostic radiology departments of every hospital, and radiation therapy units of every cancer treatment center.

And it all began with the dream of a thinker who changed our world.

"All the great minds, from Pythagoras and Archimedes, to Graham Bell, the Wright Brothers, and Einstein, were dreamers at heart."

David was at a loss for words, an avoided eye contact with Margo.

"Now, to your question concerning the practicality of the core of my doctoral thesis the answer is, I don't know.

"Imagine; maybe in the future, hundreds or even thousands of years from now, if we could, before birth, make safely a miniscule change, sort of a *tagging*, in a precisely predetermined section of the DNA of the fetus, that shouldn't have any influence on physical or intellectual development. The change would be recorded and registered with a universal DNA bank. Do you follow me?

"If this ever became possible, the genome-the entire set of DNA-of every new born would be different, never existed before and never to be replicated in the future. Every man or woman would be born with his or her genetic identity eliminating all odds, not only one in a billion or trillion, but even not one in a zillion!"

Margo stayed at Caltech and had been promoted to the tenured rank of associate professor. Although enamored with math and probabilities, she continued to practice and play the cello with the same enthusiasm and dedication.

The importance of music, that connected the trio to begin with, had never diminished, and remained an integral part of their lives.

She celebrated her thirty-third birthday eight moths ago, with no prospects of any serious and meaningful relationship on sight, at this time of her life. Was she waiting for another *freak*?

Five months ago Margo met Fred Hassenbruck, an astrophysicist-eight year her senior, when he came to Caltech to be interviewed, as one of the candidates, for the position of Chairman of the Department of Physics and professor of Astrophysics.

Fred was originally from Germany and got his undergraduate degree in physics from the University of Munich. He was a brilliant student, graduated first in his class, and was offered a full scholarship at MIT, where he got his Master's degree in astrophysics in one year instead of two, and the expectation was that after he was accepted, he would stay for his doctorate.

He met with the department chairman unexpectedly, without any warning and out of the blue two weeks before he was to start, and requested a two year leave of absence. He said the reason was something personal, and definitely planned to return and continue with his doctoral studies.

Fred's exceptional performance had impressed the entire faculty of the department, and everyone agreed he was a brilliant student. The concern was that he was quiet, withdrawn, introspective, disassociated at times, rather distant, and always serious. His infrequent smile was enigmatic, and no one from the class ever remembered having seen or heard him really laughing! He was polite, rather reserve, and not easy to make or be friend with.

In the classroom was a different story, when he was given the opportunity to speak. He was eloquent, analytical, precise, exhibiting a critical mind with apocalyptic fervor that shined above par and peers.

His performance had raised the bar for the other students, and some were greatly relieved when heard of his plans. He returned to MIT two years later, as scheduled, and got his doctorate degree in three years. He was asked to join the faculty, and at the age of thirty-four became a full professor.

Margo interviewed Fred and spent with him close to three hours as a member of the search committee, which included a total of nine members, all professors, with the Dean as chairman.

Through a nationwide search, fourteen candidates were recruited and asked to come and meet with committee members. The entire process took over one year, and the committee would meet soon to make a decision.

All candidates were renowned scientists, reputable academic scholars, teachers, and published authors of plethora of articles and several textbooks.

All member of the committee, before confirmed, were asked to sign a confidentiality agreement that barred them from discussing among themselves or others any of the candidates, their qualifications, and personal preferences.

Each member was requested to personally deliver to the Dean's office a sealed envelope with the name of the candidate he or she thought was the best for the institution.

The idea was to ensure complete objectivity and impartiality, and avoid any discussion and opinions based on individual perceptions that may exert some influence and even pressure from the more senior members of the committee. After the last candidate was interviewed, the committee was given six weeks to come up with its choice.

It was late Friday afternoon.

The search committee was to meet at 6 o'clock in the small conference room, adjacent to the dean's office. Everyone was on time.

The dean came in holding a letter opener and an office tray with the nine envelopes inside. He methodically opened each envelope and read the name of the candidate. The choice was unanimous! Every member had voted for Fred, who from that moment on would become head of physics and professor in one of the most prestigious universities of the nation, if not the world.

Margo, from Fred's resume, knew that he had spent one doctoral year at MIT under the tutelage of Lesley Wilson, when he was a professor there, and before his appointment as president of Trinity University.

She would call Lucia to get some scoop out of Lesley concerning Fred. He was such a unique mind, but he came so reserved on one hand, and so indifferent and blasé on the other during the interview.

Lesley and Lucia had become good friends, and trusted and respected each other. He slowly, and everybody knew that, was grooming her to be the first dean of women, whenever the position was finally established by the board.

Lucia's commitment and dedication to counseling, deep understanding of female student issues, the trust she emanated, and respect she got from all students made her contribution and leadership appreciated by all.

After Margo's call, Lucia mentioned to Lesley during lunch that Fred, one of his ex-students, who later became professor at MIT, was appointed head of the physics department at Caltech.

"I'm not surprised at all; he is brilliant, and it was a matter of time.

"He worked with me for one year. I got to know him well, and we became close. We still correspond during holidays; he still addresses me as *Uncle Les*, and I'm considering him as one of my nephews. He is a straight shooter, reliable, and a man of integrity.

"I was the first one he called after he was informed of his appointment. Socially, he might come on as an *odd ball* or strange when you first meet him. This perception became more believable after, for no apparent reason, he disappeared for two years. Some thought he would never come back.

"Being his confidant, I was the only one, who knew what happened those two years; and I was sworn never to mention it to anyone under any circumstances. Once you got to know him, you would be surprised with his gentleness and sensitivity.

"Fred had an unusual childhood. Some might perceive it as tragic but not me; sad would be more appropriate, for he is at peace with himself and never complained or felt deprived.

"He became an orphan at the age of four, after his parents were killed in car crash. From then on, his mother's older brother, Paul, took care of him. There were no other close relatives.

"Paul was a priest and Paul grew up in the rectory. All the parish's mothers adopted him as another son, and he was surrounded by countless brothers and sisters. And as he grew older became the altar boy in *residence.*

"Father Paul realized how intelligent Fred was, and made sure that he would get the best education possible. He died ten years ago and Fred has no close ties back home. He traveled to Munich every two to three years primarily to go to the cemetery and visit the family plot, where his parents and uncle were buried, and meet with a few friends from high school and college."

Margo got a call from Lucia in the evening with all the information concerning Fred's background.

She was intrigued with the secrecy of the two year hiatus. What could have been the reasons? Her probability oriented genius mind immediately tried to figure out the odds of what could have happened those two years.

It looked as if he could have some kind of behavioral or psychological problems. Did he have any special treatment? Two years was a long time, unless he had to be hospitalized for a while or undergo psychoanalysis.

In his resume concerning health history and in his employment application nothing was listed except for appendectomy when he was in college. As a student and faculty member at MIT, there was no indication of any sick leaves for hospitalization or other treatments, and he stated his health status as excellent.

Margo's mind was moving too fast, and she thought definitely was out of line.

What is the matter with me? Am I nuts? Here is a guy with an extraordinary mind, our new head of the physics department, and I think, without really knowing him, that he maybe a cuckoo; shame on me.

❧   ❧   ❧

Three years ago, Margo's father was nominated for Justice to the U.S. Supreme Court, the first Hispanic, ever. The Senate hearings went smoothly, the vote was unanimous, and history was made. Her parents relocated to Washington D.C. and her mother sold the art gallery business.

With Pedro, her brother, working in the same city, would be much easier for the family to get together; Margo was only one non-stop flight away.

Pedro was one of most eligible bachelor of the city; a Yale Law School graduate, an associate in one of the most prestigious and reputable international law firms specializing in banking, and as of late, the son of a Supreme Court Justice! That didn't last for too long.

Two years ago, he met Elizabeth Whealer, a beautiful and smart English girl in her late twenty's-a graduate of Cambridge with a Master's degree in Communications from George Washington University.

Her father, back in London, was the president of International Trust and Banking Company, and Elizabeth was responsible for running the PR (Public Relations) for the Washington office. Pedro's firm was representing the banking company in U.S., and he was extensively involved with acquisitions and expansions in South America, Argentina in particular. His command of Spanish made him a formidable negotiator and an extremely valuable and irreplaceable asset of the law firm.

Pedro and Elizabeth met through work, and had lunch together once in a while.

When the Argentina project came along, they saw each other much more frequently and twice flew to Buenos Aires together.

Pedro flew to England to finalize the Argentina project. Elizabeth had left two weeks earlier to arrange several important meetings, and especially prepare the formal presentation to the stockholders representatives.

It had been a hectic ten days for Pedro, Elizabeth, and her parents. With all formal dinners, club meetings, presentation, speeches, etc. done, the Argentina project had finally come to a successful conclusion.

It was Friday, 5 o'clock in the afternoon.

Pedro was in his hotel room lying down almost completely exhausted. He was flying back to Washington on Sunday, and was relieved to have one full day to recuperate. On Saturday, he was invited for lunch at the Whealers' summer home, thirty miles outside of London. Chester, Elizabeth's father, had made arrangements with his chauffer to pick-up Pedro from the hotel around 12 noon.

It was a beautiful sight of early fall countryside, and Pedro was enjoying the Bentley's softly cushioned ride.

Elizabeth and her mother, Anna, greeted Pedro at the door when he arrived.

Chester, her father, was waiting in the sitting room.

As soon as he heard the doorbell, opened a bottle of champagne and poured it in the four long stemmed crystal glasses, and placed them on a silver tray. When Pedro came into the sitting room, Chester passed the silver tray and each one took a glass; then he raised his to a toast.

"Pedro welcome to our home not as our banking company's lawyer, but as our friend. You already got your accolades and appreciation from the board. Everyone involved in the Argentina project was so impressed with your professional skills. Your analysis and deep knowledge of Argentina's banking laws gave us more than we ever expected.

"Professional skills alone are not enough to project one's character.

"What Elizabeth has told me about you is nothing but praise. You have been a perfect gentleman. I'm also so thankful to your parents for having opened their home to Elizabeth; being alone in a big city, and away from home, is not that easy for anyone no matter how confident."

All brought the glasses to their lips and after sipping, Pedro spoke.

He was cool, and his appearance exuded confidence.

"Mr. and Mrs. Whealer; I like to thank for your invitation amid ten days of havoc, and with so many issues at stake. Thanks to God, everything turned out well for our law firm in Washington, and your company in London, in the process of expanding. We're both winners and I hope our successful association will continue in the years to come.

"On a personal note, I would like to thank Elizabeth for her contributions and especially for educating and providing me with the feedback I needed to deal with the local market.

"I have visited your company before, but there were certain sensitive issues that had to be addressed extremely carefully, without offending or even compromising the culture of your company, with a proven record of long and exemplarily successful tradition in the banking and financial world.

"Please, allow me now to say something important, more personal, and I hope appropriate under the circumstances.

"I met Elizabeth a little over a year ago.

"For the past six months, working close with her, I got to know her better, and through her, I got to know you and your values as a family.

"Elizabeth and I started on the other side of the fence but ended up on the same side. She came, way back, from a family of privilege; I did not. With hard work, tenacity, perseverance, faith, fortitude, and use of God given talents, I humbly realized that I have come from a family of privilege, too. The essence of difference is simply chronological and not substantive. That's why you honored me and invited me to your house today.

"I would like to ask you for something that should be of unique importance to Elizabeth, you, my family, and me.

"Elizabeth and I, in passing, discussed it only once. No one is aware of what I'm about to ask you, although some family members and friends back in the States subconsciously might have thought of.

"I hope I'm not presumptuous, and I, definitely, wouldn't like to be perceived as exerting a preemptive and manipulative effort intended to compromise your free will and intellectual honesty, in considering my request."

The Whealers and particular Elizabeth were overtaken by Pedro's commanding presence, composure, and control of language.

His sparkling deep blue eyes, an accentuated trait from his Anglo mother, contrasted his darkened Latino skin even more, and gave his facial features the courageous expression of a worrier, fighting for honor and freedom, with unabated valor and passion until the end.

Pedro put his champagne glass back on the silver tray, and moved next to Elizabeth. He took her left hand with his right, looked Chester and Anna directly in the eyes, and continued;

"Mr. and Mrs. Whealer; I love and respect Elizabeth and the values she was brought up with; the same values my family brought me up with. I humbly ask for your consent and Elizabeth's hand in marriage. I promise to love and honor Elizabeth until the end of my life."

Pedro hugged Chester and Anna, then embraced and kissed Elizabeth.

The parents, as well as Elizabeth were dumfounded.

The last four months of the Argentina project, Pedro and Elizabeth, slowly but surly, came to realize that were deeply in love. Pedro wanted to get married soon. There wasn't any reason to wait. Both were mature, with excellent education behind them, and successfully employed.

Elizabeth wasn't ready and wanted to wait for a while, but she never said for how long, and what the reason was for waiting. Pedro had observed that Elizabeth, out of the blue, sometimes was sad, preoccupied, and as if she was trying to hide something.

Pedro remained supportive and patient.

She finally opened up and hoped he would understand.

Elizabeth's marriage to him would require permanent relocation to U.S., and long separations from her parents.

Even working in Washington, every five to six weeks, combining business and pleasure, she would fly to London to spend a few days with her parents.

Their lives had changed so dramatically the last two years. If they were married, wouldn't be fair to leave Pedro to visit her parents that often.

Two years ago, the Whealers experienced a tragedy that affected the entire family.

Philip, Elizabeth's only sibling, and two years her senior, was killed in a riding accident while playing polo. One year earlier, he graduated from the London School of Economics, after attending and graduating from Oxford University law school.

He was being primed to eventually head the law department of the family banking business.

Pedro decided to gamble and let the parents know of what was going on.

He was sure Elizabeth loved him and would like to get married now. On the other hand, she felt it was too soon to separate from her parents. If she were willing to wait for two more years, so should he.

Pedro's only concern was not to upset Elizabeth by going ahead with his marriage proposal, without discussing it first with her.

Chester and Anna kissed and embraced the already embraced Pedro and Elizabeth. All eyes wept; all hearts beat to the same beat; and all minds were taken by the same thought; everlasting happiness, love, and a life of blessings.

Chester, after drying his eyes, in an emotional but controlled voice said,

"Pedro is our honor and privilege to give away our daughter Elizabeth to be your wife.

"The last two years have been so difficult for us. Now I feel so different, as if lost happiness is flying back to nest in our home and hearts, again. Looking at Anna and Elizabeth's eyes now, I see sparkles that were missing for so long.

"Pedro, my son, welcome to our family. Bringing the word *son* to my lips after two years resurrected my hope to live a more fulfilling life."

Pedro took out of his pocket a small red velvet box and gave it to Elizabeth. Once she opened it, there it was a two carat solitaire diamond engagement ring inside!

Three days before she left for London, Elizabeth took Pedro to Cartier's looking for a pair of earrings for one of her girlfriends who was getting married.

Accidentally, her eyes caught the same ring; she thought was exquisite. While she was looking for earrings, Pedro passed a note to a saleslady asking her to lay away the ring for him, without even asking for the price. Next day, he went back and bought it.

Elizabeth took the ring out of the box and asked Pedro to put it on her finger. It fitted perfectly as if it was sized for her.

"Pedro, it's so beautiful; and I thank you for your guts, and for what you did today. Sometimes, thinking of protecting others, we do nothing else but covering our own insecurities, fears, and doubts. I've never seen my parents so happy for the last two years."

The lunch and all preparations became a casualty of today's event; Pedro and Elizabeth's engagement.

Everybody was on the phone calling everybody. All lines, from London to London, London to Washington, and London to California, were busy carrying the good news.

For the X generation, cyberspace was the cool way to communicate the happy news attaching to E-mail funny faces, pictures, and singing messages.

The circle of happiness is closing in; will be completed soon?

CHAPTER 8

The Calling Came: The Circle was Complete

It was the first Monday of September; the beginning of the new academic year, and the first day of Fred at Caltech, as Chairman of the Department of Physics.

Fred parked his car and walked trough the corridor connecting the garage to the main lobby of the Sciences Building.

The lobby was dimly lit with the emergency exit lights on.

The reception desk was closed, and the elevator and stairwell doors were locked. The clock on the wall showed 6:30. After trying, he realized that he wouldn't be able to get into his office, which was located on the fourth floor. He took a seat and waited patiently. Clipped to his jacket, was the official ID faculty card, which was issued to him last week, when he went through the University HR (Human Resources) office.

At exactly 7 o'clock, the elevator door opened, and the third shift security supervisor walked out. He went directly to Fred, who stood up. He checked Fred's badge and introduced himself.

"Dr. Hassenbruck, my name is Captain Jim Stevek, from security.

"I'm sorry; you're early.

"The elevators, doors, and offices are centrally controlled and timed to unlock at 7:30 in the morning, and lock the same time in the evening. If you plan to come early or like to have access to your office twenty-four hours a day, including weekends, wouldn't be any problem at all. Security already has your name on file.

"Once you're in your office, access security through your PC; you already know your screen name and password. After you enter your password, ENTER PIN will appear on the screen. Enter a six letter word or six digit number; click OK and you're all set. The PIN is cancelled the first day of every month, and a new one must be activated. There's a keypad by the elevator and stairwell doors to enter your PIN to unlock them. I'd be more than happy to take you to your office now."

"Thanks, Captain Stevek. I'm an early riser.

"You cannot teach old dog new tricks! As far as I remember, from my early days at MIT, I was in my office no later than 6:30.

"There's something intriguing and even mystical about early mornings; either anticipation or impatience or both, driven by the predicament of the cyclic nature of time impart certain degree of urgency and energy."

Both went to the elevator door. Jim unlocked it, let Fed in, followed him, and pressed the button for the fourth floor. Fred's office was three doors down to the left. Jim opened the office door and let Fred in.

"Welcome to Caltech, Professor. Sylvia, your secretary, usually gets here around 8 o'clock. Have a nice day, Sir."

"You, too, Captain. Thanks for your help."

"You're welcome."

Fred met Sylvia Bowlan, when Margo showed him around the first time he visited Caltech for his interview, and two weeks ago, when she brought him back to his office, after he had moved to the city; he was staying in a hotel for now.

With the help of the housing office he found a nice two bedroom apartment close by, and bought all the furniture he needed. He moved nothing from back east except for his car, personal items like clothing, and books. Fred expected to be moving in as soon as the furniture was delivered, probably around the end of the week.

Margo, who unofficially had become his welcoming committee and guide, told him that as department chairman, according to the University's policy, had the prerogative to bring or hire his own secretary, either now or later. Sylvia was aware that she would serve at the chairman's will.

In case of a transfer to another department, she wouldn't lose seniority and her salary and benefits would remain the same.

Fred's first impression of Sylvia was positive.

She was in her mid-fifties, almost fifteen years older than he, nicely dressed, thin, about five feet six inches tall. Her voice was soft, but well projected. She never married and lived with her mother, who was in her late seventies, and in good health.

She had been an employee of the university close to twenty-five years, the last ten as an executive administrative assistant.

The office had two sections: The reception-sitting area, with a desk where Sylvia sat, and the chairman's office to the left.

When Fred entered his office noticed a beautiful bronze plaque, with a walnut base, on his desk. The plaque was engraved with: Frederick H. Hassenbruck, Ph.D., Chairman, Department of Physics. This was a surprise. No one had asked him if he wanted a plaque. He was admiring the nameplate when there was a knock at the door behind him, and Sylvia came in.

"Good morning, Sylvia; please, come in, how are you?"

Fred walked to her and shook hands.

"Good morning Dr. Hassenbruck; I'm fine, and welcome to Caltech. Can I get you a cup of coffee? You're an early bird. I just saw Jim from security leaving, as I was coming in; he said you were here at 6:30!"

Fred asked Sylvia to sit down, walked around the desk, and sat on the desk chair, right across from her.

"Sylvia; we met, briefly, twice before, but I don't think we had the opportunity to get to know and get used to each other. I've a gut feeling we're going to do just fine. I hope, I don't sound offensive.

"Please, don't ever ask me again about coffee. It was kind and courteous of you; I appreciate it, and thank you, but I don't consider this to be part of your job. Did you order my nameplate? It's beautiful."

"I got a copy of the list of supplies and stationary you requested. They were delivered to office last week, but your name plate was missing. Apparently, you weren't asked. I took the liberty to order one; it's the standard nameplate that the engraver makes for the faculty and department heads."

"My goodness! Your mind works really fast; you're way ahead of all of us. Thanks."

The phone rang; Sylvia excused herself, rushed to her desk, answered, and came right back.

"Sir, Dr. Martinez is on the line. She is asking if you're free; she'd like to come to see you sometime this morning."

"Sure; I'll be more than happy to see her. She can come any time. I'll be waiting for her."

Half an hour later Margo came in; Sylvia took her to Fred's office, and walked out.

Fred was sitting by his desk, taking out of his briefcase a framed photograph. When Margo walked in, he got up, put the picture down, and greeted her.

"Good morning Dr. Martinez. What's going on? You look different, sort of happy!"

"Good morning to you. You're right; everyone I see this morning tells me the same. Somehow, it must show.

"Saturday, early in the morning, I received a call from my brother Pedro, from London, where he flew on business ten days ago. He got engaged!

"Pedro is an attorney with a firm in Washington, DC. He met Elizabeth, his fiancée in Washington, where she works now as a PR person for her family's banking business. Pedro and his firm do all the legal work for the banking company. They got to know each other well, while working on the Argentina project, the company's expansion to South America.

"I've met her, and so have my parents. She is nice, kind, and a down to earth person considering where she is coming from."

"Congratulations! This must a happy event for the entire family. When and where are they getting married?"

"After Christmas; the wedding will be in England, and they'll be back in Washington to live, where both work.

"Now, I have a request.

"When I walked in, you addressed me as *Dr. Martinez*. Margo would be fine with me. You're not my boss, and I'm in a different department, although we share lab space, classrooms, and students. Formally addressing each other would be more appropriate in the presence of students."

"Okay, Margo! I have no problem with your request; and of course you'll address me as Fred from now on."

"Absolutely, Fred. Now, after resolving the *name calling* issue, let's get down to business. What time would be convenient for you to get around and meet people? I'm free until lunch. Then we'll have lunch together; you'll be my guest. There's a nice restaurant close by, we can walk to."

"Thanks, maybe in an hour. My first priority is to go over the file from HR that Sylvia has to take back before lunch; and sign on, so I can get my PIN to access after hours my office and the Sciences Building."

"Bye-bye Fred; see you later."

Margo noticed on Fred's desk the framed photograph of a priest. She presumed was Paul, Fred's uncle. She didn't want to prey on his privacy; she might ask him some other time.

From the information she got from Lucia, personal perceptions notwithstanding, if nothing else, Fred was apparently a loner. Was he a loner by his own choice or by circumstances? He was such a brilliant mind; no argument about that. Was his intelligence intimidating, even to his peers?

The fact remained, that during his growing up years, he was sheltered, emotionally isolated, and deprived of every child's expected warmth and affection; that could have inhibited or altered his pathways of communication with others, and the development of social skills.

Maybe, relocating from the thick, impenetrable and unforgivable to the sun pitch dark clouds, and dreariness of winters of the northeast to sunny Pasadena, could change and light up his mood.

The impressions of people who came in contact with Fred might have been presumptive, for no one really got to know him well, with possibly the exception of Lesley Wilson, his mentor at MIT and current president of Trinity University.

Lesley, being a priest himself, reminded Fed his uncle Father Paul. Maybe it was Fred's fault.

He had never come forward to respond to overtures to any kind of friendships, either from men or women, and the notion that he might be gay was quickly dispelled. Did anybody ever ask Fred if he was happy? Was his self-induced isolation a sign of faultiness of his character and personality or a sign of inner peace and serenity?

Is any kind of socialization or personal connections, of any nature, with others a prerequisite for individual happiness? Maybe, he was a loner and an oddball to others, but happy with himself and his life. How is possible for anyone to know and judge someone else's inner existence and feelings?

A perceived fool can fool confident fools with impunity, and catch them with their pants down!

After Margo left, Fred asked Sylvia to hold all his calls for the next half an hour.

Back in the office, he sat down and looked at the picture of his Uncle Paul. He was the one person Fred remembered having consciously loved. His parents had died when he was very young—too young to have a memory of loving them. The few photographs of them he had seen made him more curious than sentimental. Uncle Paul had given him anything he needed and made him what he was.

Fred was not only thankful to have lived with his uncle, but also to have been part of his of uncle's life and work. He experienced, in real time, the life of a priest with all challenges, trepidations, sacrifices, and around the clock demands.

Every since he moved into the rectory to live, hardly four years old, he was never left alone; his uncle took him along everywhere he went, days or nights, until he was old enough and able to take care of himself.

He went to hospitals, and homes to visit the sick and the dying. He attended weddings, baptisms and christenings; visited funeral homes and stood by burials. He had seen, and as he grew older, experienced every human condition possible; tears and laughter; hate and love; faith and indifference; abundance and poverty; charity and selfishness. As an altar boy, he became a participant of every service: Matins, Vespers and Liturgies.

Fred's uncle had been dead closed to ten years.

Every time he looked at his uncle's picture, the smile on his face brought him back to life. He never saw him sad. He never heard him complaining, or expressing any anger. His face radiated serenity and always was framed with a smile of happiness and contentment. That face depicted the essence of his uncle memory that vividly was imprinted on Fred's mind to stay for ever.

Children, during their formative years and especially in their upper teens, can sense whether their parents are happy with their chosen profession. A child is unlikely to follow in the footsteps of a parent who is openly dissatisfied professionally. Conversely, a child whose parents express satisfaction with their career paths will probably be influenced to pursue the same or a similar profession.

Because his Uncle seemed to have found in the priesthood the happiness and fulfillment for which every one strives, Fred was seriously thinking of going to the seminary himself.

For his part, Father Paul had recognized early on that his nephew was exceptionally bright and had made every effort to help him develop his cognitive skills. Fred's teachers said that he was bored and frustrated, which Father Paul took to be a sign that Fred needed, and was capable of mastering, a more advanced curriculum than the school had to offer.

Two of Father Paul's parishioners, both professors in the science department at the University of Munich, tutored Fred in math and physics. By the time he finished high school, he had already completed all the required courses that would help him to obtain his degree from that university in two years rather than four.

When Fred mentioned his desire to become a priest, however, Father Paul was not encouraging.

"Look; I'm happy with my work Fred, and if I had to do it all over again my choice would have been the same. With God's will and help my commitment to the priesthood becomes more and more relevant and my joy and satisfaction in my work grows deeper and more rewarding.

"As servant of God, I have accepted these gifts with humility. I had hoped you would be inspired by the substance, content, and power of the priesthood, not just by me as your uncle. But you must realize that the priesthood is a *calling* and you must wait to sense the genuineness and the sincerity of your commitment before choosing this path.

"You are only 18, and I believe you are too young to make such a profound decision now. God has given you a unique mind and talent, and he will demand accountability from you, as he does from us all, for the gifts he bestows. You should be prepared for this.

"In my teens, I was fascinated by the military, the intent and strategies behind old and new conflicts, and the seemingly mighty concepts and philosophies behind planning for victory but never for defeat.

"I entered Army Officer's School as a cadet and, after four years, graduated third in my class. Tradition all but dictates that the top twenty graduates will go on to become generals, but two weeks after I was promoted to Captain, I resigned my commission and entered the seminary. I was 28. What made me change, I don't know, but I sensed my *calling* to the priesthood. The rest, as they say, is history."

Now, years later, looking at the picture of his uncle—Father Paul—Fred smiled. He was sure his uncle was smiling at him, too, and proud of what he had become. Father Paul's wisdom had guided him and remained an integral part of his life.

The appointment at the University would give him the opportunity to use his talents wisely and to inspire new generations of scientists to help make the world a better, safer, more knowledgeable, and more tolerant place.

A few minutes later Margo came by. With her as his guide, he visited several offices and was introduced to other faculty members. Everyone was friendly, open, informal, and welcoming. Although Fred was well known for his work in astrophysics, many on the faculty had ever met him in person.

Margo, on a second thought instead of going to a restaurant, quickly arranged an informal luncheon-reception in a small conference room. No formal introductions were planned. Everyone introduced him or herself.

To Margo's surprise, Fred was talkative and appeared comfortable. Perhaps he realized that, as head of the department, he would be working more closely with people and would have to be more approachable. He was, after all, wearing two hats now: the scientist and the administrator. The dual responsibility could initiate changes in his approach to life, even in his thinking, and his response to his environment both inside and outside of his work.

After the luncheon, Margo and Fred walked back to his office.

"I know the relocation office has been working with you to find an apartment. Did anything happen over the weekend? Did you see something you liked?"

"I was lucky. I found the ideal place—a two bedroom unit on the sixth floor and close to the school. Nobody even knew there was a vacancy in the building. Maybe it was intended for someone else."

"What is the address?"

"1231 Pine View Towers."

"I can't believe it!" Margo exclaimed. "I live in the same building. We're neighbors. My apartment is on the same floor at the other end of the hallway facing yours. Your apartment has been vacant for so long that the other tenants thought there was something wrong. There's no number on the door or on the mailbox."

"It looked fine to me. It was clean, newly painted, and the floors were waxed. If something was wrong must have been fixed."

"When are you moving in?"

"The furniture will be delivered sometime Saturday afternoon. I'll check out of the hotel where I'm staying before noon on Sunday."

"I remember the day I moved into my place. It was a mess. Would you like to come for dinner on Sunday, say, around 5? I'm right across the hall. Come earlier if you like, if you don't mind seeing me in my apron working in the kitchen. Dress casually. You've probably had enough of the formalities."

"Thanks. That's nice of you. But you've spent so much time with me already. I don't want to interfere if you had other plans for the weekend. We can always plan dinner for another time."

"I had no other plans and it's no bother at all. See you Sunday."

On Sunday, around 5 o'clock, Fred ringed the bell at Margo's apartment door.

He was wearing a dress shirt, but no tie, a light color fall suit, and brown wingtips shoes.

Margo answered the door. She had blue jeans on, a light brown sweater top, and gym shoes.

"Hi Fred; how are you? Has all the furniture been delivered? I said dress casual. You didn't have to wear a suit."

"I dressed casual. You see? I don't wear a tie."

"That's fine. Don't worry about it. Give me your jacket. Please sit down and relax."

Margo took Fred's jacket and hung it the closet, and as he sat down on the sofa said,

"Thanks for asking. The lady from the department store, whom I worked with, came with the delivery crew to make sure everything was all right. She was kind enough to make one of the beds. I'm all set for tonight.

"She's coming back tomorrow to measure for drapes and check if there's something else I may need. I'm not good at taking care of apartments after moving in. Your place is nice; and tastefully done. It looks bigger than mine. May I look?"

"Sure; I'll show you around. You're right. My apartment is bigger. It's a three bedroom unit, and the living room is larger."

Fred got up and followed Margo. She showed him the entire unit. The last stop was the master bedroom where Margo slept. He looked around and noticed the picture of the three girls on the desk, which was taken the first year they met at the Academy. He moved closer, looked at it a little longer and asked,

"Who are the other two girls?

"My sisters; Lucia and Barbara."

"Wait a minute! You don't look like sisters, and the other day when you talked about your family, you only mentioned your brother, Pedro. You said nothing about having sisters."

"Oh, my God! If there was ever a Freudian slip, that would be it! We met as juniors at the Academy, a boarding preparatory school, close to eighteen years ago. We became close and have been like sisters every since. Nobody really, not even our own families, can comprehend our bonding."

"I know what you mean, and how it feels to be close to and love someone. The only person I have ever been close to and loved was my uncle Paul; he was a priest. He passed on ten years ago, but I can still feel his blessings and love. With your girlfriends is different. You became so close, but you're not even related."

Both returned to the living room. Fred sat on the sofa, and Margo went to the kitchen. She came back carrying a tray, with cheese and crackers, put it on the coffee table and asked Fred;

"Would you like something to drink? I have soft drinks and white wine."

"Water would be fine for now. I'd like to save my wine for dinner."

Margo was somewhat surprised with Fred.

He appeared much more at ease than she thought he would be as a guest. There was no question. His social skills weren't up to speed, if he thought not wearing a tie, was dressed *casual*. Maybe this was the way he grew-up in Munich.

Some exceptional and disciplined high schools back in Germany, designed for bright students-called Gymnasiums, are strict and demanding academically; maybe they required a more structured dress code Fred was used to.

After dinner, Margo and Fred went to the living room, sat down, and talked…and talked…and talked. When the time came to say goodnight, it was 3 o'clock in the morning!

For the average mind this was absurd, if not insane.

Here, you have a woman thirty-three years old, the hostess, and a man forty-one year old, the guest invited by the hostess's prerogative, both single and attractive, meeting for dinner. What could they have been talking about for so many hours? What did they see or say to each other to keep it going? Were they insomniacs, freaks or a couple of homos? It was a total waste of time, if not a disaster! They never touched or kissed; and forget about scoring!

For the exceptionally intelligent minds this was an intellectual feast of the highest caliber possible that could have lasted for ever, if there weren't for physical needs built into humans to remind them of their mortal nature.

It's amazing, that creations of minds destined to live for ever came out of mortal flesh destined to corrupt in death. In the passage of time, from the beginning to the end, flesh was meant to be a mere host to the mind that was the only endowed with immortality through its concepts and creativity.

When brilliant minds meet, the outpouring of knowledge can be breathtaking. If brilliance of the minds is intertwined with spirituality and faith, the outcome could generate cosmic energy.

Two brilliant spiritually enamored minds met; a man and a woman, notwithstanding. What would be the expectations? What rules of human and social laws would be enacted? The rules of mortal flesh, with its corruptive, fleeting, ephemeral, and capricious nature, or the rules of immortal mind, with its creative thoughts and intellectual curiosity concerning the beginning and end of life, redemption, and the concept of good and evil?

Margo and Fred really enjoyed each other's views and conversation, and never bothered to check the time. Many a time dealing with concepts and trying to understand them, you could stumble and even reach an impasse. This became apparent when the origin of *evil* came up.

"Fred, the belief is, in all monotheistic religions, that God is *Holy, Good, Mighty,* and *Immortal.* Where did *evil* come from? God being *Holy* and *Good* couldn't have created evil. We all know evil exists. Did evil create itself? That couldn't have been possible either, for only Good is *Mighty,* and *evil* couldn't overcome God's power and create itself. Where did *evil* come from?"

Fred smiled and pointed his finder first to himself, and then to Margo.

"*Evil* comes from me, you, and all humanity. *Evil* came, comes, and will come out of the free will of every man and woman who ever lived. Let's use the Judeo-Christian paradigm of creation.

"God in His wisdom, created a *free* man and a *free* woman, in His own image, and not zombies. From the onset in the process maturation on this earth, men and women would be given a *free will* to make choices and say yes or no to any challenges, temptations, and evil acts. If they make the wrong choices become *evil.*

"Civilized societies function under the same premise. If the wrong choices were made, the rule of law was violated, and evil acts were committed punishment must be carried out. People become evil by committing evil acts. The difference is that God always gives a second chance through redemption, for as long as we live, provided we exercise, again, our own *free will* in asking.

"God respects our free will, and redemption was never intended to be attained by either force or coercion, ever. God knows what is good for us, but the choice is ultimately ours. The ball is always in our court, and it's up to us, whether we win or lose, rise or fall, become evil or good."

"What about the images of *fallen angels* and *demons*? Where do they fit in, if ever did exist, in the origin of good and evil? Are they real? Are we stretching the imagination a little bit too far?"

"Not at all; fallen *angels* and *demons* are as real as you and I! We all are born *angels* with a free will to choose. If we choose *good,* we remain *angels.* If we choose *evil,* we change and become *fallen angels* and *demons.* The change is reversible by exercising our free will to seek redemption. Unfortunately, sometimes arrogance and ego get in the way of asking for redemption, and the condition becomes permanent."

After Fred left, Margo sat down and thought for a while.

Oh my; Fred is really a smart guy and deep thinker. He maybe an astrophysicist, but could pass as a theologian, too. I can tell from my own personal experience; scientists somehow, from ancient times, gravitated and were drawn into metaphysics.

Intelligent minds are always uneasy, on the go, and never rest. Even if they have found the answer still look for a better or a different one. If minds indulged and were captivated with present knowledge would regress, and progress would be impeded.

Fred and Margo bumped into each other frequently in the hallway, coming and going to their offices, and met for lunch in the dining room with other faculty members, several times.

Fred seemed to be adjusting well and the department and faculty were elated to have him as their leader. He appeared to be getting more open and friendlier, and frequently visited offices of other faculty members unannounced, just to say hello.

Margo, as the fall semester progressed, became busier. It wasn't only her academic work, teaching, and seminars that kept her busy, but also the upcoming Pedro's wedding.

Thanksgiving week, she flew to Washington D.C., and stayed with her parents. Thanksgiving dinner was special for the Martinez family, this year; Elizabeth, Fred's fiancée had joined them. Elizabeth, with her blue eyes and natural blond hair looked more like Clara's daughter than Margo did.

The wedding day was set for the 27th of December. Besides the groom, the Whealers invited his parents and sister to stay with them in the country house, outside of London, and spent Christmas together, as a family. The house was large enough and accommodating, and with extra help, wouldn't be any burden at all for Elizabeth's parents.

Both families decided not to send any wedding invitations back to U.S., to even close friends. They had planned a formal dinner-dance reception in Washington, D.C., during spring break, when Margo would be free.

The private wedding ceremony of Pedro and Elizabeth, for immediate families and close relatives, took place at St. Andrew's Church. A small country chapel close by the Whealers summer home, where they were married, and Elizabeth and her brother was baptized.

Following the ceremony, a dinner-dance for three hundred people was held at the Savoy Hotel, in London. The newly-weds, after a two-week honeymoon in Australia and New Zeeland, returned back to Washington., DC.

It was the 8th of January, and one week before the spring semester was to begin.

Margo was on her way to the office to check the mail. She was rested, and had a good time in London. The wedding and all were so well planned.

Elizabeth's parents were seasoned hosts, and every detail was addressed unobtrusively with class, and no fanfare. She stayed with her parents in Washington for several days, before returning back to the west coast.

It was a beautiful sunny southern California morning. What a difference from London! The wedding though, with all its festivities, had changed everything to sunshine, and the weather became irrelevant.

The last envelope Margo came to was intriguing by its appearance alone, contents notwithstanding, which weren't known at this juncture. Her full name was printed on, with no sender's name, or stamp. Apparently, it came from the university and was left with the rest of the pile.

She opened the envelope, took a letter out, and read it.

Margo,

Welcome back home. I wished you and your family the best for the New Year. My sincere congratulations on your brother wedding, and may God bless him and his bride, and make all their days, for the rest of their lives, as happy as the wedding day.

Before the new semester starts, knowing how busy we all will be, it's important for me that we meet. I would like to visit you at your apartment, sometime after supper, just to talk. Please, call my apartment. If I am not in, leave a message with my voice-mail.

Sincerely,

Fred.

Margo became curious.

The little she knew of Fred, she could tell by the tenor of the letter, that there was a certain degree of urgency. What could be? Was he unhappy with the school? Did something happen, while she was gone? Maybe as member of the search committee, she could help.

She didn't want to wait. She called his apartment and left a message. She was free tonight, and he could come over any time, after 7 o'clock.

Exactly at 7 o'clock, Fred rang the bell at Margo's apartment. She opened the door and asked him to come in.

"Happy New Year, Fred; how are you? How were your holidays?"

"Happy New Year to you, too; Christmas was rather unusual for me this year, if not strange."

"What do you mean?"

"The weather! There has never been a Christmas season for me, as far as I can remember, without snow. It'll take sometime to get used to this kind of climate, I guess.

"Thanks for finding time to meet with me so quickly. You were out of town for two weeks, and I'm sure, there're other things you'd rather be doing."

"Don't worry; it worked out fine with me. I've plenty of time, and so do you. School won't start for another week. How is your work coming along, so far? Are you happy with your decision to come to Caltech?"

"I'm happy and honored, and I'm sure, it's going to work well for all concerned. The reason I'm here is because I want to talk to you. There's something personal and sacred that has entered my life, and maybe will enter your life, too."

Margo was at a loss.

Her mathematical genius, expertise, and probabilities acumen were put on hold. Her female intuitive power had taken over, but stumbled. The sincerity and power in Fred's expression and directness in his eyes emanated a puzzling, if not frightening, dynamism and sincerity.

His piercing eyes were trained and attuned not only to detect brilliance in the skies and galaxies, but also in earthlings.

"Margo, what I want to tell you now, wouldn't make any sense at all, unless I go way back and reflect on my life. There's something in my past that you should know, which would make some sense of my present. What you're about to hear, only one other person has known; my mentor at MIT. I trust you, and I hope it stays with you, at least for the time being.

"When I was in my senior year in high school, back in Munich, I had a long talk with my Uncle Paul, the priest. I don't know if you noticed; I have his picture on my desk. The conversation lasted for hours, and became a legacy that has followed me for the rest of my life.

"At 18, I had a burning desire to enter the seminar and become a priest. But my uncle convinced me that priesthood was a revelation, a *calling*, sort of an epiphany from God, and if that was to be my path, I would know when the time came. He was concerned that his own life had influenced me, and felt that I was too young to make such a lifetime commitment.

"I followed his advice and continued my studies, while waiting for my *calling*. After I got my Master's from MIT, and two weeks before I was to begin my doctoral studies, I decided I needed to get away for a while.

"I spent the next two years at the Harvard Divinity School working on a Master's degree in Biblical Studies and Sacred Theology. It was during those two years that I realized that my *calling* was not to the priesthood, but to continue my studies in physics and astrophysics.

"My *calling* was to look at the Universe, study God's wonders and creations, and disseminate knowledge that would glorify His Wisdom and Might."

"Wow! What a story. Now I know where you came from, that would explain your analysis of the origin of *good* and *evil* we discussed the last time, when you came over for dinner. If I had to define your mind with one word, would have been the word composite."

"You still remember our last conversation? It was several months ago."

"Of course, I do."

"It was dumb of me to ask. I'm sure; your brilliant mind has its own web of memory, with unlimited capacity.

"Now, it's time to talk about another *calling* that was revealed to me and feels so right. I'm not good at this, and I haven't done it before. I hope the words, coming out of my mouth, are the correct ones and appropriate for the moment.

"Margo, I would like much us to get married, and become husband and wife whenever you're ready. I feel connected with you."

Fred remained cool and collected with an as matter of fact expression on his face. He fully understood the seriousness, hastiness, and even abruptness of his proposal, most probably devoid of any romance, but he didn't know any better.

He was determined to pluck the heaviest cord possible and make a sound strong enough to be heard loud and clear.

Margo's jaw dropped. Her skin turned white. Everything around her started spinning faster and faster. The floor began to sink, and slowly a hole opened ready to swallow her and the chair she sat on. She excused herself, and quickly disappeared into the bathroom.

She felt sick to her stomach and dry-heaved several times. She washed her face with cold water and put a wet towel on. She looked in the mirror; the color of her skin had almost come back to normal. She put fresh makeup on, and felt composed enough to return to the living room. She was upset and maybe angry, but she didn't want to show it. When she came back, Fred was standing by the door ready to leave.

"I'm sorry; I didn't mean to upset you. I'll live right now, if it'll make you feel better. I told you what was in my mind. The rest is up to you."

"Please, sit down; you don't have to go. It's my turn to talk now, and you have to listen to what I'm about to say.

"In your own idiomatic way, and out of the blue, you proposed and ask me to marry you. That is totally absurd, to put it mildly, if not insane.

"We hardly know each other, and we aren't in love; at least speaking for myself, although flattered by your proposal. Your move, to put it mildly, was presumptuous, preposterous, ill-timed, and impulsive. There was neither logic nor decorum behind it, and the lack of knowledge of social standards, etiquette, and awareness were obvious."

Margo tried to conceal her bewilderment, annoyance, and anger, but the tone in her voice and choice of words betrayed her. She intended to make Fred understand and question the appropriateness of his behavior, his intentions notwithstanding.

He took her for granted and available for keeps, without considering her own feelings, preferences, and without even thinking if she was seeing another man.

Fred remained calm and composed. He thought there was no reason for Margo to be upset. She could have said *thanks but no thanks, goodbye and see you around.* Maybe her reaction, subconsciously, was compensatory for feelings she wanted to avoid, ignore, and even suppress.

"Margo, you said *we weren't in love.*

"What did you mean by that? What's you concept of love? Where does love begin and come from? Do desire, passion and lust precede love or follow love? What is the compelling force of love? Where is home for love? A beautiful face and body, or a beautiful spirit, mind, and soul? Can love survive, and make it only on sensuality alone, devoid of spirituality and commitment?

"I seldom watch television. The other night, I saw a movie that probably depicted how love is perceived nowadays.

"A professional man-out of town and separated from his wife, and a professional woman-divorced, met in her office for business for the first time. The man, being a gentleman and appreciative of her services, invited the woman to meet him for dinner at his hotel, later in the evening. During dinner, they admitted that were attracted to each other.

"After dinner, they talked for a while in the lobby, and finally ended up in bed, in his hotel room. The experience, both admitted, was extraordinary.

"The affair continued for a while. The last time the man was back in town for business said he *thought* he was falling in love; so did the woman. Is love an after thought of a habit, no matter how powerful and pleasurable might be, or the beginning of communion and glory?

"The affair eventually ended, when the man went back to his wife for the sake of the children. I'm sure this was not the love you had in mind, irrespective of the ending, and even under more favorable circumstances.

"What's your definition of love? How and when love maturates to empower and unite? Please, anoint the ignorant; and educate the naïve, and the socially challenged!"

Margo detected a certain degree of sarcasm in Fred's comments. She new, he was smart, but his directness caught her by surprise; his points were well taken and supported, but didn't change what she felt inside.

Her mind was burning with curiosity. She wanted to find out what was the breaking point and when it happened, that made Fred aware of his feelings for her? He was so direct and uninhibited. Why shouldn't she be, too?

"Fred, when you had the long conversation with your uncle, way back, he said you should know and sense when your *calling* for something unique had come. When and how your feelings for me overwhelmed you? There must have been be a defining moment of awakening, worthy remembering."

"When you invited me for dinner; the first time I was in your apartment, and you took me around to show me your place.

"I noticed the picture of the three girls on your desk in your bedroom.

"You told me how immediately, and out of nowhere, the three of you got connected, the first day at the Academy, and became sisters every since. This was a sign to me that you not only believe in *callings*, but also you were the beneficiary of a *calling* that had changed your life dramatically and irrevocably for ever.

"What draws one person to another or others, like in your case, it's a mystery. You know the connection is right, but you don't know why.

"Next to the photograph on your desk, I noticed a small painting of Virgin Mary. That triggered cascades of feelings and thoughts in my heart and mind, going all the way back to the rectory, where I grew-up.

"That small painting spoke volumes for you. It was a witness and acknowledgement of your spirituality, faith, and values that are my values, too.

"I don't really play an instrument-my uncle helped me fool around with the organ in the church, but I appreciate, love, and understand music fairly well for an amateur. My uncle loved classical music and opera, and took me to many performances from early on. This continued when I came to a MIT, with the Boston Symphony and other ensembles close by.

"Next to your desk I saw a cello case, behind the music stand. And what was on the music stand? The score of one of Bach's Suites-Saraband, for unaccompanied cello!

"He took an old folksy free-spirited Spanish dance, and his genius transformed it to an artistically idealized piece of music, with not only esoteric, but also joyful quality, that could fill your being with grace, happiness, and contemplation. The choice and willingness to learn and play this kind of music demands not only dexterity and intelligence, but deep spirituality and a refined musical instinct that projects the richness in one's soul and existence.

"That was the straw that broke the camel's back, and convinced me that you and only you, not even someone like you, was for me.

"My awakening and *calling* had come, and I had to look no farther. I got connected. I hope, I answered your question.

"Before I go, I'd like to make something clear.

"What happened and what was discussed tonight, as far as I'm concerned, should remain within these walls, never to be repeated or mentioned by me to you. Whether you want to bring the issue up with someone else, would be strictly up to you and your judgment.

"There would be no pressure for a time frame from me. The next step should come from you; maybe tomorrow; maybe never.

"If you decide, that you'd like us to start seeing each other, that's fine; if you change your mind, you can stop anytime, with no questions asked. You're free to conduct your personal life as you wish, and change nothing on my account."

Fred got up, took Margo's right hand with both of his unexpectedly, kissed it gently, said goodnight, and left rather hurriedly.

❧   ❧   ❧

After Fred left, Margo took a deep breath relieved, and sat down.

She tried to objectively reconstruct and analyze Fred's visit. To say the least, he had guts. When determined to reach his goal, he was shy and withdrawn no more. He exhibited coolness in articulating his feelings and was in complete control and command.

Besides being a brilliant mind, he possessed unlimited internal resources, like spirituality and faith that made him secure and resolute; and his instinct for music was uncanny.

His appearance, manners, demeanor, body language, and physical characteristics projected austerity and conservatism that were notable and well suited for him; and he wasn't bad looking either.

What was Margo to do? Fred was an all-around good guy, but she wasn't attracted to him. At least for the time being, she would do nothing.

Margo, after sorting out her thoughts, got up and went to her bedroom to pick up her cell phone. She wanted to call Barbara and Lucia right away. They would be the only ones to know.

The trio had recently acquired the latest in cell phone technology that allowed them instant communication: the PPT (push to talk) cell phone. Just by pressing a button, the three were instantly connected and could hear each other.

Margo talked for sometime and gave the entire scoop in detail to Barbara and Lucia. She was anxious to hear their opinion. Both were surprised, listened attentively, and without interrupting.

Barbara, known for her astuteness, boldness, and dry sense of humor, was the first one to respond, rather bluntly.

"What's your problem? You said you weren't attracted to him, period; the man put no pressure, and left the ball in your court. What's the big fuzz all about? The case is closed, and that's the end of the story. Why are you calling us? Your mind is all made up.

"I'm sick and tired of your shenanigans when it comes to men. You see every man as a math problem and theorem that you have to solve and find the answer. You're so picky; you make me mad. Pretty soon you're going to be thirty-four years old. You let so many good men go by.

"Wake-up and smell the coffee, princess; unless you want to join Lucia, and become a nun! No offense intended, Lucia.

"There're no more princes left to go around. And if you find one, aged and all shriveled-up, he has horse no more to sweep you off your feet and away; for his horse preceded him in kicking the bucket! That's all I have to say to you, sis."

They all laughed hysterically, until Lucia cut in.

"Barbara, you're so good! I'm glad you're a doctor and not a lawyer.

"Margo look; I don't blame Barbara for being upset. I completely agree with her. Here is a man, a brilliant mind, a man of spirit and faith by your own admission, who fell in love with you; he said he connected with you. So what! He didn't say he loved you, but that's what he meant, for he didn't' know any better.

"Are you allowing euphemisms and romanticized frivolity to blind the vision of you consciousness? Even if you aren't attracted to Fred, what's wrong if you go out with him a few times to get to know him better; and again, by your own description, he is not bad looking, either.

"Are you afraid of him and his commitment? Are you subconsciously concerned that he maybe smarter than you? I know you inside out, like you know me and Barbara; we're sisters.

"I never met Fred. From your description of him, I can clearly see that you have so many things in common.

"You're both exceptional scientists. You're a classic cello player, and he has an instinct for understanding and feeling music. His spirituality, faith in God, and values not only match, but exceed ours. His connection with you would be the best compliment a man could ever give you in his own unique way, despite that societal semantics and etiquette may have been ignored and forgone.

"The essence of this man is substance; he is a diamond in the rough, with a brilliant honesty, and merits your attention. That's all I have to say to you. Barbara, is any thing else? Goodbye from me, and keep us posted."

"Listen you, blue eye Latina beauty; don't be stupid, and get the ball rolling. Nobody tells you to marry the guy. Just let your intellectual curiosity and intuition look around and search. If nothing is found, you lose nothing; but if there's something, you could lose everything, if you don't try. You can't live footloose and fancy free for ever. Goodbye, Margo; we love you, and keep in touch."

After the call, Margo was happy and settled. She thought of, and reflected a lot on what Barbara and Lucia had said.

My goodness; I am so blessed. It's so helpful to have two sisters to talk to. When in need, we become a sounding board for one another. We don't only hear what we like to, but also what we don't, avoid, or are afraid of. I think, they have assessed Fred, whom never met, much more objectively than I, based on the information I have given them.

Maybe, being involved in the selection process, as a member of the search committee, I blinded my female intuition; I was so overtaken by his brain power, and never saw him as a man, to say the least, and even much less a as potential suitor.

The situation is precarious and has to be played out with the utmost caution. Fred put the burden entirely on me. If I ask him out, I have to make sure I don't convey the wrong message and give him the impression that his proposal for marriage has been accepted.

It's really funny, awkward, and unheard of; for a woman to ask a man out for a date that has been preempted by the man's proposal to marry her! That's Fred I guess. It can't get any stranger, but interesting for sure.

OK sisters; you got your wish and God bless! I hope none of us would regret it.

❧   ❧   ❧

Two weeks went by, but nothing happed.

Margo and Fred crossed each other's paths at school, talked business, and had lunch together as usual with other members of the faculty several times.

When Margo returned to her apartment from school, it was late Thursday evening, hoping that Barbara and Lucia wouldn't call again.

For the past three days she was thinking to find something that would be appropriate for Fred and her to do, and get together over the weekend; she promised it to Barbara and Lucia. She threatened to change her phone number if they didn't stop pestering her! They called every day, and last night, the trio spent almost two hours on the phone.

Next day, as soon as the ticket office of LA Philharmonic Orchestra opened, Margo called and charged two tickets for the Saturday's evening performance; fortunately a few good seats were still available.

Both were experts and lovers of classical music from a different perspective. She, as an advanced amateur performer and he, as an educated listener with a critical ear.

Margo after supper, around 8 o'clock, called Fred. She never thought of asking him before getting tickets. If he couldn't make it, she would take one of her girlfriends. She doubted, though. As far as she new, Fred hadn't shown any signs of active social life during the first semester.

"Hello Fred; Margo calling. How are you?"

"I'm fine. I started getting used to the sun, this time of the year."

"Listen; I didn't ask you. I hope you're free. I got two tickets for tomorrow, for the Philharmonic. Would you like to be my guest?"

"I'd be delighted; and thanks for inviting me. I'd like to ask you for a favor. I hope you wouldn't mind. I'd like us to have dinner, before going to the concert. You're native to the area. Choose a nice restaurant you're familiar with. What time the concert begins?'

"8 o'clock; I wouldn't mind it at all. I'd love to. It's so kind of you to ask. We have to leave no later than 6 o'clock. If you don't mind, I'll drive? It'd be much easier."

"That's fine; it's your town. Do you want me to wait downstairs in the lobby, or pick you up from your place? My door faces yours; we live on the same floor; remember?"

Margo didn't respond for a second or two, thinking.

"Sure; come to my place, and ring the bell. I'll come right out. Goodnight; I'll see you tomorrow.

"I'm looking forward to. Thanks for inviting me. Goodnight."

It wasn't that bad, Margo thought after hanging up.

She was amazed how polite and considerate Fred was. He took absolutely nothing for granted. The way he asked her for dinner was refreshing, as if she'd do him a favor, if agreed to go. No pressure at all; and he was willing to wait for her in the main lobby, if he rather not pick her up from her apartment.

Saturday, around 4 o'clock in the afternoon, Margo's phone rung.

"Hello; Margo speaking. May I help you?"

"Ms. Martinez, this is the reception desk downstairs.

"A young lady, from the florist down the street, has a delivery for you. I let her in; she is on her way up to your apartment.

'Thanks."

Margo was surprised. Who would have sent her flowers?

She went to her bedroom in a hurry and took out of her wallet some cash to tip the delivery lady. On her way back, the door bell rung; she answered.

"Dr. Martinez, I have these two packages for you. Would you please sign?"

"Thanks; please wait. I'll be right back."

Margo took the packages inside. She returned, signed, tipped the lady, and closed the door.

One package was three feet long by one foot wide, and the other ten by ten inches square. Both packages were wrapped with fancy paper and tied with a golden ribbon, ending in a large bow.

Margo first opened the larger package.

After removing the wrapping paper, there was a white box with the florist's name on. Her large blue eyes sparkled with surprise when she removed the cover. There were twelve long stem red roses, as fresh as if they were just cut from the rosebush.

Fine droplets of dew on the deep red color petals gave them a silvery chromatic texture, as the afternoon sun, penetrating the window facing south, had welcomed them to their last residence before the final doom, death, and destruction. There would be neither celebration of joy, nor expressions of gratitude and love, unless someone-the bouquet of roses in this instance-was willing to pay a price; perhaps the ultimate price.

Margo, impatiently looked and looked, but to her chagrin, couldn't find a card to tell who had sent the roses. She went to the kitchen and brought a vase filled with water. She put the roses inside and placed the vase on the oval coffee table, right across from the sofa.

When Margo opened the smaller package, became even more surprised, if not anxious. From the transparent plastic cover, after removing the white envelop on top, she could see a beautiful and delicate corsage made of white orchids. The envelope was addressed to her by first name only, and inside was a card with a short note:

Dear Margo,
Just a token of appreciation, to celebrate your kindness.
With many thanks,
Fred.

Margo's knees buckled; she sat down. She couldn't believe it.

Fred, the asocial, the loner, and all other epithets he was describe with, with the possible exception of being a *misanthrope*, could be so overwhelmingly generous, sensitive, and kind. She took the corsage and put it in the refrigerator, right away, to keep it fresh, until ready to pin it on.

By 5:30, Margo was all dressed and ready to go. She had an ankle length black sleeveless silk dress with random silvery embroidering on the top above the waist to match the lapels of the long sleeve black jacket. Margo dressed sharply and elegantly, like the rest of the trio.

Margo, like her brother, had inherited the deep blue eyes of her *Anglo* mother that even made the color deeper, when her wavy shoulder length of deep brown shiny hair locks accidentally crossed them at random.

At exactly 6 o'clock, Fred was outside Margo's door.

He was dressed in a black-with fine deep burgundy stripes-vested suit, white poplin French cuffs shirt, and a black, with small burgundy dots, tie.

His straw blond hair, deep blue eyes, and whiter than white skin, unquestionably heralded his Teutonic, if not Germanic origin.

When he rung the bell, and Margo opened the door, the contrast was breathtakingly phenomenal and made each one shine even more.

Margo's Latina's beauty, radiant face, and care-free smile softened Fred's gothic austere expression, as the only common physical denominator-their deep blue eyes-stared at each other in an astonishing, and mutually restrained admiration.

"Hi Fred; thanks for the roses and the corsage. There're so beautiful and fresh.

Come in; let me show you."

"You're welcome. They look nice. Let's go. I don't know how far the restaurant is from the music hall."

"Don't worry. I made dinner reservation at the music hall's restaurant; it's convenient. Just one place to park and the food is decent."

The evening went well. Both were comfortable and enjoyed each other's company. Margo was surprised how relaxed Fred was the entire evening. By the time they returned to the apartment was 11 o'clock. Fred walked Margo to the door, and she asked him to come in for a glass of wine, or just to talk.

"No thanks. It's getting a little too late. I don't know about you, but with the new semester starting and all, tomorrow after church, I have to go back to my office. I would like to thank you for the evening, and like to see you again; if and when, would be entirely up to you. Goodnight, and thanks again."

Margo, once inside her apartment, took her jacket and shoes off, sat on the sofa, and stared at the beautiful bouquet of red roses on the coffee table; still lively and alive, unconcerned of their eventual doom and demise.

The corsage, on the lapel, began to show signs of wilting, reminiscing of the ephemeral nature of matter over mind and spirit, irrespective how promising and youthful the beginning was. Any regrets? Absolutely, none; for the message was delivered!

Margo's mathematical mind, with its probability dynamics and ratios, was stunned tonight, and couldn't come up with any rational figures and measures to account for Fred's behavior.

Out of nowhere, unexpectedly and unaccountably, from early on in the evening, he exhibited standards of social awareness and grace that would not only match, but even surpassed anyone's she had ever been out with.

The flowers, opening the car door, helping her to sit down at the restaurant, taking off and putting the jacket back on, holding the elevator door, etc.; just name it. He did it all, and he did it all, right!

Where did this come from?

Certainly not from the rectory and his uncle Paul, a smart and dedicated, but humble priest. Maybe his connection with her, Margo thought, unleashed traits that he had always been within him, but he never had the chance to use.

Maybe, his *calling* directed him to adjust his social awareness in order to meet the needs of the moment.

Intuitiveness, monopolized by the female psyche, could be part of the male psyche, too; teaching and leading to new paths that could make a man conscious and aware of circumstances, dictating and compelling him that his modus operandi better be altered, in order to accommodate new and important entries in his life, in the pursuit of happiness and personal growth.

Margo had learned a valuable lesson today that she should never forget.

To *box in* anyone, man or woman, on perceptions and information provided by others, or early undocumented personal impressions, to say the least, was unintelligent and intellectually fraudulent.

What had happened to exercising unhurriedly cautious and objective judgment in assessing and adjudicating one's virtues or flaws in general?

Fred wasn't a diamond in the rough; he was a priceless, highly polished, brilliant stone covered with dust. His connection with Margo became the dusting cloth that brought unabated and everlasting brilliance back to life. She was more humbled than proud thinking;

OK; I am smart, good looking, unattached. Fred must have come across some other women.

What was so special about me that really shook Fred's existence? Spirituality, destiny, fate, mutual faith in God, and values we share? Could be a calling for both of us? An awakening? Who knows? Maybe the combination of all.

Objectively speaking, Fred and Margo had so many things in common.

Both were brilliant scientists, faculty members at one of the top schools in the world, and endowed with internal richness that would keep heart, mind, spirit, and soul fortified and united.

With love or connection, individual definitions notwithstanding, Fred and Margo could reach an endearing and empowering level of unprecedented interdependent happiness in their life's journey.

Early Sunday morning, Margo called Barbara and Lucia. Both were ecstatic with the good news.

"I thank you my friends. I have to admit it; I was wrong. If you hadn't pushed me, nothing would have happened. It's early to tell, but the first experience was unquestionably revelatory."

"Look baby blue eyes; don't waste any valuable time. You should get together at least one day every weekend; and fly with him, in about month, to Washington, so that he can meet you parents."

"Barbara, aren't you rushing me a little bit?"

Lucia cut in.

"Barbara's right. From what you have told us, Fred's mind is all made up. That's why you have to meet often to make up your mind, too.

"In my book, from what I can sense, your mind has already changed after the first date. I think you're made for each other. He's so sincere and honest with his feelings, and especially with you, from day one.

"I can hear wedding bells. Maybe Fred is the other *freak* you were looking for all your life. Remember? I'm using your own words."

"Lucia your memory scares me! Thanks again. You've been so fantastic. What could we have done without each other? I don't even want to think about it. Have a nice Sunday. I'll be calling you soon, bye."

As the day went on, Margo thought more and more about Fred.

Objectively speaking she wasn't in love with him, now. Could she fall in love, if she would know him better? After last night the answer was, yes. The dynamics had changed precipitately.

Already she liked him more than she did before going out. Her sisters were right. She should start spending more time with him and avoid being so blasé and casual.

Around 8 o'clock in the evening, Margo called Fed.

"Hi Fred; this is Margo. How are you?"

"Good evening Margo; I just came back from the office. I went after church, and practically spent the entire day there."

"I'm sorry; if this is not a good time, I can call tomorrow."

"Not at all; I had dinner out, after I left the office."

"I had a wonderful time last night and enjoyed your company a lot. Since you put the burden on me for us getting together, I have an idea for Saturday.

"How about driving south and going to San Diego? It's an easy and relaxing ride. We can leave in the morning and spend the entire day. There're nice places to see, like the Balboa Park, where the 1916 World Fair was held. We can talk, walk, relax, and have fun."

After the Saturday outing, Margo admitted, whether she liked or not, that she was attracted to Fred. She had never met a man with such a depth. She couldn't believe that people like him existed.

They continued to see each other more often, and after two months, Margo finally accepted Fred's proposal. Two weeks later, they flew to Washington for the weekend, and the rest of the Martinez family met Fred for the first time. They were all thrilled and happy for Margo.

Saturday evening, after dinner at the Martinez apartment, Fred presented Margo with a beautiful marquise diamond ring she had chosen before leaving LA.

The wedding day was set for the first weekend of June.

Margo insisted to have the reception for Pedro and Elizabeth the same day with her wedding reception, instead of the spring break weekend; logistically, it made more sense. Elizabeth was adamant that the day should be only for Margo, but Margo prevailed. The Four Seasons Hotel Ballroom was reserved for the reception, to accommodate a larger crowed.

The wedding ceremony was celebrated at the Washington Cathedral.

Barbara and Lucia were maids of honor, and Margo's brother and his wife stood as best man and woman. Janice, Barbara's almost three year old little girl served, admirably poised, as the flower girl.

The Trio, after dinner, amid festive moments of wine, music, song, and dance found time for themselves.

With Margo's wedding, everything had come to a *complete* circle, and each one of the trio was secured and accomplished in her own niche.

They hugged, cried, and laughed. They were so blessed; and used their God given gifts wisely, and most of all had each other for life, with no interruption or any ugliness that could have compromised the sanctity of their vows.

Margo's wedding brought them together early this summer, and they wouldn't be meeting again until next year to renew their vows, as they had done since graduating from the Academy.

The trio, embraced and with their heads bowed, recited their *Vows* not only with emotion and tears, but also with resolve, commitment, and fortitude.

The power of love and magnetism that had drawn them together remained as strong, deep, mystical, spiritual, divine, real, and fresh as ever.

It's amazing that the trio, so far, encountered no obstacles. It had been like a dream.

Why some are given everything in this world? Nobody knows; that's the mystery of life.

Was the dream going to last for ever? Were they lucky? The fact remained that although gifted never rested on their laurels and never took anything for granted. Did spirituality and faith empower them with more determination to try harder?

Their *Vows* have stood the test of time so far, but were never really challenged. If they were, could have survived and made the bond of the trio even stronger?

CHAPTER 9

Catching-up, Near Death Experience, and Survival

Barbara, Lucia, and Margo, a few months apart, celebrated their forty-second birthday this year. Time really flew.

They met twenty-five years ago as seventeen year olds, nonetheless extremely intelligent and gifted. As time passed, the three women had shined in their chosen fields, kept their spirituality and faith, applied their intelligence wisely, and were blessed with success.

Barbara, known for her strong personality and leadership, had become the leader of her Ob/Gyn group practice. The group had grown from five, when she joined, to twenty. She continued her association with the clinic of the City Hospital, and provided prenatal and obstetrical care for indigent patients.

With so many physicians in the group, Barbara was on call only once or twice a month; that allowed her to spent more at home with her family, and practice and play the piano she so loved. Janice, her daughter, approaching her ninth birthday, started piano lessons two years ago and was doing pretty well.

There was a little rivalry, sort of, between Barbara and her father, who retired several years ago. She, being a disciplinarian and a devotee of serious piano music, wanted her daughter to stay and follow the strict classical pedagogy of the instrument.

On the other hand, her father Centric, the jazz pianist, with his uncanny improvisational skills, sneaked in the process and taught his granddaughter to play some fun tunes she quickly picked up.

That scene was so familiar! It happened with her so long ago, when her mother walked in unexpectedly and found father and daughter playing jazz for four hands. But Barbara, at this stage of her life, was mellower than her mother.

It was so endearing to see grandfather and granddaughter sitting on the piano bench, playing together.

There was a brief interruption in Barbara's happy life.

When her daughter was five years old, she became pregnant; the entire family, including Lucia and Margo, were excited. Unfortunately, her pregnancy developed inside her right tube—ectopic pregnancy is the proper medical term-and she underwent emergency surgery to control life threatening bleeding. She would like to have another child, but was content and thankful for what she did have, and not sorry for what she didn't.

❦   ❦   ❦

Lucia continued her monastic life with commitment and dedication, and especially the mission to help young women, particularly students at Trinity University, to develop skills and critical thinking in facing the demands and challenges of their personal and professional lives.

Some students, even after finishing graduate school and getting married, continued to see her; she had become their *special* friend and mentor.

Two years ago, Lucia was appointed Dean of Women at large, at Trinity.

She taught, across the board, philosophy and applied sociology to undergraduate and graduate students, with emphasis on women's issues, relationships, and family.

Everybody was amazed with the number of male students attending her classes. Her seminars, bringing men and women, married or single from the outside world, were successful. The lectures were televised to several classrooms to accommodate the large number of students interested in attending.

Lucia was known to all as *Mother Hope*; always with a smile in her face, ready to listen, never to judge, and never tired to help. If you never believed in angels, just follow Lucia for one day only; you might change your mind. And if you didn't, you were either a fool or a human with no heart.

Putting God and angels up in the clouds and away from us, we forget kindness present among us mortals, every single day.

John, Lucia's brother, got his wish.

Last year, after being promoted, he was transferred to the American Embassy, in Tokyo as Consul General.

Lucia, whenever talked to him on the phone, called him jokingly, *Mr. Ambassador,* his next rank of promotion! His wife was pregnant with their second child. They had a four year old girl, Theresa, named after his grandmother. Her parents had retired, and were busy looking after the charitable foundation they had endowed.

❧   ❧   ❧

Margo and Fred were nick-named love birds with *brains* by Barbara and Lucia. They were suited so well for each other. They had corroborated in two books, combining astrophysics and probabilities!

It's phenomenal what brains could produce sleeping together. The bodies weren't left behind, either.

Margo, at the age of thirty-seven, became pregnant and had a boy. And of course, he was named Paul, after Fred's uncle, the priest.

The summer before Margo became pregnant traveled to Munich with Fred.

It would be a homecoming naturally for him, but for her as well. They visited the rectory where Fred grew up, and the cemetery, where his uncle was buried. Fred fell on his knees, and Margo followed him in a silent prayer.

For sure, Fred thanked God for Uncle Paul, his wisdom, and advice to wait for his *calling*, and so did Margo, for raising Fred with such spirituality and internal richness.

Pedro, Margo's brother, had become an international finance attorney of renown, still with the same firm in Washington, DC. Elizabeth, his wife, loved living in the US, and had become the all American wife, with the exception of her clipped accent that was still traceable back to the old Union Jack. They had two children, a boy named Julio Pedro, and a girl, Anna Elizabeth.

The unbelievable happened with Margo's father.

When the Chief Justice of US Supreme Court retired, the President nominated him as the new Chief Justice. He was unanimously confirmed by the Senate. A second first for him; not only was he the first Hispanic in the highest court, but also the first Hispanic Chief Justice.

Her mother enjoyed staying home, playing the cello, and spending time with the grandchildren.

❧   ❧   ❧

Barbara, Lucia, and Margo wanted this year, the silver jubilee of their vows, to be something special.

They promised each other, when they met last summer, to practice and practice, and by hook or by crook be ready to play Tchaikovsky's Trio in A minor for violin, cello, and piano in its entirety, for their twenty-fifth anniversary. After all, this is what brought them together and made them sisters for life.

The meeting was set for the second weekend of June, and would be at the resort up in the mountains where they met twenty years ago, the summer they graduated from college.

Barbara and Margo would arrive on Friday, late in the evening, and planned to leave the following Saturday. Lucia, free from any family constrains, would be there two days earlier to ensure that all arrangements requested had gone through.

The smaller conference room, with a seating capacity of one hundred, was reserved for the trio's concert. On Thursday morning, the grand piano from the ballroom was to be moved to the conference the room where the performance would take place.

The piano tuner was scheduled for Thursday afternoon, and Lucia, with her violin, planned to be with him to make sure that the pitch was correct. Brochures and information concerning the free concert would be distributed by Friday noon; and the trio planned to start rehearsing Saturday morning, after breakfast.

It was the third week of May.

Lucia had a light supper; she wasn't hungry at all.

For the last three days she became nauseous, and vomited in the morning. She made an appointment to see a doctor, the first thing in the morning. She had been always healthy and felt well otherwise.

With traveling plans for the upcoming reunion with her sisters, she wanted to make sure that everything was OK. Maybe, it was some kind of intestinal flu. She hadn't seen a doctor for several years. It would be a good opportunity to have a complete physical, and also a mammogram done.

Lucia was on time for her 9 o'clock appointment.

She underwent a complete physical examination, and the nurse took blood and urine specimens for lab work. Mammograms had to be scheduled for another day; besides the doctor wanted to check all lab results before any further testing.

The doctor reassured her, that she was in excellent health, and advised her to call the office tomorrow afternoon, to discuss the lab results. Lucia was happy nothing was wrong that would have interfered with her travel plans.

Next day, later in the afternoon, Lucia called the doctor's office and asked to speak with him.

"Hello Doctor; I'm calling for my lab tests...all were negative except for one...is it serious? Oh my God...how can this be possible? You double-checked...and you're sure...I'll call your office, after my trip to get he name of a specialist...could be a mix-up in the samples? My urine...and blood...were sent to the lab together. Thanks...Doctor...Goodbye...so am I."

Lucia closed the office door, locked it, and sat down.

She became totally disassociated and felt as she were floating higher and higher, finally hitting the ceiling that was as impenetrable, cold, unforgiving, and heavy as a tombstone.

She was conscious, but the desire to escape reality and disappear into oblivion was overwhelming.

Sweat from her forehead, eyebrows, and face cascaded in lumps down to her face, and the collar of her blouse stuck to her neck like a hungry leach.

Reason and logic would be totally useless, for neither the rule of moral law was violated nor was the rule of physical law enacted. To even think of divine intervention would be not only blasphemy, but an unforgivable mortal sin.

Fortunately, Lucia had a light raincoat in her office.

She waited until dark, and after all had left the building and before the cleaning crew showed up, put the raincoat on, went to her car in a hurry, and drove away.

By the time she arrived at the House of Hope, was 9 o'clock. Everybody was concerned that she might have been involved in a car accident; they were happy to see her, although she didn't look too hot.

By the time she got to her room, she was having chills and her teeth were chattering. She removed the raincoat; the sweat had gone through the entire blouse, upper part of the skirt, and underwear. She got undressed and took a shower.

How long did she stay inside the shower stall? She didn't care to know and never bothered to check the time.

Time was of no essence to her any longer, for it would never change the present that was destined become part of all the tomorrows to come.

She mechanically dried her body and hair; put a nightgown and robe on, and as she brushed her teeth look in the mirror.

Her face, from now on, would never be looked at as before by others. The truth must be buried for ever, and only her sisters would know; and she hoped they would believe in her. After all, this was the meaning, and what their vows stood for; *trust and faith, above and beyond logic, and circumstance.*

Lucia sat in prayer for a while. Was her faith being tested? Was this going to be her cross? Had her calling been challenged? Could she continue, with her credibility and moral standing in question?

Without a doubt, the time of crisis had come; and for the first time in twenty-five years, the *Vows of Three Sisters* would be challenged to the core. Fortunately, there was plenty of time for Lucia to sort things out before leaving for the reunion in the mountains.

An hour later, she purchased plane tickets on the phone. She planned to take the first morning flight out to Washington, DC next day, and return the following day.

❧   ❧   ❧

Barbara and Margo arrived at the resort Friday evening. Lucia came two days early, to take care of business, and was waiting for them in the main lobby. Once, she saw the van from the airport, came outside to greet them. They hug, kissed, and embraced one another, with deep love and affection.

Intuitively, Barbara and Margo knew right away, that there was something profoundly different with Lucia; she held on to them so tight and appeared somewhat withdrawn.

The accommodations were the same, as usual.

The trio had adjoining rooms, with Lucia in the middle. After unpacking, they met in Lucia's room and tried to catch up with a quick update of what was new, since they met last year; it would be plain of time to go into details later.

For Barbara and Margo, it was another banner year; marriages, family, personal, and professional lives had progressed as expected and were happy, thankful to God, and counting their blessings.

When Lucia's turn came to talk, Barbara and Margo's initial impressions were confirmed. They knew that something big was inside her.

"I'm happy for you; you and your families are always in my prayers. I'm sure you're anxious to hear from me. Let's have some fun now. We can talk after the concert.

"The Grand piano was moved to the smaller room and tuned to perfection. There's quite a bit of interest among the guests, and two additional rows of seats were added.

"The hotel management, gratis, has planned a reception, for the patrons and us, to be given immediately after the performance. When I paid the balance for renting the room, the management said would be available, all day long Saturday, for us to practice."

The trio rehearsed all day Saturday, with a long, two hour break for lunch. They would never be happy with their technical skills, for the music was so demanding and fearsome.

Nevertheless, as amateur performers had accepted a certain degree of compromise. What it meant to them, especially this year, was more important; the growth of a sacred, divine, and mystical love that had connected them with divine power for a quarter of a century, and made them sisters for life.

Sunday after lunch, the trio split. They would rest for a while, and meet all dressed-up for the performance in Lucia's room, around 2:15 pm. Margo had left her cello in Lucia's room after the rehearsal.

When Barbara and Margo, dressed in formal long black gowns the three had agreed on, entered Lucia's room, were taken aghast and looked at each other in a state of bewilderment!

Lucia was wearing a beautiful long white organza gown and satin white shoes. She looked so serene and beautiful. The color of her green eyes had never been seen as deep and bright.

"Please don't be mad at me. I can tell from your looks in your eyes, you think I'm nuts, and cheated on you. After agonizing for several days, I returned the black gown last week and exchanged it for this one. I had to do it for myself, and for my own peace of mind. I hope, you'd understand.

"That's fine with me," Barbara said. "I am sure Margo feels the same."

"I do; I respect Lucia's choice. She looks so lovely."

Barbara and Margo's suspicions were again confirmed; something was dramatically different with Lucia. She definitely was making a personal statement. Could be something unique, that Lucia was trying to convey to her sisters and assert the state of her own frame of mind? They were sure, eventually, would find out. The trio never kept any secrets from each other.

The performance was splendid.

The cohesiveness and rapport among the three players was unprecedented; and they had never attained before such a degree of depth and connection.

Barbara and Margo never saw or heard Lucia to play like she did this time; they responded and complimented her accordingly.

Her face had an angelic and radiant expression that emanated inner peace, reconciliation, acceptance, and hope. Her violin really sang majestically with perfect intonation, controlled breathing, and redeeming passion.

She wept once, and the moist made her big green eyes sparkle with luster that made the color more luminous. When the unattended tears reached her upper lip, a hint of a smile was noticeable.

The audience, its chamber music understanding and knowledge notwithstanding, roared and applauded, and the trio courteously responded with several bows.

At the reception, the trio mixed with the audience and thanked them for attending. Some were even more surprised when they learned the background of the performers; a university Dean and philosopher; a mathematician and university professor; a physician specialist, and civic volunteer. And to top this all, a nun and two wives/mothers.

That was amazing! Was it? Not at all, if intelligent and gifted minds were guided by discipline, perseverance, patience, pride, confidence, and faith and trust in one anther.

The trio went back to the hotel rooms to change.

Later, after dinner, they took a long walk. They talked about the performance and admitted that the playing this afternoon was the best, ever. It had come together as never before and became a witness and acknowledgement that the three sisters had reached the point of no return. The union was unbreakable, unyielding, unexplainable, and not subjected to any laws governing human relationships.

By the time they returned to the hotel, it was 9:30, and as usual, gathered in Lucia's room. Everyone was quiet and said nothing, but the eyes spoke volumes.

Barbara and Margo constantly thought of Lucia; and Lucia was constantly wondering what Barbara and Margo were thinking of her. The trio's intuitive power ball was relentlessly bouncing back and forth with accelerating energy, ready to burst. The guessing game must end, if dethroned inner peace was to return and reign again, uninterruptedly.

Lucia broke the silence.

"I know well what's bothering you and has been in your mind since Friday. You look at me asking; *what happened to Lucia? She looks so different.* You're right. Please allow me to talk and don't interrupt me. I'm sure you'll have millions of questions. I know and understand what your questions would be, and preemptively, I will try to answer them, as I go along. Whether you believe me or not, would be a different matter, and entirely up to you.

"We know each other so well; we're sisters. You're right; something happened to me, and I look different. I'm pregnant!"

Every joint in Barbara and Margo's body disarticulated. The bodies became limp, heavy, and immobile. The faces turned white. The eyes couldn't see, nor could the ears hear. Lucia, the sister they loved, 42 years old-a celibate nun for twenty years-was pregnant!

Their senses were blunted to oblivion, lest they feel the pain of betrayal of her vows, loss of respect and dignity, but not love. The promise of love was for ever. What about their vows of trust, faith, and truth for each other? Were still relevant and could they survive?

Lucia remained poised.

"I know exactly how you feel. I went through the same thing, when the doctor told me. The pain was excruciating and visceral. Your insides are being eaten up, and you want to lose your existence into nowhere, and disappear from the face of the planet earth; and if you could go to another planet, would be even worse, not better; for the hope of love you needed so badly, was left behind.

"For the past eight months, I noticed my period, once or twice, was a little late. I felt fine; I thought probably menopause was on sight.

"Three weeks ago, after getting up in the morning, three times in a row, I became nauseous and vomited several times. My bra felt a little tight, like when you expect your period; for the first time my period was three weeks late. I went to the doctor to make sure that everything was OK and wouldn't be any problem traveling. He must have suspected I was pregnant.

"When he examined my breasts asked me if I noticed any changes in the color of the skin around the nipples. He ordered lab work, and when I called next day to get the results, I got the news.

"I know what's in your mind; say it; ask me."

Neither Barbara nor Margo responded. Both sat quiet in disbelief.

Lucia continued asking questions, she expected to come from Barbara and Margo.

"Who is the father? Whom did I sleep with? What happened to me and my vows as a nun? In the name of the Lord, we all love and worship, there is no father; I slept with no man, and my vows of chastity weren't violated. God is my witness."

Barbara and Margo looked at each other wondering;

Is Lucia mad? Is she in self denial? Could she be in a state of conversion hysteria, where her mind had blocked events and circumstances too traumatic to enter consciousness, and contradictory to her sense of righteousness, moral fabric, and commitment?

Lucia got up, went to the closet, and took out of her briefcase, what appeared to be a folded document, and gave it to Barbara.

"Please wait; don't open it, yet.

"When my brother John decided to join the US Foreign Service, among other tests, had to undergo an extensive lie detector test. I was impressed and fascinated by it. The Polygraph Laboratories, Inc., in Washington, DC is a private company, well known, that follows the same standards, like the US Government. It's probably the most reputable organization the private sector uses, like lawyers, industry, etc.

"The next day, after I was told I was pregnant flew to Washington, DC, took a lie detector test, and I passed it with flying colors. They asked me if I had a boyfriend, how often I had sex, when was the last time I had sex, and if I was on birth control pill, etc.; of course, my answer to every single question was a categorical, no; which's the absolute truth!

"Barbara, go ahead; read the report, and pass it to Margo."

After Barbara and Margo read the report looked at each other thinking;

That's preposterous! Was Lucia's denial in her mind so overpowering to alter the tracing of the polygraph to record a false negative result? If she were telling the truth, what would be the implications? Don't even think the unthinkable! Another Immaculate Conception? That's blasphemy. Oh God, forgive us for impulsive and impure thoughts.

"I better stop for now; I'd like to know what you think; Barbara, you first."

"I'm shocked and confused. Who wouldn't be; my mental capacity to reason is diminished, if not completely gone. I can't think straight. My heart and mind are split and mock each other.

"I reject the human motion and inclination to make a moral judgment for you, Margo or anybody else. But we're sisters; and every year we meet to renew our vows. We have done this for a quarter of a century. The third and last paragraph of our vows clearly states:

Above and most of all, our communion under any circumstances irrespective how demanding, challenging, and unexplainable might be, shall always be guided by absolute and unconditional faith, truth, and trust in one another, so help us God.

"I'm in a moral dilemma; I don't know about you, Margo. It'd have been much easier for all of us if the natural law was acknowledged. I'm not just only a physician, but an Ob/Gyn specialist! There're only two ways for a woman to become pregnant. Either by sexual contact with a man, or by artificial insemination.

"If physical law wasn't invoked, how did Lucia become pregnant? Was the result of something supernatural that could be connected to metaphysical law? A miracle perhaps? That's crazy? Isn't?

"On the other hand, our vows unquestionably compel us to believe that Lucia is telling the truth. If we don't, our vows are null, void, dead, and buried for good. We're finished, and the last twenty-five years were a big lie. That's all I have to say for starters. Margo is your turn, now. What do you think?"

"Well; let's think rationally, now.

"Lucia ruled out natural law and you, by using common sense I hope we all have, ruled out supernatural intervention and a miracle. Could be another alternative or option? What if probabilities would come with odds that could explain *parthenogenesis?*

"As you know probabilities and biostatics are my life's commitment and expertise. I'll have my graduate students do research, as a matter of intellectual curiosity and mental exercise.

"*Parthenogenesis*, commonly know as virgin birth, is a composite Greek word for parthenos-*virgin*, and *genesis*-birth. If I can find another probable natural law of conception, then we're all home free."

"What if you don't?" Lucia asked. "In the name of God, I don't feel any different or *chosen*. I'm the same old Lucia, the nun, and nothing special. How and why this happened to me? I don't know. My belief in God, and the *Immaculate Conception* as a miracle and unique event in history, never to be repeated, would remain unshaken, I hope. And if I have to go through this ordeal alone, I would it gladly. God will give me strength.

"Maybe my pregnancy was meant to test not only my faith, but also test and challenge the existence of our vows. We have been so smug and proud of our vows for so long. The time to show the true colors has finally come."

Barbara and Margo, in the twenty-five years had known Lucia never saw such a sparkle in her eyes and conviction in her voice.

When the dynamics in one's life are abruptly changed, strength, tenacity, perseverance, resilience and power could surprise not only the individuals involved, but also others surrounding them.

Lucia, as a woman of faith, was convinced that God would be with her all the way, and help her overcome all future eventualities and adversities. God would never have allowed her to carry more burden than she was able to.

"I have an idea," Barbara said. "Both my parents are retired. My mother's expertise and research background were in reproductive embryology and medical genetics. Margo will do research to find out what are the probabilities and odds concerning virgin birth. I'll ask my mother to do the same to find out all embryological and genetic information available up to date, relative to virgin birth.

"And something else; regardless of what my mother or Margo will find our vows stand unshaken.

"I've to admit; I got a little uneasy, if not skeptical. I'm sorry Lucia. I trust and believe in you, no matter what. Our Vows were destined for eternity, during our lifetime, not death. Usually, we renew our vows the day before we leave. If it's OK with you, we should do it right now."

The trio embraced, and with their heads bowed and tears flowing, renewed the *Vows of Three Sisters* for the twenty-fifth consecutive year. They had survived the first crisis and were ready to face all challenges together.

Lucia was moved and happy. Her sisters would be with her every step of the way.

"I'm grateful to you. Your trust would give me strength. Who would believe me?

"I would be a fallen woman; the nun, who betrayed her vows, a demonized hypocrite deserving to burn in hell. Even if there were another physiological explanations for my condition, who would have the patience and the time to listen?

"When I face my confessor, what should I tell him? That I slept with a man, sinned, yielded to evil and ask for forgiveness? That would be a lie, and the easy way out to avoid scandalizing the priest and faithful. It would make a mockery of the sacrament of penance, for God knows that no sin was committed.

"Do I have to follow semantics and meet perceptions to satisfy structure versus substance and truth?"

"Look; you talk like a philosopher," Barbara said. "Your life has been consumed with physical laws and metaphysics. You're a brilliant mind. Let's be more practical. I have an idea.

"Many a woman, later in life, develop a compelling desire to become mothers. The same happened to you. You decided to go ahead with artificial insemination and you finally became pregnant. What's wrong with this? There's no lie, scandal, or deception. As long as you're in peace with yourself and your maker, there's nobody's business."

"You're so clever Barbara," Margo remarked. "You talk like an Ob/Gyn doctor, and you make sense. What do you think Lucia? This would the secret of the three sisters. No one would ever know."

"I don't know; I'll think about it; it's true, maybe could save face, but in the long run wouldn't make any difference. My life as you know it, it's over.

"I have to leave the House of Hope and resign my position from Trinity University. Single motherhood, by any means, wouldn't meet the conduct requirements of the school, let alone The House of Hope.

"I'll ask for leave of absence pretty soon or resign altogether, for personal reasons, as soon as I get back home, and eventually teach in a small college.

"Thanks to my father and the trust fund he has set up for me, I don't have to work.

"The artificial insemination scenario would be good for my parents and brother, and give them some logic that can live with. In actuality, it's still a lie. I'll think about it, or say nothing, and let the chips fall where they may.

"If I'm asked anything about my pregnancy, I'd simply say that it's something personal, and rather not discuss it.

"If intellectual honesty and truth have to be brutalized to protect one's ego, pacify others, and make appearances more palatable, is not worthy. If deep in your heart you know you're are right and your conscious is clear, contempt and wicked judgment by others are irrelevant, for only God is your witness. Peace with Him defies all the outcries and condemnation of humans."

Barbara and Margo were speechless. They had never seen such a dynamism and command in Lucia. Her presence was overpowering projecting leadership, tenacity and fortitude.

Lucia's analytical, critical, and philosophical mind was always expressed in a rather subdued and enigmatic genre provoking more questions than providing answers in searching for the truth. Her motto was that the more you ask, the more you learn; and the more you learn, the wiser you become.

But not any more. Knowing the truth had given her the power to come up in front with passion and valor.

Lucia, all of sudden, had been transformed to a warrior with her shiny panoply on, ready to face her destiny no matter where would take her.

By the time the trio retired was 6 o'clock in the morning. The "Do Not Disturb" sign hung on the three doors.

The events of the last twenty-four hours were extraordinary for the three women. They made music and were tested as never before; renewed their vows with ferocious commitment, and they were determined to fight to the bitter end. Lucia's condition wasn't by choice or free will.

In certain instances, destiny, fate, or even the unknown create unforeseen events and circumstances that were forced upon. Choices and free will would be an option to be exercised afterwards, but not before. What choices did Lucia have? None, but to continue. After all, she was a nun committed to God she trusted, worshiped, and loved!

The formal white gown she wore at the concert reflected her inner world of peace, purity, promise, and commitment.

Barbara and Margo finally understood the symbolism. It meant to be a statement of purity of body, mind, heart, and spirit.

The trio spent the rest of the time at the resort celebrating love, communion, and union that were meant to be for ever, looking forward to next year.

The *Vows of the Three Sisters* were challenged by nature and physical law, but apparently survived unscratched.

As victorious, could the *Vows* become more inspirational and powerful? Where the trust and faith of Barbara and Margo in Lucia will take her?

The saga of the three sisters has reached the point of no return. The tale is fairy no more! Did the *Vows of Three Sisters* make any sense in defying nature and logic?

CHAPTER 10

Confrontation, Courage, and Pride

Flying back to the city, Lucia was thinking of strategies to handle the situation.

Perhaps for some would have been more expedient to beat around the bush to gain time, until physical body changes had become obvious; but not for her. What would be the gain? Nothing; delaying the inevitable wouldn't change its finality. She wanted a clean break on her own terms.

This was the best time, with the school being in summer recess.

She decided to write a simple laconic letter of resignation citing personal reasons and hand-deliver it to the president of Trinity University; she'd elaborate, off the record, more when they'd meet. For her sisters at the House of Hope, she planned to speak and confront them in the Chapel, after the evening prayers.

The plane landed at 2:30 pm. Lucia, after picking up her luggage, took the shuttle bus to the airport garage, where she had parked her car. She loaded the car and drove home. By the time she arrived, was close to 4 o'clock.

Roxanne, her mother, immediately noticed that something was different about Lucia. She looked unusually serious, preoccupied, and rather distant. She was surprised that Lucia came home directly from the airport; this never happened before, when she was out of town, especially Saturdays. She'd go to the House of Hope, and visit the family on Sunday, and stay for dinner.

Lucia went directly upstairs to the chapel. She closed the door, lit a candle, made the sign of the cross, knelt in front of the icon of St. Augustine, and prayed…and prayed.

She hoped her parent would understand and not think less of her. How the unexplainable could be explained and made to be understood? Who would conceivably believe that the process of natural law was circumvented, but the outcome was the same? In other words she didn't have sex, but she was pregnant! Was this insane?

She walked to her bedroom, took off her dress and shoes, and put a robe and sleepers on, washed her face, and brushed her hair. Then, she took the elevator down to the breakfast room where her parents were waiting.

"Would you like something to drink? Can I fix you a little lunch?"

"Thanks Mother; a glass of orange juice would be fine."

"How are the girls? Did you have a good time?"

"Barbara and Margo are fine; and so are their families."

"I'm amazed Margo showed up the last two years, with her son Paul, being a toddler and all."

"Before we met, Margo flew to Washington with Paul; he stayed with his grandparents. Early July, Margo and her husband will be flying back to Washington for a family get together, and bring him back to Pasadena, when they return."

"I can't believe it; you have been meeting every single year for the past twenty-five years; you never missed one. Being sort of your silver jubilee, was anything special this year? Are you planning to continue?" Lucia's father asked.

"Of course we're; as long as we're alive and in good health, nothing could hold us back. Don't ever forget. We found in each other the sisters we never had; and every time we meet our bonding becomes stronger and deeper.

"Dad, you asked me if anything special was this year; it was more than special. It was unusual, to say the least, if not extraordinary. I hope you and Mom would understand.

"I don't know how to tell you this. I have accepted it and has settled in me, but for you maybe difficult to comprehend. Please, don't interrupt me and let me finish. I'm sure, you'll have so many questions; I whished I had all the answers.

"Three weeks before my trip, and three mornings in a row, I became nauseous, felt sick to my stomach, and vomited several times. It felt like the flu, but I wanted to be sure before I left for the mountains. By the way, my period was unusually late this time.

"To make it short, I went to the doctor for a physical examination, and lab work. He found me healthy, and asked me to call him next day to discuss the results of the tests. All tests were negative, except for one. He must have suspected something to order it."

Lucia's parents became concerned and looked at each other, wondering if their daughter was found to have some type of cancer or another serious illness.

Roxanne got up, hug, and kissed Lucia several times. Her father moved his chair closer, and put his arm around her shoulders.

"What is it? What's wrong? Your Dad and I'll be with you every step of the way; we'll fight it together, as a family. How bad is it?"

"Mother, I'm not sick; and I don't have a terminal illness, Thank God."

"So, what is the matter with you?"

"Mom, Dad, hold on, keep your cool, and brace yourselves. I'm forty-two years old, and I'm pregnant!"

Lucia's parents felt as if a tornado had hit them and were sucked into a vacuum, while their daughter's expression remained unexplainably cool, serene, if not defiant.

Was she mad? Was she entirely disconnected from reality? Not at all; for she knew the truth, its complexity, and unreality notwithstanding.

"Are you still with me? Mom, you just said we'd fight it together. Dad, I'm your daughter; remember? I'm the same person you've loved all your life.

"I'm pregnant; but my heart, mind, soul, and spirit are the same, and most of all, God is, and will be with me as never before; for he knows the truth, and my promise to him was kept. It's understandable; you're shocked, and I don't blame you. The whole thing is incomprehensible."

The pressure slowly returned, and the vacuum started filling in. Lucia's parents had to face reality. Lucia needed help; they couldn't abandon her.

Lucia, the brilliant philosopher and nun, consumed with physical laws and metaphysics all her life, had reached an impasse, whose absoluteness would hover over the entire Antonelli family time and time again.

"Look; your mother and I'll love you for ever. You're our daughter; that'll never change."

"Dad, I don't want your love out of pity. I don't want you and Mom to feel sorry for me and the *condition* I'm in. I can do this on my own. I have never felt so strong in my entire life. I want you to love and trust me for what I'm, and not despite of."

Rick and Roxanne had never seen their daughter in such a state of mind. Her assertion, self-confidence, articulation, determination, and aura were declamatory, if not heroic.

Where there should be shame was pride; where there should be defeat was victory; where there should be war was peace; and where there should be condemnation was redemption.

"Of course we love you; and always we will. It was so sudden. Give us a little more time. Your mother and I'll be by your side, and help you as much as we can. How did Barbara and Margo respond to your news? What was their reaction?"

"Thanks Dad; Barbara, Margo, and I spent a great deal of time discussing my pregnancy.

"When we left, we realized that we were as close as ever, if not more. Our love and union hadn't changed, and the trust, respect, and inspiring admiration we feel for each other has matured and become even deeper and stronger, and more committed. We passed our first crisis, trial, and tribulation admirably.

"Let me give you an outline of my immediate plans. I'll drive to the House of Hope tonight. At the evening prayer, I'll confront, and talk to the nuns.

"The first thing Monday morning, I'll meet with Lesley Wilson, the university president, and hand him my resignation for personal reasons, but off the record I'll tell him the truth."

"Before you jump the gun, as your father, I have a question. I'm sure this must be in your mother's mind, too.

"We understand your leaving the House, but not the university. Why don't you marry the gentleman, and go about you business. Nowadays, many brides are pregnant.

"Our society is becoming more and more forgiving and less condemning, which is the right thing to do, and in accordance with the teachings of the Bible."

Lucia started laughing hysterically and uncontrollably!

Her parents looked at each other in dismay; they were confused, if not scarred. Was Lucia losing her mind and going crazy?

"What's wrong with what your father asked you? What's so funny?"

Lucia tried to regain her composure, lest she be perceived disrespectful and insensitive.

"Mother, what Dad asked would be impossible. It would be much easier to change water to gasoline by adding a pill in your gas tank!

"I honestly said everything that could be said; there's nothing left to say now or in the future. We all have to start from here. I'll try to find a small furnished apartment, prepare for motherhood, contemplate my life's commitment to philosophy, pray, and practice my violin. Maybe, you and I can learn and play music for two violins. How about that?"

"Wait a minute; this is your house, too. Why don't move in with us."

"Mother, for the next three-four months, I'd like to be alone. Later in my pregnancy, I'll move in with you. Thanks for your support and understanding."

It wasn't that bad of a confrontation; two more to go. The sisters of the House of Hope this evening, and the university president on Monday.

Lucia arrived at the House of Hope right before 9 o'clock. The evening prayers usually lasted for about fifteen minutes. After the prayers, open time was available, if one of the nuns wished to share her experience of the past week, had something unusual or extraordinary happened.

Lucia was the first to speak.

"My dear Sisters; my life has gone through three phases:

"1. The phase of being taught of the importance of values and spirituality in life; the time I spent with my family from birth until I went to boarding school.

"2. The phase of intellectual curiosity; to ask questions, look for answers, develop my mind, use my mental gifts, and understand the complexity of thoughts and ideas; my last two years of high school at the Marie Curie Academy.

"And 3. The phase of virtue and expansion of spirituality that helped me integrated as a person, empowered my commitment to God, and gave me strength and wisdom to help others in the process; the last twenty years I've spent in this house.

"Phase 1 and 2 directed me to seek and find what I needed to be what I am today; but phase 3 made me what I'm today.

"I joined the House of Hope twenty years ago.

"With your support, I felt strong and never looked back to entertain tempting questions of leisure and abandon, like what could I have become if I weren't here, or how would my life have been any different if I were married?

"I'd like to thank you all, from the bottom of my heart, for giving me the best twenty years of my life; nothing and no one would ever replace or take them. There're inherent to my being, and amalgamated into my heart, mind, soul, and spirit, in designing, hammering, and polishing the most priceless jewel in this life's journey; peace and contentment within one's self."

The nuns, all intelligent and accomplished professionals, looked at each other dumbfounded. They had tasted Lucia's mind before; the mind of a philosopher with critical thinking combined with the burning desire to reach a higher level of creative thought, and challenge logic.

Where was she going with all this? What was she driving at? Was this an exhibitionistic speech and display of self-serving outpouring of mental power? Could be a farewell, an epitaph, or both?

"To expose and confess in public, condemnation, decry, and punishment notwithstanding, the state of one's soul, he or she must have some degree of courage, especially if the revelations would be shocking.

"I could have walked away and let everything go. I couldn't have done that; it would have been intellectually dishonest and out of character.

"What I'm about to tell you, will shock you; I'm sure. You'll make certain assumptions based on physical law and nature, and no one could argue. Let's leave it that way; I won't corroborate any further.

"Effective immediately, I'm resigning from the House of Hope; I'm with child!"

Every nun present in the chapel froze to her seat. Heads became fixed, and so were the eyes that stared at Lucia.

Eve, a bank vice-president, asked,

"Lucia, you're pregnant. Why did you use the expression you're with child?"

"I don't know. That's all I have to say. I love you, and think of me in your prayers; and God bless us all. Goodnight."

Lucia left the chapel immediately.

The rest of the nuns slowly and silently started moving toward the exit, but had the same question in mind. What would make a dedicated and intelligent woman at the age of forty-two, a Dean of a prestigious university and a nun for twenty years, to succumb to temptation? What Lucia, a fallen woman, would have expected from the nuns? Forgiveness? Only God could really forgive.

Wicked human impetuousness would push for condemnation, ostracism, and even burning in hell, for sacred vows and promises made to God were violated.

If God is always ready and willing to forgive, why humans are hesitant or wouldn't? Is it part of human vanity in assessing self-worthiness?

Why God should reward the repentant sinner the same or even more-like the prodigal son-as the one who never violated vows and promises made to Him? The answer is simple: God is devoid of human pettiness.

❧   ❧   ❧

One more meeting to go and Lucia would be free as a bird. She survived the trio, her parents, and the nuns. Only the university president was left; Lesley Wilson, she planned to meet the first thing Monday morning. Lesley was usually in his office no later than 7:15 am.

Lucia arrived five minutes earlier and was waiting outside.

"Good morning Lucia. What are you doing up so early? Don't you know we're on summer recess? How was your trip?"

"Good morning; I wanted to meet with you early, and before you got busy. There's something personal we've to discuss."

Lesley unlocked the private side door of his office, let Lucia in, and closed the door.

"Have a seat; what's on your mind?"

Lucia opened her briefcase, took out her resignation letter and handed it to Lesley.

"Les, I'm resigning as Dean and professor."

Lesley red the letter; it was so unreal. There must be a way out of this, and make Lucia change her mind. What about his proposal to the Board of Trustees?

"You; resigning for personal reasons? You must be kidding! No matter what it is, we can fix it.

"You're aware that this coming fall, the administrative changes the board approved will be fully implemented.

"The search committed has been interviewing candidates to fill the newly created position of executive vice-president/provost.

"Last week, while you were away, I sent a memo to the search committee asking that no more candidates be interviewed. My suggestion was to consider you, although you hadn't applied. The vote was unanimous.

"At the next board meeting, you name will be on the agenda for official approval. Are you willing to pass this opportunity for whatever *personal reasons* you may have? I'm sure, you understand. Your appointment was strictly based on merit, academic excellence, scholarship, contributions, and commitment to the university, and had nothing to do with the financial support the university has been receiving from your family and the Antonelli Foundation over the years."

"Les, I'm flattered; I'd like to thank you and the University for thinking so highly of me, but my decision is irrevocable. In my letter I cite personal reasons, but off the record, I'd like to be more specific.

"I'm aware you're wearing two hats. That of the president of Trinity University, and the collar of an ordained priest. What you're about to hear is not a confession and not protected by sacramental sanctity and secrecy. You're free to use the information as you see it fit.

"I'm pregnant! That's all there's to it. I've nothing else to say or explain.

"You may assume whatever you're comfortable with, and I won't blame you. Perceptions, in such instances, would ran wild, for human thoughts are bound by the inevitability and understanding of natural law. To argue would either insane or blasphemous. I'm not here to rewrite the *Good Book,* if you know what I mean. Goodbye Les and God bless."

How could Lucia make Les or anyone believe she was pregnant and a virgin? What would be the implication? Blasphemy? Self-denial? Lunacy?

She got up and left the office in hurry.

Lesley was completely taken by Lucia's last statement. The surprise and bewilderment concerning her pregnancy and resignation had completely dissipated, and had become completely irrelevant. He was wondering;

What did she mean she wasn't here to rewrite the Good Book? Oh my God; was she thinking what I'm thinking? Is she gone mad? Oh Lord, help us, and don't tempt our faith. On the other hand I know Lucia well. This won't be the end of her. She has guts and may come back to haunt us all in her own way!

CHAPTER 11

Vindication

As soon as Barbara and Margo returned from the trip started their research project; they were obsessed to find out everything the scientific world had done research on, observed, and published concerning *virgin birth.*

To begin with, *virgin birth,* i.e., the development of an egg into an embryo without sperm fertilization, was a well-known biological fact; an aberration perhaps, but still part of natural law. It had been observed in several inferior species, like insects. Eggs of bees and ants could produce female workers, with no father involved.

Virgin birth had been observed in larger animals, like lizards, and was artificially induced in frogs and snakes.

On September 26, 2002, the National Geographic News published on the Web another case of virgin birth, in higher animal species-mammals, documented for the first time.

A female white spotted bamboo shark at the Belle Isle Aquarium in Detroit surprised the zookeepers two months earlier by giving birth to two babies. What was unusual about this birth was that no male shark had been in the tank that housed the female shark for over six years.

In the same venue, a human egg cell could develop into an embryo without genetic input from sperm cells; in such a case, the embryo should always be female, with the identical genetic information of the mother; in reality, a clone of the mother.

In Lucia's case, amniocentesis would confirm the sex of the embryo and the identical genetic structure of embryo and mother. The procedure was also recommended for pregnant women over the age of thirty-five to detect any developmental or genetic abnormalities.

While Barbara was busy gathering genetic and embryological information of virgin birth, Margo was dealing with statistical probabilities and the scientific possibility of virgin birth.

Margo found out that one in five million women carried both X (female) and Y (male) chromosomes. In such a case virgin birth of a male couldn't be ruled out as scientifically impossible.

Barbara and Margo called Lucia and gave her the good news.

Lucia was happy her sisters were convinced she was telling the truth after all. Her pregnancy was a variation of natural law.

She ruled out amniocentesis, for it wouldn't change the course she was committed to, no matter what the finding were. Could she ever be able to convince others? She wouldn't even try; she could be mocked and ridiculed for nothing. It wasn't worth it, as long as God and her sisters new the truth.

Lucia rented a small, one bedroom, furnished apartment, where she planned to stay for a while. She enjoyed doing nothing, and being away from pressure and responsibilities for the first time in her life.

She spent more time practicing the violin and was freer to attend church more often. She loved the vesper services; they were so southing and pacifying to a clean soul, so condemned by others, but loved by God, and her sisters, who knew the truth.

One evening, as Lucia was leaving the church, made the sign of the cross, while looking at Virgin Mary holding in her arms the infant Jesus.

All of a sudden something came over her. Her knees buckled and almost fell.

She recalled what Margo had told her of the probabilities of virgin birth of males. If virgin birth of a male in one out of five million women was scientifically not impossible, could this challenge the church doctrine of *Virgin Birth* of Jesus as a *Miracle?*

As a life long scholar of physical laws and metaphysics, she must also have a clearer view of her believes as a Christian and nun; mentally she was still a nun.

She would call Fred, Margo's husband, and ask his opinion, when she got home. He had a Master's degree in Biblical Studies and Sacred Theology from Harvard Divinity School.

As soon as Lucia got to her apartment called Margo.

"Hi Margo; is Fred home? Can I talk to him?"

"Hi kid; how are you doing? He's; I'll get him."

"Hello, Lucia; how can I help you?"

"I'm sure Margo discussed with you our last trip, and the research she and Barbara did concerning virgin birth. How the doctrine of the church could be challenged by the possibility of the virgin birth of a male? The virgin birth of female wouldn't be any challenge at all."

"Faith is faith, and shouldn't make any difference.

"Theologically and dogmatically, the church, from the beginning had a clear view that hasn't changed.

"There're two historical events and miracles, that if they hadn't occurred there would be neither Christian Faith nor Church, period; *Virgin Birth* and *Resurrection.*

"Virgin birth historically, especially in the Middle East, was viewed as extremely offensive, out of wedlock, and many a time punishable by death known as *honor killing.*

"How anyone, in his or her right mind, would have accepted this concept and preached it in such a hostile environment and make it one of the foundations of the new faith? It must have been an *Inspiring Miracle* to the faithful that gave them the strength, to even defy death. I have read your doctoral thesis. It's brilliant and you got it right; the blurring of physical laws and metaphysics.

"Greeks philosophers were never happy, always searching for answers and the truth. And Metaphysics were something to fall on for comfort when logic became illusive.

"Paul, the Apostle, was smart.

"When he visited Athens, where did he go to preach the Christian faith? He went to the cream of the crop and the elite. He visited the Areopagus, the hill west of the Acropolis, the seat of the City Council members, the Supreme Court justices, and the gathering place of all intellectuals bred, bathed, and inspired by the ideas of Plato, Aristotle, Socrates, Pericles, and all others.

"He didn't mean to ignore the common people, but he wanted to challenge the intellectuals and wise. They would understand more the perfunctory limitations of physical laws in the vastness of the universe.

"When Paul saw the altar to *The Unknown God*, read the Greek mind well. Their gods had, to a certain degree, all human virtues and vices; the difference was only in power. The Athenians believed in, worshiped, and envisioned a deity that existed beyond of what was known. The Greek mind, through generations of great thinkers, was always open, searched for the metaphysical, and went beyond physical law to find the truth; and Paul challenged them real well, and to the limit. Imagine; he spoke to them of *Resurrection*. Why? Intelligent minds love to be challenged! There would be no more intelligent if shut out ideas and concepts that challenged them and were difficult to comprehend.

"That was the fundamental principle of *inquiry* introduced and championed by Aristotle. Challenge your mind and search!

"Paul succeeded and was convincing.

"Dionysius, a Supreme Court Justice became a Christian, and so did Damaris, a woman in the audience.

"It's was interesting to witness the presence of these events, which are chronicled in the Acts of the New Testament, in real time twenty centuries later.

"When I was a senior in the Gymnasium, back in Munich, we traveled to Athens, Greece, and visited museums of renown, and other historical sites.

"In one of the most affluent and older neighborhoods, in the center of the modern city, we found a church dedicated to, and named after the patron of city of Athens; the Church of Saint Dionysius of Areopagus, commemorating the Supreme Court Justice and the first Athenian to become a Christian.

"The Columns of he Temple of Olympian Zeus, a twenty minute walk from the foothills of the Acropolis and the Parthenon, were archeological landmarks of the ancient city, and a point of topographic reference of the modern one. Two miles north of the temple, and by an old cemetery, there was a narrow street running through a residential area.

"Can you guess, whom the street was name after? Would you believe it? Damaris! The first Athenian woman to espouse Christianity.

"I've discussed this with your sister Margo, *Dr. Probabilities*, several times.

"Metaphysics in any size, shape, and form shouldn't be expected to complement physical law, but go beyond; if they did, there should neither mystery nor miracle any more and faith would become a mathematical equation and formula, devoid of mysticism and spirituality.

"The miracle of *Virgin Birth* will be challenged by physical law in perpetuity to no avail, until the end of time, but the faithful will keep it alive until the end of time. If they don't, their lives will be lived wasted; and there would be neither hope nor redemption."

Lucia wrote a long letter to her brother John concerning her pregnancy. In the letter the same vague language was used, like when she revealed her pregnancy to others. There was only one undisputable fact; she was pregnant, and there was nothing else to say or explain.

For some reason, John was the only person Lucia informed of her pregnancy by correspondence. If he were living in U.S., she would have talked with him directly, like she did with her parents. She could have called, but she felt more comfortable, writing about.

John, in his response, was understanding and never pressed for any details; he respected her privacy. He reassured her that his love for her hadn't changed and trusted her judgment. He, being a trained diplomat, understood crises, of all kinds, well. You gain more by listening than arguing.

Lucia was in her third month of pregnancy. The morning sickness was all but gone, and her clothes started feeling tighter. Today, she unexpectedly received a letter from John. It was amazing! She had the same thing in mind. Was ESP, or a coincidence?

She was looking for an Ob/Gyn specialist for prenatal care and delivery. She wasn't adamant about it, but her first choice would be a female physician.

John, in his letter, mentioned Dr. Emily Rugger, the fraternal twin sister of his friend Eric. They all met in college, at Georgetown. Eric went to law school and Emily to medical school, both at Georgetown.

They caught up with each other at their tenth reunion, where John found out that Emily's office was only seven miles away from the house the Antonelli kids grew up. Emily was married, and the mother of two children.

Once more, Lucia realized how much her brother loved her.

In Japan, and thousands of miles away from home, married and with kids, he was still concerned for his forty-two year old baby sister. These were trying times; they needed each other more than ever.

Next day at 9:00 am, Lucia called the doctor's office to make an appointment; an office visit was scheduled fifteen days hence.

Later in the afternoon, Lucia's phone rung.

"Hello; who is calling?"

"Ms. Antonelli, this is Dr. Rugger's office. Would you like to come to the office tomorrow at 4 o'clock for your visit?"

"Tomorrow is Wednesday. I thought the doctor was off."

"That's fine. We'll see you at four."

"Thanks; I'll be there. Goodbye."

Lucia was on time. She was the only patient in the waiting room.

The nurse took her to the examining rooms, helped her undress, and put an examining gown on. Then, she took her H&P (History and Physical), vital signs, wrote everything down on the chart, including demographics. She put Lucia on the examining table, with her legs on stirrups, and called the doctor.

"Ms. Antonelli, I'm Doctor Rugger. How're you?"

"I'm fine; thank you. You didn't have to come for me, your day off. I could have waited. I'm pregnant, not sick."

"That's fine; don't worry. I drop in the office on Wednesdays, to check my mail, unless I'm out of town. Before I leave the office, I always check the list of new patients. When I saw the name Antonelli, I though you must be John's sister. Where is John now?"

"Tokyo; he loves it."

Emily first examined Lucia's abdomen. Then she put a pair of gloves on and proceeded to do a vaginal examination. Lucia grimaced and slightly moved.

"I'm sorry; we're all done. I hope didn't hurt you much. Please get dressed and come to my office."

The nurse untied the gown, helped Lucia put her clothes back on, and took her to Dr. Rugger's consultation room.

"Lucia, have a seat; you don't mind if I call you by your first name. You can call me Emily."

"That's fine with me…Emily!"

The nurse came in and handed the doctor the folder with Lucia's medical record.

"Lucia; you're forty-two years old, single, and this is your first pregnancy.

"I've seen in my practice many single professional women who decided to become pregnant in their late thirties but not forties, opting for motherhood primarily through adoption.

"When I examined you, I found you're still a virgin. There're two possibilities: Either you were artificially inseminated or was an accident; penetration isn't always necessary. Ejaculation outside the vagina could result in pregnancy. I've seen it several times."

"It wasn't planned for sure; you can call it an accident. It was the biggest surprise in my life, but I'm getting used to."

"Is the father aware you're pregnant? Will he be involved in the delivery? Is he going to be present in the delivery room? In my fourteen years of obstetrics I've seen everything."

Lucia smiled with confidence and pride.

"The Father knows I'm pregnant! You won't see Him here or in the delivery room, but in spirit we're always together. The strength I get from Him keeps me going.

"One of my closest friends, Barbara, is an obstetrician; we're like sisters and see each other every summer."

Emily couldn't tell whether she was confused or Lucia. Her reference to Barbara was a hint that she wanted to change the subject. Emily, out of respect for Lucia's privacy, obliged.

"As your physician, I'd like to discuss a few things with you. You don't have to decide now. You can tell me when you come back for your next visit, which will be in about six weeks.

"For women thirty-five or older amniocentesis is recommended, in order to detect fetal defects or any other abnormalities. The incidence increases with the mother's age."

"I've already decided against it. Barbara and I talked about it; would be of no value to me. I'll continue with my pregnancy, regardless."

"There's a good chance, you'll have a C-section delivery; the incidence is higher in older women, especially with the first pregnancy. An advantage is that the delivery can be scheduled electively."

"That I like. It would be convenient not only for the expectant, but also for the doctor. I have a request. After the baby is born, I'd like for both of us to have a DNA test done."

"Any particular reason?"

"No; I'm just curious."

"I'll take care of it; I'll make a note on your chart."

"Thanks Doctor; and thank you for seeing me so quickly. Goodbye."

Lucia left the office and on the way out, the secretary handed her the doctor's business card, with the date and the time of the next appointment written on. Driving back to the apartment, she felt more serene and happy.

The visit and examination by the doctor had settled in Lucia's mind the undisputed reality of her pregnancy. At times, it was so unreal, but not any longer.

For the first time in her life, she heard words like *older women* and *mother* directed to, and intended for her. The sound was so unfamiliar, if not strange; but the tightness around the abdomen had become a resounding reality she had to live with from now on.

Reconciliation had finally had set in.

She wasn't a *chosen* woman for a miracle birth. That happened only once, never to be repeated; her weakened faith, after all she was only human, had returned with more strength, resolve, and commitment. Her analytical, critical, and philosophical mind, confused and bewildered at the beginning, had reached the point of reason.

Lucia accepted her pregnancy as part of physical law and nature, maybe an aberration, and nothing miraculous; otherwise she could have handicapped, risked, and even lost her faith in God, her life long commitment.

❦   ❦   ❦

Lucia reached the seventh month of pregnancy, uneventfully.

Her slime figure, little weight gain, radiant face, and smile made her more attractive and looking younger than forty-two.

The lack of a wedding ring was noticeable, but explainable to the casual busybody; it was too tight to wear! Last month, she moved in to leave with her parents.

The anxiety, shame, and embarrassment were all gone. The anticipation of the arrival of a new child made Lucia's parents happy. Both, in their early seventies, enjoyed good health and remained active.

The Antonelli Foundation to the surprise of both-Trinity University and the House of Hope-continued to provide financial support to both institutions, following Lucia's resignation.

After Lucia moved in with her parents, her father changed his will.

Following the death of both parents, she was to inherit the house. It was big enough to be used for any worthwhile causes; like retreats.

Lucia's interest in counseling and mentoring young women hadn't changed.

Her status, as a single never married mother, could be perceived as hypocritical and question her credibility. She thought of this, but she didn't care.

There was something positive, that she would use, silently and unobtrusively, as an example what to avoid in life; out of wedlock pregnancy and single motherhood.

There would never be a greater sacrifice ever, than the humiliation and worthlessness one bestowed upon oneself, in order to benefit others and the common good.

The unheralded heroism of self-deprecation to enlighten others denotes a person acting not because, but despite of human nature.

If all brave wars fought internally in the mind, heart, spirit, and soul to free others were chronicled, there would be no paper left to write, print, or wrap.

Barbara and Margo admired Lucia's forthrightness and her decision not to use artificial insemination as a cover-up for her pregnancy.

She remained unflappable, indifferent, and let the imagination of others conclude whatever were comfortable with. The trio was on the phone on daily basis, even for a few minutes.

Suddenly, they had discovered another commonality that gave more depth to their union; motherhood.

For the past twenty years, since Lucia entered the House of Hope, Barbara and Margo-eventually both got married and became mothers-had seen her as a virgin nun. Now in the trio's mind, she was a virgin expectant mother.

The change would be descriptive of an anatomical reality. That had settled Lucia's pregnancy for good, and the three sisters were happy with this concept.

Several times, while on the phone, Barbara and Margo asked Lucia if she, under the most favorable circumstances, would reconsider and get married; the answer was a categorical and resounding, no.

Mentally and spiritually, and before God, she was still a nun.

The vows of chastity and her commitment as a nun were still in full affect, as far as she was concerned. She felt more comfortable than ever with the decision she made twenty years ago, and there was reason to change.

She would be responsible for another human being now, but that shouldn't impede her spiritual growth, along her chosen path. God allowed the physical law to work in a mysterious way for some reason. Her faith and hope were strong enough to envision a future full happiness and blessings.

Lucia entered her ninth month of pregnancy uneventfully.

The sonogram and all lab work were normal, and she had gained only twelve pounds. She and Emily, her doctor, became good friends, and comfortable with each other. Barbara and Margo insisted on flying in for the delivery, no matter what.

Lucia would be closer to her fortieth week of gestation the first week of April, the time Emily had planned for C-section.

Everything went according to schedule.

Barbara and Margo flew in two days before the delivery, and stayed at the Antonelli house. The trio relived and reminisced the first Thanksgiving they had spent together with their families, after taking the *Vows of Three Sisters*, when first met as juniors at the Academy.

Twenty-five years had passed.

There were so many changes; personal and professional growth, marriages, children. At this moment, everything seemed to be so distant.

Lucia had become the epicenter of Barbara and Margo's attention. They loved her so much; she had been an inspiration for life. Her spirituality, faith in

God, devotion, and sacrifice to help others, without being judgmental or critical, humbled them, and made them feel inadequate. She was so unaffected, pure, and gentle; a real angel of a woman.

Lucia's surgery was scheduled for 7:30 am. She was to check in at 5:30 am.

Barbara and Margo drove her to the hospital. The parents would come later and wait in the maternity surgery lounge.

After checking in at the admitting office, a volunteer put Lucia on a wheelchair and took her to maternity surgery, which was on the third floor. Barbara and Margo followed her. The volunteer pressed the door switch and automatically the double door opened.

A nurse, in a scrub suit came out, took over, and wheeled Lucia into the holding area. Barbara stayed with Lucia, and Margo went to the maternity lobby to wait for Lucia's parents.

The nurse helped Lucia get undressed, put a hospital gown on her, laid her on a cart, and started an IV. Later, the anesthesiologist came in and asked her certain questions concerning allergies, medications, previous surgeries, etc. At 7:o'clock, Emily, Lucia's doctor walked in.

"Good morning Lucia; how are you?'

"I'm fine; thank you."

Emily extended her arm and shook hands with Barbara.

"You must be Barbara, the doctor friend; nice meeting you. Lucia has spoken so highly of you. I think I know you well by now."

"Nice meeting you, too, Emily. I hope you don't mind; I'd like to be in the OR (Operating Room) with you."

"Not at all; let's go to the doctor's dressing room to change, and put scrub suits on."

Barbara, hugged and kissed Lucia, and quickly followed Emily to the dressing room.

Shortly, Lucia was premedicated, transported to the OR, and moved from the cart to the OR table. The anesthesiologist checked the IV to make sure was open and running.

He helped her sit on the table, inserted a needle in her lower back, passed through a small catheter, and injected an anesthetic solution to numb her abdomen and pelvis.

After the injection, Lucia was helped lie down again. The abdomen was prepped with an antiseptic solution and draped appropriately, exposing only the site of the incision, in the lower abdomen.

The C-section was performed quickly, and within minutes the baby's crying was heard.

"What a beautiful girl," the doctor said.

Lucia, still sedated, could hear Barbara's voice.

"Can you hear me? Can you hear me Lucia? It's a beautiful health little girl."

"I can hear you; and my baby well," Lucia answered, sleepily, as tears started flowing from her eyes.

Barbara left in a hurry and went to the maternity lounge, where Lucia's parents and Margo were waiting, and gave them the good news. Lucia had a baby girl, and both were doing fine.

All were ecstatic, crying and laughing at the same time.

One would wonder; why people cry when happy? When unhappy is understandable, for tears were meant to cleanse sadness. But why mixing laughter with tears when happy? Would this suggest a damaged emotional grid by overloading?

Nobody knows. Coexistence of contradicting sentiments is a fact of human nature and experience, like drinking wine; a glass to celebrate happiness or a glass to drown sorrow!

Following the procedure, Lucia was taken to the recovery room and after the anesthetic wore off, she was brought to the maternity suite, where her parents, Barbara and Margo were waiting.

Later on, a nurse from the nursery brought the baby girl in the room all dressed and wrapped in a pink blanket, and put her in Lucia's arms.

Everyone was moved and happy.

It wasn't the arrival of a new life per se, but the improbability that Lucia was connected with. Who could have ever imagined, being in sound and rational mind that Lucia, a dedicated nun for twenty years, would be a mother out of nowhere in the future, holding her new born baby girl?

If one believed that you should never say never, that would be it!

Lucia's mother stared at the baby, shook her head, and smiled.

"I can't believe it. As soon as I get home I'll look for your baby pictures. It has been forty-two years since you were born. A mother never forgets the face of her newborn child. Your daughter looks exactly like you did, when you were born. That's uncanny!"

The unit secretary came to the room and asked,

"Have you decided yet? The birth certificate is complete except for the first and middle name. Your doctor told me you wanted the father to remain anonymous; the last name will be the same as yours. What about first name?"

"Damaris; the baby's full name will be Damaris Roxanne Antonelli."

"Damaris…Damaris…that's an unusual name. I've been a secretary for maternity for over twenty-one years and have written on thousands upon thousands birth certificates, but I have never come across the name Damaris; thanks. I'll take care of it," the secretary said, and left the room.

"I have," Margo said enthusiastically, "When an astrophysicist, Dean of Physics at Caltech and theologian-my husband Fred, and a philosopher and nun-my sister Lucia, talked over the phone about the dynamics between physical law and metaphysics.

"I wasn't ear dropping. I picked up the phone, and I was asked to listen. That was the most uplifting, analytical, philosophical, and spiritual conversation that anyone would have ever heard on the phone.

"If talking dirty on the phone, to titillate senses cost several dollars a minute, that call by comparison, to titillate the mind and spirit should have cost thousands. Of course you can't be impartial when you talk about your husband and sister, but honestly that's the truth.

"Damaris was the first Athenian woman to become Christian. She probably was a smart, intelligent, and intellectually curious woman to be found where the action was; in the center of the government, law, politics, and debate; and I'm sure she could bake cookies, too!"

Barbara and Margo had planned to be with Lucia around the clock.

They had reserved a room in a motel near by and would be alternating the night shift. Lucia was upset with the arrangement, but she had no choice; her sisters wanted to be with her and the new member of the family.

Lucia and the baby were discharged from the hospital the forth post-operative day. Barbara and Margo stayed with Lucia, in her house, for two more days before flying back home. They would return for Damaris' baptism, after the 4th of July.

The big mansion on the hill, the Antonelli house, was slowly being transformed, and going through a period of unexpected and unfamiliar changes to become home of a beautiful newborn girl!

When the Antonelli family moved in, right after the house was built, Lucia was nine years old, and her bother John eleven. Computers, bicycles, games, erectors, waterslides, dollhouses, and happy, bubbly, shrieking kids, and loud music were all over the place.

What a difference! None of that any more; for lullabies, chimes, diapers, formulas, bassinets, infant car seats, perambulators had invaded by storm and taken over.

But something was strange.

The owners, instead of being upset, were elated. The rush, competing with each other, which one of the grandparents would get to the baby girl first and hold her longer, made them look younger, more energetic and vibrant.

Lucia had the time of her life.

The circumstances were unusual for sure, but she never felt as happy and accomplished. By her own volition and design not to become a mother, could she have missed something that would have ended up in a vacuum later in life?

As a woman of faith, and trusting Divine Providence, Lucia had accepted everything as a gift from God, whether was dedication and surrender to him or motherhood. It wouldn't have been within her domain to assign degree of value and find which one was more virtuous.

In Lucia's mind, *Axiology,* the philosophy of weighting values and virtue, for the faithful was the prerogative of God, not humans.

A month had gone by and Lucia and the baby were doing well.

Two days ago, Damaris saw the pediatrician for the first time, since she was discharged from the hospital. Growth and weight gain were normal; she didn't have to go back for three months. Lucia was due for her first postop/postpartum visit this afternoon at 4:00 pm.

Emily examined Lucia and was happy with her progress. The incision was healing well. She could resume all her daily activities, and with some caution and moderation, could start certain exercises, like swimming.

After the examination, Emily asked Lucia to wait in her office; she wanted to talk to her. It wouldn't take long. She had only one telephone call to make.

Emily returned to her office, shortly, and sat on the desk chair right across from Lucia.

"Everything looks great, considering you age, and the fact that this was your first pregnancy; we were both lucky. All went as planned without a hitch. I don't like to bring the age issue again, but it's a reality we cannot ignore it. I'd recommend that you be careful from now on.

"If you become pregnant again, couldn't be as easy. Unfortunately, you didn't follow my advice to have your tubes tied, just to make sure, and be on the safe side."

Lucia tried to control herself, lest she burst into a hysterical laughter.

"Emily, I promise; I'll be a good girl and take all precautions!"

Emily detected some inflexion of sarcasm in Lucia's voice, but tried to ignore it; maybe her reaction was from bitterness and unhappiness that the unexpected pregnancy had caused her.

Suddenly, there was a knock at the door. The door opened, and Emily's secretary walked in.

"Doctor, sorry for interrupting; the courier from Biological Lab just delivered a lab report for Ms. Antonelli. You may want to discuss the results."

The secretary handed the opened envelope to Emily, left the consultation room, and closed the door.

Emily took out of the envelope the report and red it several times.

She looked Lucia directly in the eyes for a few seconds, and read the report again, and again.

"Is it anything serious? Please, tell me; I'm ready, no matter what."

"Lucia, remember? The first time you came to the office you asked me, after the delivery, to order a DNA test for you and the baby. No patient of mine, so far, has ever asked for this kind of testing. When I asked you why, you said you were just curious.

"There is nothing wrong, either with you or your daughter.

"If you were curious before, now I'm baffled and confused. The more I read the results, the more confused I become.

"My first reaction would be that there was some kind of a mix-up and repeat the test again. The lab was surprised, too, and repeated the test once; the result was the same. Samples were sent to two independent laboratories, and all came up with the same conclusion."

"What is it? I've to know; forget about me. I've an infant, I'm responsible for."

"Well; *genome* is the full set of chromosomes that contain the DNA macromolecules responsible for all inheritable traits. You and your daughter have identical genomes; your daughter's DNA mirrors your DNA; they're exactly the same. What does this means? Your daughter is a *clone* of you! I don't believe it; there is no male genetic trait in your daughter's DNA structure.

"You must have had a hunch. Since I first met you, the response concerning your pregnancy was queer. Now, going back, everything you said, it's coming into focus and makes sense."

"Can you explain this to me, Doctor? What do you think happened?"

"Female eggs can be tricked or duped to multiply, and become embryos without male genetic input. That's virgin birth.

"On 5/5/03, CBS News reported on the Web, that Advanced Cell Technology, Inc., a biotechnology company based in Worcester, Mass, through various techniques, used virgin birth to produce human embryos and stem cells that were identical to the donor's cells.

"Of course, this creates a plethora of ethical, legal, philosophical, and social issues, but this is not the place and the time to discuss them. Besides, these issues fall within your expertise, as far as I know. The question is; what happened to you? Can this be explained as something natural? I think so.

"Your egg, fresh out of the ovary, and through one the tubes, traveled to the uterus waiting for male genetic input; sperm. Your daughter's DNA ruled out one hundred percent *male* input. Your egg spontaneously started multiplying for some strange reason, without stimulation that is used in the laboratory, and changed into an embryo that fully developed!

"Your innuendos you made concerning your pregnancy, I can understand now. You wouldn't blame me for being skeptical. Would you? I thought something was mentally wrong with you."

"Not at all; nobody would have or ever will."

"Even now, with a reasonable explanation possible, would be futile and mentally fatiguing, if not exhausting, to go through all these facts to convince others. Personally, I'm vindicated! My sisters, who loved and trusted me, believed in me. That's all that counts."

"As a physician, I wonder, how often could something like this happen? We'd never know, unless we conduct routine post-partum DNA testing on all, which would be unpractical and expensive."

"I agree with you; and thanks for understanding."

The baptism of Damaris would bring the trio back together, this summer; it would be a double feast. The baptism of Lucia's daughter, and the renewal of the *Vows of Three Sisters*. And something else that never happened before. The kids of the trio would meet each other.

Janice, Barbara's daughter, two month's ago celebrated her ninth birthday.

Paul, Margo's son would be four in two months. Lucia had planned a party for *after* and *before* birthdays, after the baptism, to welcome the two kids, who came from the south and west to meet the new cousin.

Paul was fascinated with the new baby; and being an only child, wanted to be with her all the time; and under strict supervision, he was allowed to take her strolling.

The baptism took place at Holy Trinity Church.

A retired bishop, close friend of Lucia's father officiated, with the two parish priests assisting. Godparents were Barbara and Margo, with their kids holding nicely decorated white candles during the service.

Before leaving the church, the trio sneaked quickly to a corner towards the exit and renewed their vows silently.

Rick and Roxanne, after the baptism, gave an elaborate catered dinner party, held in the gardens of their large home, for over one hundred guests.

A string quartet and a trumpet player, old friends and colleagues of Roxanne's from the Institute of Music, played baroque and other celebratory tunes appropriate for the occasion; it was a smash!

Lucia was surprised with her parents, and especially with her father's enthusiasm.

He wanted everything to be perfect; the day before, he was on the phone constantly to make sure all his orders had gone through.

"Dad; don't you think, you're overdoing it? This is a baptism, not a wedding!"

"Lucia, my dear; I love you for what you're and have become. On the other hand, all fathers dream of their daughter's wedding. You brought that up and not me; let me do my thing."

Lucia could hardly hold her tears.

She hugged and kissed her father with the abandon and impetuousness of a little girl. What a great man he was; and what a great father he had been; full of love, understanding, and foresight. The tenderness, comfort, and warmth of his touch were left unchanged by the passage of time.

Rick, after Lucia became pregnant, saw qualities in her that he might have let go by unnoticeable, under more acceptable circumstances.

Lucia was in total control, with her convictions and leadership left intact.

There was something heroic about her, especially after Damaris was born. Where would she go from here? Would she be happy to be a mother only? She was endowed to excel to whatever she would choose, and at the same time be the best mother possible.

What would the future hold for her? What was her destiny? Only God, she unconditionally believed in, knew and time would tell.

Lucia's idea to teach in a small college faded away pretty fast.

For the next five years, she planned to stay home, take care of her daughter, practice the violin, read, and who knows? She might write a book.

She had become a mother, but deep in her heart, had also remained the nun she was before.

Lucia had heard of mothers of grown children who chose celibacy and monasticism, later in life, after the death of their husbands. Her reversal of fortune made her no lesser of a nun.

She was fortunate, and thanked her father everyday for his foresight.

The chapel he built in the house had become her sanctuary for prayer, concentration, thanksgiving, and dreaming; not the afterlife, but the present life she was part of and committed to.

One day, she should be accountable for her gifts; motherhood shouldn't be used as an alibi and excuse to abrogate tasks, vision, and dreams that she knew she had the power to fulfill.

CHAPTER 12

Triumph and Victory

The trio continued to meet every summer to renew the *Vows of Three Sisters*, and to experience closeness, warmth, and love for one another.

For the past four years the trio met at Lucia's house. She had the youngest child-Barbara and Margo's were older-and she didn't want to be away from Damaris. This was also a good opportunity for the godmothers to see their goddaughter growing up.

This time would be different.

Damaris was five years old, independent, mature, lovable; she liked to be with her grandparents, who spoiled her to death. Ten days apart wouldn't be that hard for either Lucia or her daughter.

This year, for the thirtieth anniversary of the *Vows of the Three Sisters*, the trio forty-seven years old by now, decided to visit the mountains again, and stay at the same resort; it would be the third time. The last two were carved in their memories profoundly.

The first one was the summer after graduating from college, at the age of twenty-two. Choices had already been made that would determine the intellectual development, professional directions, personal commitments, and the over all quality of life for each of the three sisters.

Dramatic deviation from the expected norms challenged the trio's survival, and the ability and power of the vows of the three sisters to keep them together.

The announcement of Lucia to become a nun still generated memories of separation anxiety that eventually proved to be as steady as bubble that unceremoniously burst into nothing. They survived; and the decision of one enriched the lives of the other two.

The second time was to celebrate the twenty-fifth anniversary of the vows, when they were forty-two years old.

Maturity, spirituality, faith, accomplishments, and love shared by all, had made the trio secure and happy.

The time of trial and challenge of the vows, for validity, power, spiritually, truthfulness, trust, and relevancy had finally arrived.

It was like the thunder and blast of a comet possessing meteoric power: Lucia's pregnancy; the pregnancy of the celibate nun!

Would the *Vows of Three Sisters* survive?

Everything that had inspired the vows and stood for would be on the line, and the values of the trio would come under scrutiny; morality, ethics, promises, faith, church doctrine, trust, truth, natural law, metaphysics.

The vows were shaken to the ground, bent to the winds, drenched by hurricanes, hit by tornados, but never were uprooted. Why? For the trio's faith and trust for one another were deeply rooted. Twenty-five years of greatness couldn't have been sustained by lies and deception.

Eventually reason and natural law gave the answers. The vows survived though, because faith, truth, and trust had remained unshaken and strong irrespective of reason, and not waiting for the logic of proof.

Faith of any kind, to loving humans or a loving God, wouldn't be faith at all, if verification, tactile evidence, and reasoning were prerequisites.

Faith devoid of wonder and mystery would be a fake faith devoid of redeeming power. Real faith has no face value, for its value is undeterminable and unknown.

The third meeting on the mountains, for the thirtieth anniversary to renew the *Vow of Three Sisters*, was several months away.

The trio was excited and looking forward to see each other again, be together, and most impotently renew their vows.

Was anything unusual in the works? Who could guess? Only time would tell. One thing was for sure; the celebrity Lucia had become after her book titled *Persona, Person and Personality: Perception and Reality* was published two years ago.

The premise of the book was that *Persona* was only defined by looks and appearances that were subjects to individual perceptions.

It was a philosophical, psychological, and sociological study of how behavioral, societal, and circumstantial changes in people's lives altered the reactions of others surrounding them strictly based on perceptions.

If one would be judged on *perceptions* only, the search would never go beyond the *persona* of an individual, leaving the wealth of a person's character and its *personality* untouched and unknown.

Lucia had lived the paradigm and was judged by what showed, and not by what actually was. Her study was objective and impersonal and no one would have ever guessed her personal experience, except for her sisters.

Barbara and Margo were so proud of Lucia.

She had become an excellent mother and her commanding presence and leadership shined as never before.

Last summer when they met, Lucia's future came up. She would never go back to teaching, but she was so talented; she could still affect people and her communication skills, especially with young people, had been so effective in the past.

Lucia was aware, that in the long run, would be accountable for her gifts. She would think of something; her *calling* to serve hadn't changed; maybe needed redirection and change of venue.

The trio arrived at the resort late Friday evening.

They were exhausted, and quickly went to bed. The arrangements were the same as the last two times. Lucia's room was in the middle, with Barbara on one side and Margo's on the other. They were to meet around 9 o'clock in Lucia's room for breakfast.

Lucia was up at 7:30.

Motherhood and domesticity, she never thought would be part of her life, had upped her energy level.

After showering and getting dressed, she called room service and ordered an elaborate brunch for three to be delivered to her room, ten minutes to nine. They skipped dinner last night and would be hungry.

The centerpiece of various colors carnations and gladiolas complemented the white tablecloth, napkins, silverware, and china to perfection, and made the occasion not only formal, but also festive and cheerful.

A large silver bucket prominently displayed the neck of an uncorked champagne bottle buried in crushed ice.

Lucia took out of her suitcase a rectangular, two feet long by ten inches high sign, and taped on the wall: *Brunch for the Hungry Bunch*, was written on.

When Barbara and Margo walked in, the screaming and yelling was phenomenal; they were really surprised. It was unreal.

The trio met thirty years ago and a few months apart had celebrated their forty-seventh birthday, this year. Time had taken its toll; its futility and fleeting nature were visible. A few wrinkles here and there, a few pounds here and there, but something hadn't changed though, and was as youthful as ever; the sparkles in the eyes, and the exuberance and enthusiasm of youth.

The trio kissed, hugged, sung, and danced.

"What's going on? Everything looks so nice and elegant. What's all for? What're we celebrating?" Barbara asked.

"Lucia, I can tell; There's something on your mind," Margo said. "Why are you doing all this?"

"Because I love you, and you're my sisters; I wanted to surprise you. Besides, we're all hungry. We didn't have any supper last night; remember?"

"Oh my gush; with an empty stomach we'll all get drunk in no time!"

"Don't worry, Barbara; we're going to sleep in Lucia's bed, if too drunk and unsteady to walk," Margo said laughing.

Lucia poured champagne in the three long stemmed glasses. She gave one to Barbara, the other to Margo, and raised hers to a toast:

"To my faithful sisters; the sisters I have loved for so long; the sisters that never lost trust and faith in me; the sisters that never abandoned me."

The trio brought the glasses to their lips and sipped. Champagne wetted the lips, but tears wetted the eyes.

Lucia tried to regain her composure first.

"Wait a minute; this is supposed to be a happy occasion. Let's stop. You're my guests. We all became emotional for a moment; that's enough."

They started eating like hungry lumberjacks; they hadn't put anything but liquids in their mouths, since yesterday afternoon. Halfway through the meal, and with the champagne almost gone, Lucia served coffee.

"Lucia, the brunch was an excellent idea; Barbara and I'd like to thank you. I don't know about you, but we were hungry. We're all set until suppertime. For a nun, I think you have become a hostess with *pizzazz!*"

"Thanks; it was my pleasure. Who knows? Maybe, I have to sharpen my social skills and be out with people more often. There should some dramatic changes in my life pretty soon."

"I knew it! I knew it! As soon as we walked in, I could sense there was something special on Lucia's mind; we can read each other's so well by now. We've been sisters for thirty years; and the champagne? Must be something special. Barbara, are you thinking what I'm thinking? If you know what I mean!" Margo asked.

"Oh; no, no! How Lucia could have kept something like this from us, unless just happened. If she did, she must be a stinker of a sister!"

"What in the whole world are you talking about? Are you out of your minds?" Lucia asked.

"You said there should be some dramatic changes in your life. What else can it be so dramatic, with champagne and all? Barbara, go ahead; tell her."

"Lucia dear; somebody must have proposed! We're celebrating your up-coming engagement! You're a sneaky *ex-nun*! Congratulations! We still love you."

Lucia covered her face, bursting into a hysterical and loud laughter, and almost chocked.

"You're crazy; and you're nuts! The champagne must have banged, knocked, and shaken your noodle! I don't think you're in the mood for any serious conversation. Have more coffee; there's plenty left."

"C'mon sis; don't be so serious! Where's your sense of humor? What's the celebration all about, if not for your up-coming engagement? Barbara and I are all ears. We're not drunk! Just happy-go-lucky. Spill the beans. No matter what it is, we can take it; we're sure, must be something important to celebrate it with bubbly and all. A new beginning, perhaps?

Lucia took a deep breath and smiled.

She clasped and interlocked her hands, bent the head, and rested the chin on her knuckles. She remained silent and contemplative for a few seconds. She was thinking; could she be praying?

Barbara and Margo, for the first time, realized that something important and extremely serious was on Lucia's mind, kept their silence, and impatiently waited for her to make the first move.

Lucia raised her head, took her glass, and drunk the rest of the champagne.

"Well; the time has come.

"In the past, you were always the first ones to know of my decisions, or events that had happened to me. You were informed, ahead of anybody else including my parents, of my decision to become a nun. You were the first ones I told that I was pregnant.

"You stood by, understood, and supported me all the way. Our vows survived and we're closer than ever. Our vows of trust, faith, and truth, miraculously, have been the guiding force in our lives. Today is another *first*."

Barbara and Margo looked at each other impatiently. They sensed there was something big, not necessary bad that could definitely impact upon them.

"Take it easy; and keep you cool.

"I don't like to pat myself on the back, but my last book has given me publicity I never expected.

"Thanks to my mother's babysitting, I was able to travel and make the talk show rounds and the lecture circuit. I saw a lot of America, and I am not happy with what is out there; there's so much confusion.

"As a nation, we're becoming more and more disconnected from values that were meant to be the cornerstone of our democracy and freedom. Slowly but surly, we're getting further and further away from what our founding fathers, and what the framers of the constitution had in mind.

"There's no one I know of, trying at least to create an environment of curiosity to find out, where we started from, and what was the empowering force that had enlightened the leadership of our nation in the past.

"History has taught us that great nations eventually fell to obscurity after centuries of grandeur, mightiness, and fame. Could this fatal outcome be part in our nation's future? And if it could, who would have the guts, will, power, integrity, perseverance, courage, and tenacity to wake and shake us all up from our lethargic and comatose state of existence?

"We have to ask ourselves: when was the last time college graduates, of any age, went back and read the Declaration of Independence? And if they did and had the time to contemplate, how relevant was found to be in the twenty-first century America? Did they comprehend and understand its depth? Were they moved and inspired?

"People of America let America slip away from them. People of America better hurry up to rediscover America; if they don't they will perish, leaving no legacy to speak of, except for skyscrapers, automobile factories, and Hollywood. A civilization and society and that self-destructed by cutting off the roots that fed them, by denouncing the fundamentals and the principles that had brought them greatness.

"Servants to fleeting and ephemeral vanity foolishly succumbed to the lure of self-importance, and naively surrendered to the notion that *matter* was above *mind*."

Barbara and Margo were transfixed, and neither one wanted to talk first, but had the same image on their minds. The power, leadership, heroism, and command Lucia projected, made her not a mythological figure, but a real time figure; an Amazon of the twenty-first century, with her shiny panoply on, ready to lead and fight; a warrior in the making.

Barbara shook her head. She didn't know what to make of Lucia right now, but to say the least, she was curious, if not confused.

"Lucia, we know; you're smart, intelligent, with tremendous depth and spiritually.

"When you were talking, I couldn't tell-I don't know about Margo's impression-whether you were speaking as a philosopher or politician."

"Both; I've decided to run for the office of the *President* of United States. This is what my *calling* is now, and I can sense it. Presidential elections won't be on, for another three years. We've plenty of time to get organized and get the ball rolling. Are you with me, or not?"

Barbara and Margo were catapulted and launched from the steepest and highest glider's cliff with no wings to fly. They were horrified anticipating the end, for the crash was inevitable. Fortunately, it was just a dream, but the scare and anxiety were not. Was Lucia serious? Was she in control?

For the first time, they saw in her so much power and feistiness. Where did they come from? What had transformed a brilliant philosopher, academic, and a humble nun into a politician seeking the highest office in the land, and possible in the entire world? On the other hand, was she willing to face humiliation and scrutiny of her private life?

The press, a self-appointed apologist of the first amendment, with its obsessive drive for the public to *know* would kill her.

What about experience in public life and government? She had none. What did she have? Intelligence, empathy for humanity, leadership, communication skills, values, faith in herself, and most of all faith in God.

Who, knowing her intentions, would help?

She believed that American democracy needed more sincerity, ambition, love, peace, virtue, and righteousness to survive, and less laziness, deception, compromise, indifference, hatred, injustice, and greediness, lest it perish.

Lucia guessed right.

Barbara and Margo were lost. Who wouldn't be!

What any rational person would say under these circumstances? What questions would be appropriate to articulate, without being perceived as demeaning, critical, pragmatic, and even insulting? They loved and respected Lucia so much. But this was above their heads, hardly capable to breathe, while still sinking in the sand.

"I can tell; you have so many questions, c'mon; shoot your mouth off. You think I'm crazy; maybe stupid. I wouldn't blame you, even if you think I'm at my wits' end.

"Barbara, you have never been tongue-tied.

"Since I've known you spoke with your tongue in cheek, and I loved it. What's going on? Are you lost for words? That's not you; that never happened before. Even if you don't agree, at least pray for me.

"I understand both of you have your professions and families that should be your primary responsibilities. I don't expect you to drop everything and follow me in the campaign trail. That would be selfish and foolish. I want you to be in spirit with me, and comprehend my commitment. That would mean so much to me."

"I don't know what to say, and where to start from. I can tell; your mind is already made up. What about organization, money, staff, publicity; have you addressed all these issues?" Barbara asked.

"Of course I have. It wouldn't be easy. I'm not that naïve. I'm planning to use some money from my trust fund. My strength would be my message:

Rediscover America! Come back home, where you belong, no matter who and where you're; you're welcome. You have been gone for so long, and you have been missed.

"I want to reach everyone that our system has disfranchised.

"I plan to visit every state and be with people, not just to be photographed for publicity and ask for votes, but to listen; let them talk for a change. Be humble, and not afraid to say you don't have all the answers, or you don't know. Nobody expect you to, unless you lie.

"It's sad, unfortunate, and disingenuous that politics and lies have become synonymous defining each other. Well, Margo; what do you think?"

"Lucia you're a dreamer; you're an idealist. In your heart and mind, you're still are a nun.

"How can you cut into a world of cynicism and corruption and keep your virtue and purity unblemished? Playing dirty is part of the game. How can you fight back and stay out of the gutter?

"They'd love to see you fall to their level, and say,

She is like us; she is fooling you. She isn't any better; just ignorant. Us, at least we've experience.

"How can you win a war with this kind of mentality that has become main stream American politics?

"We've seen it so often.

"It's not ideas, patriotism, ethic, and gallantry that determine the winner, but the ability to discredit, uncover dirt, humiliate, and dehumanize your opponent. They'll eat you alive!"

The remaining days were spent discussing Lucia's decision to run for the presidency. It had become the center of every conversation, but they didn't care.

With every day passing, they were more and more fascinated with the idea. Objectively speaking, the trio agreed; Lucia's chance of winning the election was down to zero; statistically, a mathematical improbability!

Lucia was adamant. Barbara and Margo admired her and slowly started seeing her point and understood her motives.

She wanted to tear down the bilious, vitriolic, vicious, and asinine sport of character assassination in politics to prevail; and to make up for lack of ideas, innovation, creativity, and faith in people and their intelligence to distinguish right from wrong, and truth from lying.

Lucia's strategy would be to stir-up the conscience of the nation and be the messenger for fundamental ideas that were responsible for greatness of the past, and legacies that were to be carried on and passed into the future. Ideas that were forgotten in the frenzy of the myopic micromanagement of Washington politics, and were victimized by the expediency of lobbyist-driven partisan agendas.

After the initial hesitations and concerns Barbara and Margo came aboard.

Lucia ruled out any active involvement that would disrupt Barbara and Margo's professional and family lives. What they could do, from their home base, was to be the contact persons for the Academy's alumni. They would get the list of all Academy graduates, with e-mail and residence addresses, and make contacts.

The trio, deliberately and wisely, decided to leave out of the campaign, Pedro, Margo's brother, a high profile Washington lawyer, and Lucia's brother John, a senior officer at the US State Department, where he was serving now, after completing his stint at the US Embassy in Tokyo.

The eve of the departure, the Trio went through its usual routine of the past twenty-nine years; the renewal of *the Vows of Three Sisters* for the thirtieth year.

This year, with Lucia's precarious dream and ambition, the bar was raised to the highest level possible.

The origin of her dream and ambition weren't generated out of vanity and self-worthiness, but out of passion, dedication, and desire to serve. Deep in her heart, nothing had changed; Lucia was still a nun committed to help and make the difference.

Lucia was driven. What she had in mind would be something unique that was destined to change American politics for ever, even if she lost.

Lucia was overtaken and constantly thinking;

There is something wrong with America today; so it seems. America has given so much to the world; means of sustenance, innovation, shelter, education, medicine, freedom, respect, and promotions of human rights.

People risk life and limb trying to come to America, and many inhumanly suffocate to death in the process of being smuggled to the land of their dreams. What did America get in return? Hatred and contempt; despising and ridicule.

America is being seen by many abroad as the village idiot of the world, with the mentality of an insecure, if not insane, Lilliputian conqueror; the flappable but hapless, confused, and diminished Don Quixote of the twenty-first century.

Why these contradictory perceptions of love and hate? Could be jalousie and detest, for America is the only superpower left in the world? What America, the land of the free and the land of the brave, needs to do to regain respect and gratitude she deserves? Is any way out? It is, but wouldn't be that easy. America has to go back and rediscover herself.

On a second thought, nothing is wrong with America; the problem is with Americans.

Americans have to reconnect and go back to their roots with the rectitude of the founding fathers, who had the wisdom and fortitude to choosing the ideas, which were responsible for the greatness of America.

The great legacy bestowed upon Americans seems to have slipped away and must be recaptured. The roadmap is still here, but the trip would be arduous, challenging, long, and fatiguing; there is no other choice left. It would be a matter of life and death.

America could follow ancient Athens and Rome's burial to the tomb of obscurity, and be a victim of historical certainty; for no great power lasted for ever.

The responsibility to escape death and demise would rest with all beneficiaries and citizens of this great land; the Americans. Americans could be either the hangmen of death or the angels of resurrection.

This is my calling; to mobilize Americans for America that is still blessed, but her blessings are ignored, questioned, rejected, despised, and even betrayed by those she loves and protects the most; the Americans.

It would absurd to expect respect for America from abroad, if Americans are forgetful, ungrateful, divided, and even ashamed of the wisdom and legacy of the founding fathers.

　　　　🍁　　　　　🍁　　　　　🍁

Lucia, after returning home, waited for a week before discussing her decision with her parents. She was astonished how receptive and proud they were, especially her father-still sprite at the age of seventy-seven.

The family home, surrounded by seven acres of land, was humongous and would be the campaign headquarters. It was ideally located in a city right in the middle between the western and eastern section of US.

Lucia's father suggested building in the back of the house a furnished portable self-contained conference room to be used as pressroom.

The company that built his supermarkets had a division specializing in building potable classrooms, additions for convention centers, exhibits, etc. He promised he would underwrite the project that would be his and her mother's contribution to Lucia's election campaign.

Lucia knew her father was a smart businessman, but she was amazed with his foresight to think of a pressroom that would be so necessary since the house would be designated as the center of operations.

Barbara and Margo were elated with the response they got from the alumni. They contacted over four hundred graduates of the Academy and every one responded; some even inquired information concerning money contributions.

Laura Dillon, a classmate of the trio, the president and CEO of the second largest software company in the US mentioned that the *Prophesy* of Martha Fuller, the director of the Academy, was coming to fruition. When Martha welcomed the junior class, thirty years ago, said one of you could be, some day, *President* of the United Sates.

Mary Fertis, the owner of a large advertising agency in New York City, volunteered to be the PR consultant.

Lucia's father contacted the construction company for the press conference room. The company could deliver and assemble the unit within ten weeks. That would be fine with Lucia. She planned the first press conference the weekend following Labor Day.

❧   ❧   ❧

From now on, time would be the essence.

Lucia had only two months to prepare for the first meeting with the media.

She must be ready to demonstrate fundamental knowledge and be comfortable with addressing constitutional, foreign and domestic policy, economy, defense, and other social issues like abortion and affirmative action.

Her background, as an *ex nun* and *single*, never-married mother, that were on her back, could play an important role in the campaign, handicap her credibility, and overshadow the core of other issues.

She was ready and would welcome attacks on her personal life. She was committed to fight perceptions in American politics, eliminate, and bury their destructive and character assassination agendas for good.

One of the most powerful tools in marketing a competitive product is differentiation.

The strategy would be to put emphasis on certain properties of the product that the customer wants, but the competition overlooked. If the strategy is correct, methodical, and of clear vision, the customer would be willing not only to buy the product, but also pay a higher price.

That was exactly what Lucia had in mind; differentiation.

I would come across entirely different from the banality and tiresomeness of every-day politics. Politics and politicians that lacked not only vision, but also were overtaken by self-importance, unwillingness, arrogance, and stubbornness never to look back to America's illustrious past for inspiration, hard-taught lessons, and mistakes not to be repeated again in the future.

I, Lucia Antonelli, a philosopher and social psychologist running for president of United States? How could this be possible?

At stake is the governing of a complex twenty-first century America and not a utopian state of Plato's Republic!

Intellectual power in the White House and the virtue of truth in the Oval Office would be in? What an anachronism! And hardcore cutthroat demagoguery excused only for pomposity but not for ignorance would be out? How strange!

How would the founding fathers feel? Delighted and hopeful for the country, its values, and the generations to come. I'm ready to stand for them. It's just about time; somebody got to do it.

Lucia, a philosopher and an expert in physical law and metaphysics, had to reinvent herself and be more practical, and down to earth.

She was smart enough to know, that if she were to address and articulate her ideas and vision as an intellectual and professor speaking from the lectern, would be a disaster.

The art of a great communicator rests on simplicity.

The substance, grandiosity, and passion of the message would remain intact, be better understood and retained, if delivery was simple and human, coming from heart to heart.

If intellect and mind, with their complex fabric were to prevail in communicating, passion and enthusiasm would be tempered or disappear all together; that could be deadly.

Lack of deep passion and enthusiasm in politics would transform politicians to heartless mechanical puppets and dolls.

Lucia spent quite a bit of time alone, lately; thinking, reading, speaking to herself, and writing notes.

She was in agony for days.

She wanted to find just only one word. A word of generic, timeless, global, inclusive, incorruptible, and immutable nature, that would encompass and define all her believes, drives, directions, foundation, and character as a politician and president.

The word that constantly reverberated with a deafening, excruciatingly painful, high frequency sound in her mind was no other than the universal word *Justice.*

Justice, in Lucia's critical and analytical mind, was an absolute concept with the most dividing power ever known to humanity.

Justice would reward the just and good, and ignore, avoid, silence, rebuke, and even eliminate the unjust and bad. And what would be the greatest value of *Justice?* Inconsistency and variability.

The just and good people of today could be the unjust and bad people of tomorrow, under different circumstances.

Justice would never bestow titles for life, or lifetime achievement awards.

Justice is scrupulously non-duplicitous.

Justice either would affirm or deny, or please or displease; it couldn't do both at the same time.

When *Justice* speaks, wants to make right out of wrong. Thus, *Justice* would make friends and enemies today, and change fiends to enemies and enemies to friends tomorrow, when truth is revealed.

Justice would work perfectly only by remaining constantly inconsistent and divisive, to maintain its purity and impartiality.

Lucia had finally come to a conclusion. She couldn't be all to all, all the time, and be *just*.

All politicians had one thing in common; to be elected. And once elected would support the *wants* and *perks* of some, by yielding to selfish advocacies, unconcerned how unjust might be for the rest and the common good. It they didn't, friends would become enemies and wouldn't vote for them again.

Exchanging favors, among politicians and lobbyists, is part of everyday legislative agenda on the Hill. Someone should have the guts to tell and mean it:

You were right, just, and good yesterday; but you're wrong, unjust, and bad today. What you're doing or asked other to do for you, would violate Justice for all.

❧   ❧   ❧

The big moment had finally come; Lucia's first press conference.

She was ready and well prepared. The message would so different and unique. Was America ready not only to hear, but listen? Who knows? Time would tell.

The press conference was set for the Saturday right after Labor Day, at 10:00 am; by 9:30 every seat was taken, with some people standing in the back.

Invitations to the media were sent three weeks ago, and the response was overwhelming. TV cameras and other equipment were put in certain places and ready to go.

Lucia walked in on time.

She wore a blue suit, white blouse, and a red scarf loosely tied around the neck. Between the two short ends of the bow a small golden cross attached to a chain was visible from the first rows. Lucia stood behind the podium and adjusted the microphone. To everyone's surprise, she carried no notes.

"Ladies and gentlemen:

"Good morning and thank you for coming.

"My name is Lucia Antonelli. Today, I'm formally announcing my candidacy for the office of the president of the United States of America.

"Presidential elections won't be held until three years from this coming November, but early start would be extremely important. There would be messages to deliver, places to visit, where no presidential candidates have ever been at, and hordes of people to meet, listen to, and talk with.

"Let me tell you a little bit about myself, and why I run for the highest office.

"I'm sure, by now, you must know something, if not all, about me. I think you would be better off to hear it all directly from me. I won't bore you, and I'll be brief. Then, you can ask me any questions that come to your minds. Nothing would be off limits.

"After college, I became a nun, joined the House of Hope, and went to graduate school, where I got my doctorate in philosophy. The core of my work, research and writings, have been on physical law, metaphysics, social psychology, and their impact on life.

"I devoted my entire life in academia, went trough the ranks quickly, and at the age of thirty-five, I was full professor and the Dean for Women at Trinity University.

"My life changed dramatically five years ago, when at the age of forty-two, I found out I was pregnant. Consequently, I resigned from the House of Hope and Trinity University.

"For the past five years, I've been taking care of my daughter Damaris, a spitting image of me, I've been told, pretty soon to celebrate her fifth birthday."

The reporters looked at each other with astonishment, especially the women. They had never seen such forthrightness from any politician in the past.

Lucia preemptively erased any question of morality that they might have in mind. What could have been perceived as a handicap and compromise in Lucia's moral standing came up in front so quickly, that not only disarmed, but also shut then up.

What questions could they have asked without being considered judgmental and throwing the first stone? None! There were millions upon millions of women-out of wedlock or not, single mothers in all walks of life; productive, hard-working, tax-paying women.

The media had to come to terms.

Lucia was smart, honest, intuitive, intelligent, incisive, commanding. She wasn't, and never meant to be, your father's presidential candidate.

Fellows, men and women, of the press; you better wise-up, watch out, and get your act together!

Lucia continued;

"Now, I can tell what's on your mind; the question that has been bothering you from the moment you got my invitation with the announcement.

"Why I, an academician and philosopher, want to run for the presidency? Why I, a woman and single mother with no previous experience in public office and political life, want to be your next president?

"The answer to both questions is simple and clear.

"It's my *calling* to bring back the message that has been ignored for so long. We have to reconnect with the spirit of our fathers, lest we perish to the joy of our critics and enemies from within and abroad.

"What was fought for with blood, sweat, and tears has been pushed away by triviality, expedience, skepticism, pedestrian pseudo-legalism, judicial activism, paraphrasing constitutional twist, and ineptness.

"Look at the two presidential candidates of the two major parties in past elections.

"They were driven by the same imperatives, exercised the same options, exhibited identical behaviors, and tried to sell you-*the people*, the same things; righteousness, not falseness; empathy, not indifference; prosperity, not famine; peace, not war; national pride, not shame.

"The strategy of each candidate, regardless of party affiliation, was to convince you that he or she had all the qualification, knowledge, infrastructure, patriotism, and vision to do all the right things; his or her opponent had none of those, and if elected would lead America to misery and destruction!

"Presidential politics continue along the same venue and mentality.

"How, in the whole world, one candidate would be all that good, and the other all that bad? They're both Americans. Why one wants to build America and the other wants to destroy it?

"These are, ladies and gentlemen of the press, the dynamics of presidential politics as we have seen them in the past, and at the dawn of the twenty-first century America.

"Take for example, the presidential debates; they've been a disaster.

"The winner wouldn't be the candidate with the better ideas and better vision, but the candidate with the asinine and vitriolic ability to destroy the creditability, and question the intellectual honesty of the other.

"How could be possible one party nominee to be the personification of virtue and the other of vice? This is the most un-American polarization of presidential politics of the worst kind. The passion to serve has been replaced by the enmity to divide. Personally, I have no use for presidential debates. My strategy would be totally different.

"I'd like to meet with as many people as possible.

"I'll fly out every Monday and come back home, at least every other weekend or sooner, to be with my daughter and family. I plan to visit every State of the Union, more than once, in the next three years. I want to visit not only large metropolitan and densely populated areas, where high number of voters reside, but also small rural communities, where the beacon of the American soul still flickers patiently with pride and faith.

"The first and most important words of our constitution, *we the people*, which mean all people, young or old, poor or rich, rural or suburbanites, are so often forgotten in the frenzy of fundraising and partisan pettiness.

"I think, by now, you must have an idea, where I come from, and where I'd like to go.

"Now, it's your turn; by answering your questions, you'll have the opportunity to examine and scrutinize my convictions and vision as president, and assess the depth of my leadership. I'd like to remind you what I said at the beginning; there would be no limits. You may ask me any question you feel is important for any presidential candidate to respond.

"Please, raise your hands. Who wants to start first? The gentleman to the right; go ahead, Sir; what's your question?"

"Madam; do you honestly believe, you're qualified to be the next president of the United States?"

"I, honestly, do."

"With all respect, you have no experience; never run or held any office as an elected official."

"By your response, it's obvious you didn't like my answer. Maybe, I wasn't *honest* enough for you!

"To answer any questions correctly, as a general rule from now on, exact articulation, proper language, and wording would be a must to precisely communicate with each other, and be always on the same page."

The reporter sat down in hurry.

He was visibly upset and humiliated. This was a press conference and not a professorial lecture. Lucia, with this kind of attitude, wouldn't last for too long as a candidate. On the other hand, her demand for precision would work to her benefit and make the press more alert and prepared.

Lucia continued with more confidence.

"Sir; you actually asked me two pertinent questions; the first concerning qualifications, and the second, a follow-up question, concerning experience as an elected official.

"In accordance with article II of US Constitution, there're three requirements for a candidate to qualify for the presidency;

"1. A naturally born citizen; 2. Thirty-five years of age; and 3. Fourteen year of residency in US. My answer was honest, correct, and truthful.

"Now, let's come to your second question concerning experience as an elected official in public office. I have none. What I do have is more important; leadership.

"The leadership of any presidency should be defined only by the choice, quality, and expertise of people appointed by the president to key positions to run the government.

"Let me ask you a rhetorical and hypothetical question; the answer would clearly depict my concept of leadership as president.

"Air Force One, is carrying the President of the United States to an emergency G8 meeting. For security reasons, the location of landing has been kept with the utmost secrecy, and could change, several times, during the flight. Only the President and the pilot would know the location of landing at any given moment.

"The plane has reached thirty-five thousand feet altitude and could be anywhere in the world. During the flight, who do you thing is the most powerful, and who is the most important person in the entire world?

"C'mon; let me see some hands. Don't be bashful. This is the most aggressive, respectful, knowledgeable, inquisitive, intelligent, and incisive press corps in the world. Are you lost for words? Oh; I see a lady's hand. Ms., go ahead. Who is it?"

"I assume this is a joke! The President, of course."

"Ms., this isn't a joke. Your assumption is wrong. You missed something. Your answer was fifty percent correct.

"At any second, minute, and hour during the flight, the President would be, without a doubt, the most powerful person in the world, but not the most important. The most important person would be the pilot!

"Any mistakes of his or hers, even the slightest, could risk the life of the most powerful person in the world. The pilot is entrusted with the life of the president, because he or she is the best in the field, and second to none.

"This is the kind of leadership I'm ready to pursue.

"I have a clear vision and can make the distinction between power and importance.

"The president shouldn't be an insecure journeyman or handyman preoccupied with micromanagement, but a powerful leader with the intuitive capability to find the best and the most qualified people to serve under him or her.

"Leadership of the highest caliber possible would be achieved only if *power* is complimented with *importance* at the expense of cronyism, nepotism, and size of pre-election campaign contributions.

"Past political experience would be desirable, but history repeatedly has shown that wouldn't be a guarantor of competent, efficient, and untainted administration directed by morality and ethics, and not by party politics, and self-serving interests."

"Madam, the American political landscape has been dominated by the two party system that has served the country well. You haven't declared any affiliation with either party; the assumption would be that you would be running as an independent. So far, independent candidates have failed miserably. Why do you think, you could change the odds and win?"

"I love this question; and the timing is perfect. It'll bring us back to what we just discussed; the concept of combining power and importance in the pursuit of excellence in public life, politics, and government.

"You're so right; I haven't declared loyalty to either party. Do you know why? Because I belong to the same party that every one of you also belongs. The original, the grandest, and the most unique party; the mother of all parties; the *American Party*! The party of our land and the party of our founding fathers.

"This is what my campaign for the presidency will be all about; an outcry and call to all; come and join me. Let's celebrate in unison the legacy and the spirit of this land. Let's for once the president be a genuine American and not a committed puppet to any party.

"If elected, I'll serve only for one term. This is the way should be.

"Once the president takes the oath and enters the Oval Office becomes a member of *American Party*; any other party affiliation should be severed and voided. Power and importance take over. They must become the only priority of the president. The best, the brightest, and the most honest would be sought after to serve.

"Like *Justice*, *Excellence* in government is *blind* unable to see party banners; it's also *deaf* unable to hear party voices.

"Ideally, the president should serve only one six-year term.

"The present system violates common decency; and forgets about morality and ethics.

"The first two years of the first four year term become a duel and battleground between the president and congress; fighting for cabinet members, ambassadors, judges, etc. it's either paying back time for favors, or raunchy and spiteful opposition time, compensating for bitterness for losing the White House.

"Nominations for any positions, debates, and voting in congress should be guided by the pursuit of excellence in government, and not dirty and demeaning politics.

"And what happens when the president begins the third year of his first four year term? The fight for reelection and fundraising!

"It would be of interest to conduct a time study to find out actually how much time, out of the first four years, the president really spends governing and caring for you and me.

"You, the media, please no offense intended, when your report on the strategy of an incumbent president to be reelected, what has become the standard point of reference in assessing the chance for reelection? How much money has been already raised and the ability to even raise more!

"In the months ahead, I anticipate the campaign to be rough. I'll stay away from personal attacks. I have no intention to respond to criticism or belittling from my opponents reported by the media, no matter what they say about me.

"My strength would be the message of decency, morality, and patriotism that have defined our nation from the start. Looking at our past wouldn't be an escape from pressures of the present, but an inspiration for the future.

"Standing at the edge of a cliff, before taking a step forward, you may have to step back, take time, and think; if you don't, the next step forward could be your last one."

"Madam, considering your background and involvement with religion, what are your views on the first amendment and the effort to take the word *God* out of the Pledge of Allegiance?"

"One of the reasons our forbearers came to America was to avoid religious persecution. The first amendment of the constitution-the first article of the bill of rights that was enacted in 1791-demonstrates the wisdom and foresight of the founders of the new state not establish any religion, but, by the same token, keep the unalienable right of free expression of religion.

"With religion out of the way right now-I will come back later, let's talk abut he word *God*, you brought up.

"What document was written fifteen years prior to the enactment of the first amendment that has defined hence the existence of America and the freedoms you and I enjoy? Without this document, there wouldn't be first amendment, constitution or America at all.

"The *Declaration of Independence*; the most sacred document of our nation. The word *God* takes center stage, and is included in the first paragraph:

-*The Laws of Nature and Nature's God entitle them-*

"To some, the word *God* has become a four letter word. Are we going to rewrite the Declaration of Independence or cover up the word *God* with a strip of masking tape, lest some be offended?

"The intent of the first amendment was meant to guard and celebrate freedom of expression of religion for all and not become a declaration of the new proletariat, where a minority or a majority dictatorially takes over the law of the land.

"It would be a travesty to allow any segment of the people to dictate the free expression of another segment. Both should be equally protected, and not one at the expense of the other.

"Any expression should be voluntary, offering the option of abstaining from any expression that would be against personal believes. This is the American way, and what America was founded on. It would be an abomination of the first amendment if pornography is protected, but not free expression of religion-any religion-and the word *God*.

"I wouldn't like to be perceived as a fatalist, but when in the past we abandoned our heritage and legacy, we suffered; and the pain still continues.

"One the bleakest, inhuman, despicable, and cruelest periods of our history is *slavery*; the black eye of disgrace of America.

"Racial discrimination would have never been part of our history, if we had followed to the letter our founding fathers will, so well expressed in the beginning of the second paragraph of the Declaration of Independence:

-*That all men are crated equal, that they are endowed by their Creator with certain unalienable Rights*-

"*Slavery*, that almost destroyed America, would have ceased to exist almost two hundred years earlier from the mid nineteen-sixty's when the civil rights laws were enacted.

"If you see the actual document the words *Creator* and *Rights* start with capital letters.

"People had fought for and won these rights and no human power, be the government, racism, discrimination, ACLU, or judicial activists, should take those rights away.

"Even today, with affirmative action and all, we're still paying, maybe in reverse, the price of slavery, and discrimination.

"Activists of color would use color for their own publicity, media attention, and agenda by being biased, uninformed, and even lying, unknowing or knowing.

"We all remember the hoax of a teenager of color who cried rape, that she later admitted was a lie. Meanwhile, publicity seeking leaders of color were on TV every day screaming at the top of their lungs for justice, while holding platters waiting for white heads to roll on.

"We sinned in the past, and paid dearly; suffering humiliation, discrimination, civil war, unrest, demonstrations, assassinations, brutal killings; so unbecoming for a civilized society carrying the torch of democracy and claiming to be the cradle of freedom, dignity, and respect.

"We sinned in the past and paid dearly; for we forgot, abandoned, compromised, forged, and even betrayed the legacy, wisdom, patriotism, and sacrifices of the founding fathers.

"Let's sin no more; let's not betray our destiny for greatness.

"As Americans, we have one more chance. If we lose it, history would never forgive us; we were given it all, and could lose it all; and if we did lose it all, we would wind up being remembered as *the gluttonous over-indulging barbarians of the later days of the civilized world.*"

❧   ❧   ❧

Larry Frost and Maggie Fay, seasoned TV anchors for Transamerica Broadcasting Co., met some twenty-five years age, as young reporters, right out of college, and had remained good friends, every since. Now, Larry was based in New York and Maggie in Los Angeles. Both had covered in the past primaries, conventions, and presidential elections.

Having some three hours to spare before flying back home, Larry and Maggie had supper at the airport. After quickly catching up with each other's personal and family news, the conversation naturally turned to Lucia's press conference.

"Maggie, what do you think of Lucia? Are we wasting our time? Is she going to be the joke of the next presidential campaign? Were you impressed? Is she going to have any impact on the outcome?"

"Well; I'll tell you what I think; and forget that she's a woman and I'm a woman. I think we're for something big. She has the spirit, logic, communicating power, and a strong message:

Let's go back to the basics that made America great in the past.

"Drawing from her own personal experience, she will fight stereotyping and perceptions how people are viewed in private and public life.

"Considering the fact that there're millions upon millions of single mother voters, if she would get fifty percent of those, could determine who the next president would be; not necessary her, but one of two competing parties. Being a single mother would work to her advantage. And if the other candidates were stupid enough to bring that up would kill them."

"The president cannot be only an idealist and visionary. We have never had elected a president that intellectual and professorial. The cabinet meetings are not graduate school classrooms."

"Don't worry Larry. She's a graduate of Marie Curie Academy.

"I'm not sure how much you know about this school. She could assemble the best cabinet, ever. She could bring in expertise as we've never seen before. These women would be so passionate for one of their own. And forget about money; contributions will be coming from everywhere.

"Besides, Lucia is loaded; I mean loaded. Did you see the reception her parents threw for us after the press conference? And what a house?"

"Oh my goodness; yes. Lucia has been already living in the white house!

"Objectively speaking, she has certain advantages. She would be ahead of her opponents. With the elections being three years away, there's nothing coming out from the two major parties, but unconfirmed rumors and tasting the water.

"What would ideally work for her would be the lack of need to compete in the primaries. She would save not only money, but also energy and time.

"The strategy to be close to, and spend time with folks, would make her more human and approachable; not the hopping and itinerant politician flying from one city to the other, like a chicken with its head cut off. I'm sure the next three years would be interesting.

"Time's up; they just announced boarding for my flight. Say hello to Mark. Bye-bye."

"Larry it was nice to see you again. Regards to Esther, and have a nice flight; bye. See you at the convention!"

Other reporters, immediately after the Saturday conference was over, got busy with their notebooks. Observations, impressions, and opinions had to be entered, and transmitted back to their home bases as soon as possible.

The Sunday newspapers' headlines were conflicting but interesting, reflecting editorial philosophies and leanings; liberal or conservative.

The New York Chronicles: *From the Convent the White House: Give me a brake!*

The Washington Telegram: *To dream is innocent and innocuous: To want to do what you dream could be dangerous.*

The Dallas Press: *A breath of fresh air: Is it doable?*

The Los Angeles News: *Wake up: The first amendment is in jeopardy.*

The Atlanta Freedom: *America look back: Rediscover your values. Then move forward.*

The Boston Star: *All President's women? Please, this is not a sexist remark. The calling should be about experience and not experiment."*

Lucia remained unconcerned. Editorial opinions didn't bother her at all; the message was out, and that was what counted.

Mary Fertis, the PR person, called Lucia three days after the press conference.

"Hello; Lucia?"

"Yes; this is she. Who is calling?"

"Mary Fertis. Do you remember me?"

"Oh my goodness; how are you doing? It's been such a long time; of course I do.

"Thanks for being so willing to help. Laura, Barbara, and Margo have talked to me about you. This phone is not listed, but I told them to give you the number in case you wanted to call. This number would remain private, just for us.

"A new system is being installed to be used for all other communications. It'll have the capacity for three more additional private lines. I'll call you with the numbers as soon as the system becomes operational."

"Listen; since Barbara and Margo made the calls to the alumni, I keep receiving money. I've an idea. What about writing sort of a *manifesto*. Write down your ideas, and sent them to me.

"I'll put everything together to fit in one newspaper page. After you have seen it, I'll send it to the alumni for their signatures. Once I get it back, I'll buy ad space and have it printed in every major newspaper in US."

"That's an excellent idea. You're doing so much work for me. I'm so embarrassed."

"Don't be; and never use these words, again. There're No, No! You'll never win the White House by being embarrassed. You may stain and embarrass it after you're in, but not while you're out trying to get in, if you can get my drift."

Lucia started laughing.

"Sure, I can. You're such a smart Alec! I'll send you the transcript from my press conference. Pick and choose what you think would be the most appropriate context for the endorsement. Bye-bye; and thanks for everything."

"My pleasure. Oh, before I forget; and that's important for you to know.

"Two senators and eleven members of the House, all Academy graduates, sent contributions; they have decided to cross party-lines for the next presidential elections. This is big stuff. I'm having fun. Goodbye for now."

Four weeks later, the endorsement of Lucia's candidacy for president was published in the Sunday edition of every major newspaper across America. Who was who of women, in academia, business, professions, sciences, politics-all Academy graduates-signature was there. To make the endorsement more balanced and creditable quite a few husbands, many as prominent as their wives, cosigned it.

January 1st marked the beginning of a new calendar year, and also the year of presidential elections. The 1st Tuesday of November the new president of US would be elected; the seating president, finishing his second four year term, couldn't run again.

There were several candidates from each of the two major parties, with no clear frontrunner. Polls were inconsistent changing day by day.

With the Iowa caucuses and New Hampshire primaries coming up this month, the field could start narrowing down.

For the two parties, politics were as usual.

Personal attacks, perceptions of scandals, improprieties, hidden agendas, messianic messages of doomsdays, lies, and incompetence versus skills, honesty, prosperity, competence, and compassion all mixed together, and repeated time and time again ad nauseum.

Typical gutter politics—stereotyping, image making, and money driven.

The strategy of each candidate was the same; the monopolize good versus evil, and be the angel and not the devil.

If there ever were an absolute absurdity in self-worthiness and judgment that would be it; one candidate was the personification of all good, and the other all bad! There was only one choice. A vote could go either to an angel or the devil, depending on what side of the fence you were sitting on.

Lucia was smart enough to stay out of this menacing mess. Whenever she was asked about her opponents, the answer was the same.

"I want to be president to do good for my country, rediscover our foundation and values as a nation, and bring everybody aboard. I'm sure whoever my opponents would be, must have the same aspirations. The difference is party affiliation; I'm the candidate of the *American* Party."

The past two years Lucia visited every single state.

She was the first presidential candidate ever to visit the State of Alaska. She had no entourage, traveling alone, and she would fly back home at least every other weekend to be with her daughter, seven years old by now.

Lucia's strategy was to make as many personal contacts as possible.

The standard would be the use of sophisticated PA (Public Address) systems to speak to large crowds holding and waving banners, sings, etc. Lucia would have none of the above. She intentionally avoided any tools that had been for so long the core of organized political machines. The only tools and infrastructure that defined Lucia's campaign were airlines and car rental agencies.

Lucia carried with her one page flyers, she would pass to people she met; the text contained a short bio and her main message:

Let's go back to our roots; if we don't, we can't go forward.

She visited shopping malls, hospitals, schools, drug rehab centers, nursing homes, churches, synagogues, mosques, libraries, and prisons.

She talked to mothers, strolling babies in the park, policemen, social workers, teachers, doctors, judges, priests, ministers, rabbis, and imams. She really saw the soul of America; and America really saw the soul of one, who wanted to be the next president. Not only they spoke and touched, but they were also concerned and worried about one another and the future of their children.

The media, the first few months, ignored Lucia entirely.

As she became better known, a small number of reporters became her *groupies* and followed her everywhere she went. They became friends and many a time shared meals together. That didn't last for too long.

Two weeks ago, Lucia visited a high security prison.

When her conversation with one of the inmates hit he national news media, Lucia became a celebrity.

Debby Parker, a thirty-five year old single mother of two, was serving a twenty-five year to life sentence for armed robbery and accessory to first degree murder. She wouldn't be eligible for parole for another fifteen years. She was waiting outside and drove the get-away car after a bank robbery, where a security guard was killed.

The warden had informed the inmates of Lucia's visit. She would be in the cafeteria, and any prisoner could meet with her, if so wished.

"What are you doing here, Missy? Debby asked. "Don't you know we can't vote?"

172 Vows of Three Sisters

"I didn't come here for your vote. I wanted to meet you and talk to you."

"Why? Society thinks we're scum and maggots of stench on this earth. We're being punished. Aren't you happy and safe? The criminals are behind bars, after all. Besides, what you and I have in common?" Nothing; absolutely, nothing!"

"Debby, listen; what you did, and what you're here for, it's none of my business. The fact remains though, that you're still an American. America feeds you, provides you with shelter, and takes care and pays for the welfare of your two children. America punished you, but still loves you. America hopes the time you spend here will help you think, and be ready for a new beginning, whenever comes."

Lucia got up, walked to the bench, and sat next to Debby. She put her arm around Debby's shoulders, turned, and looked at her.

"Look; you said that you and I had nothing in common. You're dead wrong. *We're both single mothers!*"

Lucia hugged Debby. As their faces touched both started crying; and there wasn't a dry eye left around.

One woman reporter carrying a camera took a shot. The shot of a presidential candidate-a woman and single mother, hugging an inmate in a high security prison, another woman and single mother, made the front page of every newspaper and the cover of every magazine in the nation. Eventually the picture won the Pulitzer Prize for photojournalism.

The first Tuesday of March known as Super-Tuesday, where primary elections are held in ten states, was five days away. Whoever won them all, from either major party, would most likely be the party's nominee at the forthcoming conventions, scheduled for July for one party, and August for the other.

No one carried all ten states. Candidates were determined to fight to the bitter end.

Conventions started with divided parties and took several ballots, way past midnight, before finally the two candidates from the major parties were nominated.

The conventions left fractious party machines, bitterness, and many delegates left mad, peevish, and disappointed.

Letters to the editors of newspapers, from all over the country, showed that the public was fed up with both parties. Civility was replaced with hostility; decorum with unruliness; debate with screaming and yelling.

After the first debate, the candidates of both major parties left wounded; and the ratings were dismal. The next two debates didn't project any clear-cut winners, except for the diehards.

Lucia continued her low-key campaign effectively.

It was interesting that women's organizations of liberal persuasions never commented or asked to meet with her; she was completely ignored. They knew what her views would be on abortion! After all she was an *ex* nun.

On the other hand, how could they discredit a single mother, a philosopher and academic of renown, who had the guts to run for president?

Lucia could have been the poster child of what women's liberation was all about, under different circumstances.

By the end of September the polls showed Lucia equally splitting the votes with the other two candidates, a thirty-three percent.

The bickering of the nominees of the two parties continued with maliciousness, deep polarization, and hatred.

Lucia made a giant leap when she announced her choice for vice president; none!

"I run to serve and not create a dynasty.

"As I have repeatedly said, if elected, I'll serve only one term and not seek reelection.

"Nevertheless, it's important for the president to work close with congress. Let congress elect the vice president. I can work with any one they choose. I run to bring dignity to the presidency and the Capitol.

"Let's stop cheap partisanship that demeans and insults the spirit, sanctity, and purity of the values America was built on.

"Let congress become the beacon and paradigm of a conciliatory initiative that would bring the executive and legislative brunch of the government together. Amity and not embitterment should prevail.

"Diversity of opinions is necessary and would be welcomed in the debate to discover better alternatives for America. If diversity is subjected to egos, stubbornness, and party agendas, would be divisive and distractive.

"No President, Senator, and neither Member of the House nor the Judiciary should be perceived as the sole possessors of righteousness; for they all are humans. By working together, and guided by the constitution, should empower their strengths at the expense of their weaknesses, and bring virtue, honesty and trust, while exercising power from the oval office, the senate, the house, or the bench.

"Holding public office should be considered neither an avocation nor a hobby, but a vocation and *calling*, if you will, to serve.

"The only reward any politician should expect should be nothing else but the trust of *the people*, whose vote elected him or her to office. This trust demands humility and not arrogance. This trust must be honored and not disgraced. This trust must be respected and not violated."

Within a week, after Lucia announced her decision concerning a running made, the polls tilted to her favor. For the first time, she reached upper thirties, while her two opponents remained around thirty percent.

The first Tuesday of November had finally come.

Americans would vote to elect the new President, and Senators and Members of the House that were up for reelection.

Exit polls showed Lucia was ahead. By midnight Lucia was declared the winner by TV networks and news agencies. She received closed to forty percent of the popular vote, versus the equally split thirty percent of her opponents representing the two major parties.

History was in the making.

The America party, the *people*'s party, had won. America elected its first *Woman President*. Every American was a winner, for *we the people* had prevailed and not *this* or *that* party.

❧   ❧   ❧

It was the 20th of January; the day of taking the oath of office, and inauguration for the newly elected president of the US.

The stand for the ceremony was built at the West Front of the Capitol.

Lucia walked to the stand to take the oath. She looked serene. She was put up there by the people for a purpose; to link them back with America all had forgotten.

The oath was administered by the Chief Justice of the US Supreme Court Julio Martinez, still vigorous at the age of seventy-seven, while Barbara and Margo held the Bible. Lucia repeated after the Chief Justice:

I, Lucia Antonelli, do solemnly swear that I will faithfully execute the office of the President of the United States, and will to the best of my ability, preserve, protect, and defend the Constitution of the United States.

After taking the oath, the president immediately delivered the inaugural address, forgoing the traditional inaugural parade.

"My fellow Americans: Men, women, children, young, old, wherever you are.

"The message is loud and clear. America was discovered for the second time, and every one of us became a pilgrim again, ready and anxious to disembark and set foot on the land of our dreams. Today is the second coming. Today, Plymouth is being revisited with unprecedented glory.

"One of the wicked weaknesses of human nature is selfishness. Its divisive and destructive power would compromise the survival of anything worthy fighting for. No family, community, or nations would survive but perish, if not united.

"Approximately two months ago, we celebrate Thanksgiving. The unique American holiday of expressing thanks to God, for family, friends, and for all blessings and gifts received.

"I would like to remind you the definition of the word pilgrim: *a pious* person who travels to a sacred and revered land to worship, acknowledge faith and respect, and experience a spiritual and religious awakening.

"The pilgrims, people of faith, sailed to America to find a new land of worship. Unfortunately while sailing, selfishness and egos took over. The pilgrims aboard the Mayflower divided the passengers in two groups: The group of forty-four were the *real* Pilgrims, who called themselves the *Saints,* and the group of sixty-six other passengers the pilgrims called the *Strangers.*

"During the long, arduous, fatiguing, and hard voyage, supposed to be a pilgrimage, there were bickering, arguments, and infighting between the two groups; selfishness and egos had prevailed.

"Then a miracle happened!

"Once the new sacred land of dreams appeared on the horizon, the two groups put their differences behind, reconciled, and every one was accepted as pilgrim.

"If selfishness and egos were allowed to continue, both groups would have perished. There would have never been America, Declaration of Independence, and neither a US Constitution, nor Bill of Rights.

"This is the greatest lesson that we should never forget. America's power and survival in the past, present and future would always depend on unity.

Unity of depth and not convenience. Unity of peace and not truce. Unity of love and not tolerance.

"Today, every one of us became a pilgrim again. The curtains of division weren't drawn back and left opened, but were taken down and destroyed for good.

"Look; what happened today!

"A woman, hyphenated American, single mother, representing Americans, and not political parties, was sworn as president.

"The oath of the office of the president was administered by the Chief Justice of the US Supreme Court; a Hispanic, who came to US from Mexico's countryside with his parents at the age of five.

"The president took the oath of the Office by placing her hand on a Bible that long time ago belonged to a black slave. The Bible was held by the hands of my two sisters in spirit; an African-American, the great-great-great grand daughter of the black slave, and a Hispanic, the daughter of the US Chief Supreme Court Justice.

"My fellow Americans:

"This is the kind of America the pilgrims had in mind. We forsook it all, suffered, and paid the price dearly for selfishness, egos, and divisions; strangers no more we're, for we have become brothers and sisters again.

"Let recreate and keep in our minds, vividly, the first Thanksgiving.

"New land, different faces, new promises, many adversities, and even death. The natives welcomed the newcomers. No selfishness or division, but bonding, trust, and respect for each other.

"So many things to learn and so many things to teach. And prayers to overcome challenges and difficulties, in creating a new life, were never forgotten; for the pilgrims, above all, were people of *faith.*

"Praying nowadays, even as a contemplative moment, has been fought with vengeance and hatred. Why? Who is afraid, and of what?

"*Prayer* and *faith* have been as American as apple pie and the 4th of July. We have abandoned our roots. Our forefathers were people of faith and prayer from the beginning. They reaffirmed their believes in the Declaration of Independence and the first amendment of the Constitution.

"Coming from the world of analytical thinking, time and time again, I wondered, why we have taken an inclusive concept, like the first amendment, and try to make it so divisive?

"As your president, I took the oath to uphold the *Constitution* to best of my ability.

"There's something else of equal importance that as your president I will never forget. I am responsible every human life living on this land in time of war or peace, famine or prosperity, happiness or sadness.

"You, *the people* brought me where I stand at this moment.

"I owe nothing to anybody except *the people*. I want to be part of you and be aware of your concerns and worries.

"I'm not a populist, I don't know what they mean by that, but I'll come directly to you with my problems that could be your problems, too. Open, honest, and direct communication helps both; the president and the people he or she is to serve.

"Often you see the president surrounded by dignitaries, heads of Foreign States, driven in limousines, flying on Air Force One, and helicopters. All these are fine and dandy, and part of the job.

"Please, keep in mind and never forget; and I hope the president never forgets either. The president in nothing else, but *a public servant* at you disposal. If the tools of the trade substitute servitude for self-importance, the president could become and function as a *buffoon* worthless of your trust and respect.

"Today, let's all become visionaries; let's see the future through our great past.

"Let's rediscover the fervor and relentless perseverance of the pioneers to fight the elements to succeed, and the defiant spirit to create.

"Let's push divisions, egos, and selfishness aside. Only a *united* America will remain a *strong* America.

"Let's not burden our children with our sins, and give them back the legacy of our forefathers with its liberating power unabated.

"There is nobody to blame for the future, but us; for every single of our tomorrows to come, should be the foundation of the future generations to build on.

"The building of America is a never-ending process and each generation is responsible for pulling its own weight, for reinforcing our foundation and making it indestructible.

"Preserving our past will also empower us to make America of today grater and stronger. We don't live in the past, but inspired by the wisdom of our past we can make the present more glorious, enlightening, prosperous, and human.

"There is no question; America is not loved by all. To some degree, we could be responsible for that.

"We should see our mightiness with more humility and less arrogance.

"On the other hand, events like the 9/11 changed our views for the rest of the world.

"American territory was violated, and we had to respond. Certain measures had to be taken for the security of our homeland. The evil of division wearing the mask of protector of civil liberties protested.

"It has become fashionable for certain Americans to go against America. What happened to the process of critical thinking? Even civil libertarians possess it. Did anybody ask *what could I do as an American before 9/11, couldn't do after the 9/11 precautionary measurements were taken?*

"It's the duty of every American to watch the government. This has been part of our tradition and the democratic process. It should be guided by facts, personal experience, and logic, and not by hallucinating paranoia, and political partisanship.

"Demagoguery, theatrical rhetoric, and antics on Capitol Hill have tinged our political process with demeaning political primitivism and immaturity. It's time for change.

"Vitriolic vilification of any sitting president by the opposition, for party gains, has been the order of every day. It's time for change.

"Manipulating the news to advance ideological agendas has violated public trust. It's time for change.

"Policy making driven by money and self-serving lobbies have compromised integrity in government. It's time for change.

"Intellectual honesty has been replaced by duplicitous expediency. It's time for change.

"Are these changes possible? One might ask.

"Politics are not about truth or lies; politics are about getting *elected*. This is sad but true, my fellow Americans; it's the observation of a realist, and not a cynic.

"Changes are possible.

"I'm part of the change, because of you, *the people*; but be aware. Changes would never come out of Capitol Hill and Washington DC, but only from you.

"You're the only ones, who have been entrusted by the constitution to make changes. You're the only ones, who have the power to cut the Gordian knot that ties and chains change. Every single vote coming from you is more powerful than myriads of swords of Damocles in fighting to protect the sovereignty and integrity of America, and its democratic system of government.

"The Framers of our Constitution were so wise to designate the president as the Commander in-Chief. Why? To protect you; *the people*.

"We love and are proud of our military for defending our country. But governing the country is left up to you, and should be carried out by the president you elected.

"Since America became an independent nation, not even once your elected president and government were threatened by military coups and oppression;

the president you elect becomes your trustee of the freedoms guaranteed to you by the constitution. This is an example of the wisdom and legacy of our fathers, we so often forget.

"As your guarantor of the *Constitution,* I cannot be an i*deologue.*

"On the other hand nothing prevents me from being an *idealist* providing a reflection of your ideals and values that connected with mine, and inspired you to vote for me, and elected me as your president.

"That would be a perfect fit, if the people and president were sharing the same ideas and values; for both would be virtuous, loving, and proud Americans devoid of divisions and selfishness.

"My fellow Americans:

"Are we dreamers and victims of the impetuousness of youth? Absolutely, not. America is still young and must continue dreaming in order to grow.

"Our past is full of dreamers; from George Washington, to Thomas Jefferson, Abraham Lincoln, and Martin Lutheran King, to name a few.

"There is no doubt; what we see and experience across America every day, no matter where we live, affirms that dreams of yesterday became monuments of worship, admiration, and respect of tomorrow.

If there were no dreamers in America's past, legacies would have never been born, and history wouldn't have been written, as we know it today.

"I'm thankful, moved, and humbled by your trust.

"The next four years wouldn't be an experiment, but a pilgrimage to reconnect with our foundation, in order to build a better and even more glorious future.

"God bless America, and God bless the people of America."

Lucia's inaugural address was repeatedly interrupted with enthusiastic applauding.

At the end, the uproar was phenomenal.

She raised both hand and waved at the crowed. She asked Damaris to stand in front of her, after she brought Barbara and Margo on the stand.

Lucia stood in the middle, and with her right hand took Barbara's left, and with her left Margo's right.

When the president raised her hands holding the hand of her sisters the crowed went into a screaming frenzy; "Mama Lucia……Mama Lucia…We love you. Bravo…Bravo."

✤   ✤   ✤

Lucia, alone, stood on the stand for several more minutes acknowledging the enthusiasm of her supporters.

Shortly, the presidential limousine arrived.

A secret service officer escorted the president to the presidential limousine, opened the door, and helped her to the back seat. She insisted that Barbara and Margo join her.

Within a minute, another secret service officer showed up escorting Barbara and Margo. She opened the door and helped them sit. The president and her two sisters were on their way to the White House.

"What happened? I told you to follow me. When I get to the oval office for the first time, I wanted you to be with me."

"Madam President today, is your day. Margo and I thought we shouldn't be in your way."

Lucia looked at them and said nothing.

She realized, and better get used to, that once a person becomes president would be viewed and perceived entirely different by others, including loved ones. It wasn't the person per se, but the tradition, history, power, and respect the office emanated.

Shortly the presidential limousine arrived at the White House.

The secret service opened the back doors of the limousine and let Barbara and Margo out. The last to emerge was the president. She was escorted by two secret service officers to the side door of the White House, as Barbara and Margo walked behind. The marine guard saluted, and the president responded.

The president, Barbara, and Margo finally entered the oval office.

The president asked the aide standing outside to close the door. She sat on the chair by the presidential desk, and Barbara and Margo on the armchairs, right across from the president.

The three women remained silent for a while.

Barbara and Margo had planned to let Lucia talk first. They were guests of the president. The trio were still sisters at heart, but the dynamics of communication had changed precipitously, and they were conscious of the new order.

The president looked Barbara and Margo in the eyes. Her expression was serious, but not austere. She could feel the burden of the office. The love to serve and revive the values that had made America great strengthened her commitment and empowered her will.

"Well; it's has been a long journey.

"This year we celebrated our fiftieth birthday. We met as impetuous and impressionable seventeen girls thirty-three years ago. Who could have ever foreseen that from the hall of the Academy, we, one day, would wind up in the oval office of the White House! Not, us.

"How did this all happen? Where did the drive, tenacity, and inspiration come from? The answer is easy; from the *Vows of Three Sisters*.

"I went through a personal crisis that didn't make any sense at all.

"Your logic tempted you not to believe me.

"On the other hand, our vows compelled you to. You stack to them, trusted me, and had faith in me. That's why we're here to day.

"Your trust gave me the power to continue with my life, and inspired me to seek the presidency. Not only you stood by me, but also you helped me find some explanation that, at least among us, would make some sense.

"I'm the president, but we're still sisters; nothing has changed. I'll need you as never before; for you're *the people* to bring me back to reality. You, your families, relatives, and friends shall be the pulse of the nation. I count on you to keep me from going astray.

"What's going on in America today is so confusing. It could compromise the future development of our citizenry.

"We started, and still are, as a pluralistic, multi-religious, multi-racial, and multi-ethnic nation. If we're united and respect each other, no one group should feel superior to the other. There would be neither selfishness, nor disunity. We'd be all brothers and sisters.

"Every one of us has something good to offer. Why do we let the wicked part of us prevail? Has our intellectual curiosity to learn from others become subservient to insecurity?

"What is Christmas all about, America and the entire world celebrates? The birth of Christ! But the Nativity scene has been banned from everywhere, as constitutionally offensive.

"What hypocrites have we become? With this kind of mentality every faith is violated.

"What's wrong, when appropriate calendar time calls, if every faith is given equal chance to be known by others? We're civilized Americans and not religious fanatics. Our kids should grow up to know all about Christmas, Hanukah, Ramadan, Kwanzaa, and all other traditions and faiths.

"This is the America our fathers had in mind. This is the freedom of religion the first amendment meant to protect. In the privacy of our homes and the houses of worship, we can exercise our preferences.

"In public we're all Americans celebrating and learning from one another, our constitution prevails, and freedoms and choices are respected.

"My election convinced me that Americans are ready for the big picture.

"Micro-myopic politics in the age of instant information and globalization would limit our growth and influence.

"I don't expect other nations to think like us or become Americans. I want them to see that we have the same concerns they have, and our desire is to contribute to the rest of the world not as a super power, but as a nation extremely blessed and ready to assume its responsibilities for peace and all human causes.

"Americans are bombarded and pressured by so many political fronts and movements, all claiming *righteousness*.

"What happened to common sense? I hope by using common sense, we could understand one another, be more productive, and stop wasting time and money.

"I think, I was carried away and talked too much."

"Madam President," Barbara said, "You have *the people* behind you; that's all you need.

"Today is a great day for America, Americans, and we should never forget; a great day for American women. I hope women of certain persuasions wouldn't be offended that a *nun* beat them to the presidency! What do you think Margo?"

"It's amazing; your dry humor, we all have enjoyed over the years, is not abated by time, circumstance, and place. The president has a full schedule ahead of her. I think it's time for us to go. We may catch up with the president, later, in one of the receptions."

The president got up, and so did Barbara and Margo.

"Listen; before you leave there's something else.

"I'm here today, because of your trust and faith in me. You kept our vows and never looked back."

The president walked around the desk, approached Barbara and Margo, embraced them and said;

"At this moment, there's nothing more appropriate to do, but renew the *Vows of Three Sisters*."

The three women bowed their heads and recited the vows in unison:

We, Barbara, Lucia, and Margo, take the solemn Vows of Three Sisters, and promise that we shall love, respect, honor, and cherish one another like sisters, until the end of our natural lives.

Our hearts, minds, souls, and spirits shall always be in complete communion to understand one another's feelings, and provide support, help, and encouragement.

Above and most of all, our communion under any circumstances, irrespective how demanding, challenging, and unexplainable might be, shall be guided with absolute and unconditional faith, truth, and trust in one another, so help us God.

An aide was summoned and escorted Barbara and Margo out. The president was alone in the oval office, for the first time.

What a newly sworn president would do, when all alone, for the first time in the oval office? It would be hard to tell for all others, but for this one was predictable; pray!

Praying in the oval office? Would be a violation of the first amendment of the *Constitution* the president sworn to uphold?

If the walls of the oval office could talk, would speak volumes.

In times of crises, and there have been quite a few in American history-foreign wars and conflicts, slavery, civil war, assassinations, depression-the seating president must have contemplated, reflected, and even prayed in silence. If the president did pray, he simply followed the example of the founding fathers and reconnected with the roots of America.

Before the third Thanksgiving was celebrated severe drought had threatened to destroy all crops.

Famine, starvation, and death were certain. What did the pilgrims do? Prayed!

Rain fell and human life, livestock, and property were spared. Was the rain a coincidence? Who knows for sure? Maybe it was; maybe it wasn't.

Lucia sitting on the desk chair, placed her elbows on top of the desk, brought the palms of hands together, rested the chin on top of her fingers, and prayed:

Oh God, by your providence and will, I find myself in a place and position that no other American woman has ever set foot on before. Give me the strength to fulfill my mission, and the wisdom to lead America.

As the first woman president, I am a pilgrim settling on a new land. Hardships, difficulties, and adversities will be part of the territory. Like the pilgrims, I will count on your response to my prayers.

Give me the humility and patience to listen. Your answers to my prayers might come through someone else, who would be wiser than I.

We have been so blessed as a nation. Our new journey has just begun. Guide us to use our gifts and creativity to work hard and be productive, not only to help us prosper as individuals, but also united help all other Americans as well.

If we don't, we will betray America, the Pilgrims, the Signers of the Declaration of Independence, and the Framers of the Constitution, and we will be unworthy of your blessings.

0-595-66188-2